P9-CRE-327

Remnants
of Murder

Center Point
Large Print

Also by Elizabeth Lynn Casey and available from
Center Point Large Print:

The Southern Sewing Circle Series
Pinned for Murder
Deadly Notions
Dangerous Alterations
Reap What You Sew
Let It Sew

Remnants of Murder

Elizabeth Lynn Casey

CENTER POINT LARGE PRINT
THORNDIKE, MAINE

This Center Point Large Print edition
is published in the year 2013 by arrangement with
The Berkley Publishing Group,
a member of Penguin Group (USA) LLC,
a Penguin Random House Company.

The text of this Large Print edition is unabridged.
In other aspects, this book may vary
from the original edition.
Printed in the United States of America
on permanent paper.
Set in 16-point Times New Roman type.

ISBN: 978-1-61173-862-9

Library of Congress Cataloging-in-Publication Data

Casey, Elizabeth Lynn.
Remnants of Murder / Elizabeth Lynn Casey.
pages cm
ISBN 978-1-61173-862-9 (library binding : alk. paper)
1. Sewing—Fiction. 2. Murder—Investigation—Fiction.
   3. South Carolina—Fiction. 4. Mystery fiction.
   5. Large type books. I. Title.
PS3603.A8633R46 2013
813'.6—dc23

2013024398

For Jim.

I love to borrow your brain over
hot chocolate and a treat . . .

Acknowledgments

As always, writing is a very solitary profession. I spend large amounts of my time huddled over my keyboard, giving life to my Sweet Briar friends. Fortunately, I'm always surrounded by special people willing to share their expertise.

With that in mind, I'd like to take a moment to offer some heartfelt gratitude to a few of those special people . . .

Luci Zahray, thank you for answering my many poisonous questions as I began the writing of this book.

A special thank-you to Nancy M. Webster, my Facebook friend, for sharing her wonderful placemat pattern with all of us.

A huge thank-you to my cover artist, Mary Ann Lasher. Each and every cover she's drawn in this series has been spot-on, but I truly believe she's outdone herself with this book.

I'd also like to thank my editor, Michelle Vega, who has proven that change can work beautifully.

And finally, I have to thank *you,* my fans, for loving the ladies of Sweet Briar as much as I do. You are wonderful!

Remnants
of Murder

Chapter 1

Tori Sinclair heard the voice droning on in her ear, bits and pieces of the man's words mingling intermittently with the more enviable conversation taking place on the other side of the office between her fresh-off-maternity-leave assistant, Nina Morgan, and her predecessor-turned-nemesis-turned-trusty-right-hand, Dixie Dunn.

On any other day, or at any other moment, such a sight would have had her smiling and champing at the bit for a chance to chime in on her all-time favorite subject. But it wasn't any other day. And it wasn't any other moment.

"I'm sure you can appreciate our position on this, Victoria. Times are tough. Funding is being cut all across the country. This isn't personal."

The head librarian part of her knew Winston Hohlbrook was right. The board president had proven himself to be an advocate for Tori and the library since her first day on the job.

But the part of her that had gotten to know Dixie better during Nina's absence couldn't help but feel the knot of dread that had taken up residence in her stomach the moment Winston had gotten to the point of his early morning phone call.

"It's a logical move. You and Nina have always handled things fine on your own and you'll do so again." Winston cleared his throat and continued, the conviction in his voice doing little to soften the impact of his words. "Now don't get me wrong, Victoria. The board and I have greatly appreciated Dixie's willingness to pinch-hit from time to time over the past nine months. But she's—"

"She's done far more than pinch-hit," she protested before allowing her gaze to revisit the animated pair across the room, the pure happiness on Dixie's face pushing the dread into Tori's throat. "There's no way I could have overseen the floor and the renovations in my office after the fire, or pulled off either of our holiday events, without her."

"And we're grateful, Victoria. We really are. But we simply have no room in the budget to keep her on now that Nina is back."

No room in the budget . . .

"Maybe we could . . ." The words died on her lips as reality took root. She knew the library's finances. She'd personally canceled subscriptions to the major magazines and newspapers in an effort to tighten their belt. She'd seen the ever-decreasing book budget.

Winston was right and she knew it.

"Please express our appreciation when you tell her, Victoria. Perhaps at the next board meeting we can present her with a certificate in honor of her efforts."

Tori shot upright in her chair, only to curse the move when it netted raised eyebrows from the two women who'd been oblivious to her angst until that moment. "You—you want me to tell her?" she whispered as she spun her chair around to face the wall of windows that afforded a view of the hundred-year-old moss trees that dotted the library grounds.

"We think it would be easier coming from you."

Easier, she wanted to shout. *Easier for whom? Dixie or Winston?*

"Anyway, have a great day, Victoria, and we'll be talking again soon, I'm sure."

She opened her mouth to protest but was thwarted from her efforts by the telltale buzz of a dial tone in her ear.

Winston Hohlbrook had tossed the hot potato into her lap just as the music stopped.

It was up to Tori to break Dixie's heart.

Inhaling sharply, she looked out over the same grounds that Dixie, herself, had looked out over for more years than Tori had been alive. How did you tell a seventy-year-old woman who'd been ousted from her beloved job—only to be asked back a year later as a part-time employee—that her services were no longer needed?

"Victoria?"

With one last look outside, she sent up a mental prayer for guidance and then slowly spun her chair around to face Dixie.

"Nina and I have just come up with the perfect idea for the high school book club!"

Tori leaned her head against the back of her chair and silently marveled at the changes she'd witnessed in Dixie Dunn since their first-ever meeting two years earlier. Gone was the scowl from the woman's gently lined face. Gone was the near-constant fist clenching anytime the subject of the library came up in Tori's shared vicinity. In fact, the unnecessary rush to highlight her many achievements as Sweet Briar Public Library's first and only until-Tori-stole-her-job head librarian had all but disappeared from Dixie's daily mantras.

Nina moved in beside Dixie, her woolen hair a perfect casing for her dark, flawless skin. "While I wish I could take partial credit, Miss Dixie is being modest. Juxtaposing the books of today against yesterday's classics is all her idea."

"Yesterday's classics?" she echoed.

Dixie clapped her hands. "We're going to pick a single genre for half a year. We'll read three current and hip titles of the kids' choosing, and three titles of *our* choosing. Classic titles that were all the rage when they first debuted."

She tried to focus on Dixie's smile, tried to

commend it to memory for that moment when it would surely disappear, but it was hard. The roar in Tori's ears, coupled with the knot that had magnified tenfold in her stomach, was making it difficult to concentrate on much of anything besides the bomb she needed to detonate.

"I suggested we explore mysteries first. Three modern-day whodunits interspersed with three classics." Dixie smoothed back a lock of snow-white hair from her forehead then perched her stout frame on the edge of Tori's desk. "I'm thinking Edgar Allen Poe and Agatha Christie for sure. We're still debating the third. I think Sherlock Holmes, and Nina thinks we should go with Phillip Mar—"

"Dixie?" she rasped.

The woman's smile faltered ever so slightly in favor of a raised eyebrow and a worried lip. "Victoria? Is something wrong? You don't look so good right now."

In a flash, Nina was back across the room and pouring a glass of iced water from the pitcher they kept on a simple cart in their shared office. "Here, here . . . drink this," Nina said as she retraced her steps and deposited the glass on Tori's desk. "It *is* kind of hot in here today."

"That's because Winston and the board are so intent on cutting costs, they won't even consider letting us run the air-conditioning in here," Dixie groused. "They'd rather have their employees passing out from heat exhaustion than pay an extra few bucks each day in electricity."

It was the opening Tori needed, yet still, she hesitated.

Dixie lifted the glass from the desk and held it out for Tori to take, the concern in her eyes bringing a haze to Tori's. "The way they're going, it won't be long before we've got no books and no employees, ain't that right, Victoria?"

She took the glass, only to set it back down, untouched. After what seemed like an eternity, thanks to the pounding in her chest, she met Dixie's worry-filled eyes. "Dixie, I—I have some bad news."

Dixie looked from Tori to the glass and back again. "Did something happen with Milo on the phone just now?"

Milo.

For the first time since they'd met, the mere mention of Milo Wentworth's name failed to birth its usual smile. And for the first time since she'd accepted the handsome third grade teacher's marriage proposal, she knew there was nothing he could say—and no amount of emotional support or encouragement he could give—that would help her at that moment.

Dixie's inevitable heartbreak was for her to set in motion. Alone.

She swallowed and shook her head. "That wasn't Milo on the phone just now. It was . . . Winston."

And just like that, any and all concern was pushed from Dixie's face and stance in favor of something more befitting a person prepared to have a noose looped around their neck. The knowledge was there, residing right alongside resignation and a slow-boiling anger that managed to raise the temperature in the already stuffy twelve-by-twelve office. "He's cutting me, isn't he?"

At Tori's silent nod, Dixie pushed off the desk and made a beeline for the cabinet that had been cleared for the sole purpose of giving the former librarian a place to house her personal belongings while working at the library during Nina's absence. One by one, the woman removed her things—her purse, her lunch bag, and the stack of books she'd set aside for the next toddler story time.

Nina shifted from foot to foot, clearly confused. "Victoria? What's going on? Where's Miss Dixie going?"

She opened her mouth to answer but closed it as Dixie slammed the cabinet door and turned. "I'm going home, Nina. Winston and the board no longer believe I'm needed here."

Nina's hands moved from her face to her hips. "Not needed here? What are you talking about? Of course you're needed. Look at everything you've done while I was home with Lyndon . . ." The words disappeared momentarily behind lips that were suddenly pursed. When Nina spoke again, her self-discovery was aimed in Tori's direction. "Wait. They're doing this because I came back from maternity leave, aren't they?"

"They're doing this because they're cheap. You coming back from maternity leave just gave them a way to cover that fact." Squaring her shoulders against the tears Tori detected in her voice, Dixie lifted the stack of picture books shoulder-high and nudged her chin toward the door. "I'll set these up on the counter when I leave. They're good choices for the next story time."

Tori blinked against the prick of tears she felt burning in the corners of her own eyes. "You could still read to the little ones like you did before Nina went out on bed rest. In a volunteer capacity . . ."

"No."

She cast about for something to say to the emphatic response she hadn't expected, but came up empty. Dixie was hurt. And Dixie was angry.

With good reason.

"M-Maybe I could talk to Duwayne tonight and see if his mom might want to scale back her time with Lyndon to three or four days a week, instead of five. Then Duwayne and I could hire you to take care of him on the other day or two."

This time, when Dixie declined, she did so with a gentle squeeze of gratitude on Nina's arm.

"Duwayne's mama has been waiting a long time to be a grandma. She don't need me coming along and taking away her time with that precious baby of yours."

Sensing the question on the tip of Nina's tongue, Tori rose from her chair and made her way around the desk to stand beside Dixie. "But what will you do?"

For a moment, she wasn't sure Dixie was going to answer, the woman's initial anger all but gone, and in its place the kind of intense sadness that threatened to smother them all. "I guess I'll do what Winston and the board intended for me to do when they cast me aside two years ago for you, Victoria."

She tried not to take offense to the stinging nature of Dixie's words, tried to rationalize them as a knee-jerk response to current circumstances rather than a total reversion of the friendship they'd managed to forge, but her own heartache over what was happening made it hard to dismiss the latter as a possibility.

Nina reached out, took Dixie's hand in hers. "And what was that, Miss Dixie? What did they intend for you to do?"

"Go home and wait."

"Wait? Wait for what?" Nina asked.

Bracing herself for the answer she knew was coming, Tori grabbed the glass from the top of her desk and took a fortifying gulp.

Here it comes . . .

Dixie extricated her hand from Nina's hold and crossed to the door, stopping as she reached the hallway beyond. "To die, of course."

Chapter 2

Tori transferred the plate of homemade brownies to her left hand and pulled open the screen door with her right, any apprehension regarding manners bowing in mercy against the definition of futility.

It didn't matter how long she stood there, knocking. It didn't matter how many times she cleared her throat or coughed a cough she didn't need to cough. Margaret Louise Davis wasn't going to be answering the door anytime soon.

And it wasn't a surprise.

Knocks on her friend's door routinely went unheard over the near constant giggling and squealing that wafted onto the front porch at virtually any hour of the day. The sound reminded Tori of her own childhood and the countless hours she spent learning to sew under the loving tutelage of her late great-grandmother.

Stepping into the entryway and then the kitchen, she stopped and inhaled the very essence that was Margaret Louise, a much-needed smile inching across her face as she did.

"Miss Sinclair! Miss Sinclair!" Lulu Davis, Margaret Louise's fifth grandchild, hopped down from her spot between one of her brothers and one of her sisters, and raced over to Tori, her long dark ponytail swaying across her back. "Miss Sinclair, you've got to come see! Mee Maw is letting us invent a cookie or cupcake recipe for her new book!"

Tori set the covered plate on the nearest counter then threw her arms open wide. "What? No hug?"

Lulu's large brown eyes dropped to her flour-doused hands before taking in Tori's white eyelet shirt and petal pink capris. "But I might get you all messy."

"A fair price for a Lulu-hug, if you ask me." Bending forward, Tori wrapped her arms around the child and whispered a kiss across the top of her head. "Now that's more like it," she teased before stepping back and gesturing toward the table. "So you're experimenting, huh?"

"Yup. C'mon, I'll show you." Pivoting in her white and purple sneakers, Lulu led the way back to her brothers and sisters. On the far end of the table was Jake Junior, the oldest of the Davis brood. The opposite end played host to Molly, the strawberry blonde who'd recently relinquished her role as youngest upon the arrival of her baby brother, Matthew. Sandwiched between them were Sally, Tommy, Julia, Kate, and a still-standing Lulu. "Mee Maw said we could have a recipe in her book if we can make it extra yummy."

"*And* if we can all agree," Jake Junior reminded as he scooped up a handful of yellowish-colored morsels and sprinkled them into a bowl. When he was done, he grinned at Tori. "Which Mee Maw says is like waitin' to find gold at the bottom of Molly's sandbox."

Lulu slid back into her chair and pointed at various bowls set up around the table. "Mee Maw gave us all kinds of chips—light chocolate, dark chocolate, peanut butter, and butterscotch. And we're supposed to see what will make our cookies or cupcakes best."

For several moments Tori simply stood there and watched, the concentration and determination on the faces assembled around the table temporarily lifting the cloud that had hovered around her ever since Dixie had walked out of the library with a broken heart six days earlier.

Since then, she'd called her friend twice a day in an attempt to maintain contact. But each time she did, her call went straight to voice mail and was not returned. The worrier in Tori was on alert.

"Is everyone in the family room?" she asked to no one in particular.

Jake Junior nodded.

"Your Mee Maw? Aunt Leona? Everyone?"

"Everyone 'cept Mama," Lulu corrected before abandoning her bowl of chips for a closer look at Tori. "And . . . Miss Dixie, I think."

Tori's heart sank. "Miss Dixie isn't here?"

Lulu's eyebrows furrowed in thought, only to resume their normal position as she shook her head. "Nope."

"*There* you are, Victoria!" Margaret Louise breezed into the kitchen, waving a pudgy finger as she did. "Why, I was just sittin' inside frettin' 'bout everyone who ain't here and here you are." Pivoting on her Keds, the grandmother of eight peeked around the corner and into the front entryway. "Dixie? You hidin' out here, too?"

"I wish." Tori recognized the forlorn quality in her own voice right before Margaret Louise turned back with a mischievous sparkle in her brown eyes.

"Well, butter my butt and call me a biscuit!" Margaret Louise slapped her hand against her polyester-clad thigh and raised her sparkle with a face-splitting smile. "Two years ago, Dixie had you walkin' on eggshells wonderin' when she was goin' to flap her jaws 'bout losin' her job to you. Now you look like you lost your best friend just 'cause Dixie's missin' a sewin' circle meetin'." Then, with her best attempt at a whisper, the woman continued. "But don't you worry none, Victoria. I won't tell Rose or Melissa."

Tori hoisted her sewing bag farther onto her shoulder and studied her sixty-something friend closely. "Won't tell Rose or Melissa what?"

"That you ain't upset 'bout them not bein' here."

"Wait. I only knew about Melissa and that's because we already spoke on the phone about an hour ago when I called to check in on her and the baby."

At the mention of her newest grandbaby, Margaret Louise beamed with pride. "I tell you, that baby might be the purtiest baby I've ever seen."

"Mee Maw, you say that every time," Jake Junior accused before bringing his hands to his hips and lovingly mimicking his grandmother. *"I tell you, that Sally was the purtiest baby . . . Have you seen Molly Sue? She's the purtiest baby I've ever seen . . ."*

A hint of crimson rose in Margaret Louise's face just before she walked over to the table and planted a kiss on her oldest grandchild's head. "When did you get so smart, young man?"

If Jake Junior answered his grandmother, Tori didn't hear. Instead, she found her thoughts revisiting the other name on Margaret Louise's no-show list—Rose Winters.

At eighty-two, Rose was the oldest member of the Sweet Briar Ladies Society Sewing Circle. In just the two years since Tori moved to town, the group's matriarch had weathered a tropical storm that caused extensive damage to her home, as well as a rheumatoid arthritis diagnosis that seemed to accelerate the aging process. Yet through it all, Rose came to virtually each and every meeting, the edges of her bristly exterior softened by the magic of a needle and thread.

Sometimes, when Tori was stressed over budget issues or feeling blue over her great-grandmother's death, she found herself on Rose's doorstep. And every time she did, she felt infinitely better when it was time to leave.

Rose could never replace Tori's great-grandmother—no one could—but her presence in Tori's life helped ease the pain that tended to flare at the most inopportune times.

"Victoria? You okay?"

She turned to her left to find Margaret Louise studying her closely, a hint of worry on the woman's face. Tori glanced toward the table and lowered her voice to a near whisper. "Is everything okay with Rose?"

Margaret Louise's broad shoulders rose and fell in a shrug. "I asked her that when she called to decline, and you know what she told me?"

Tori waited.

"She told me to quit sniffin' 'round for somethin' that ain't there. Said she was tired and just didn't feel like gettin' dressed and comin' over here to sew when she can just keep on her slippers and sew in her own house." Margaret Louise grabbed hold of Tori's upper arm and propelled her toward the hallway, glancing back at her grandchildren with a curious mixture of affection and authority as she did. "Keep on testin' your recipe ideas while I get Miss Sinclair, here, squared away with her sewin'. Now do a good job. I can't be havin' an empty page in my cookbook, now can I?"

Once they made it into the hallway, Margaret Louise leaned her mouth close to Tori's ear, the woman's inability to whisper making the move virtually futile. "I'm glad you're here. Listenin' to my twin soap boxin' 'bout the benefits of red nail polish over pink nail polish was givin' me a splittin' headache. Why, I swear that woman could talk the ears off a dead mule."

"And give him tips on how to look more appealing in death while she's at it," Tori quipped before stopping just inside the doorway of the evening's sewing circle room of choice and taking in the faces of her closest friends.

Seated beside the rarely used fireplace was Georgina Hayes, the town's mayor—a title that had been virtually bequeathed to her by her father and her grandfather before him. Her quick thinking and tireless work ethic for the good of Sweet Briar, however, was what kept her in office after each mayoral vote.

Georgina met Tori's eye and smiled. "Why,

26

Victoria, I was just asking Beatrice if she knew whether you were coming or not tonight."

Her gaze slid to Georgina's left long enough to smile at Beatrice Tharrington, the youngest member of the Sweet Briar Ladies Society Sewing Circle. A nanny for one of the town's wealthier families, the young British woman was endearingly shy.

"I'm sorry I'm late. I got tied up at the library going over this month's budget and then had to run home for my brownies."

"We're just glad you're here, Victoria." Debbie Calhoun patted the empty sofa cushion beside her fit frame. "Come. Sit. Tell us why your eyes aren't sparkling the way they usually do."

She considered protesting her friend's observation, but opted, instead, to let it go. Debbie's bakery hadn't become the most popular eatery in Sweet Briar by coincidence. It had achieved that status because of Debbie's determination and attention to detail—qualities that also contributed to the woman's rock-solid marriage to local author Colby Calhoun, and her reputation as an amazing mother to their two children, Susanna and Jackson.

"That's easy. Victoria simply doesn't listen."

All eyes turned toward the impeccably dressed woman holding court on the upholstered wing chair beside the bank of windows that ran along the south side of the room. Leona Elkin was as different from her twin, Margaret Louise, as one could imagine. Where Margaret Louise was lovably plump and disheveled, Leona was slender and stylish. Where Margaret Louise was all about family and family-related activities, Leona was all about her hair, her makeup, and the latest uniformed male to catch her attention. And where Margaret Louise tended to focus on the stuff inside a person's shell, Leona tended to focus on the shell itself.

"Now don't you start, Twin," Margaret Louise reprimanded. "Go back to readin' that magazine of yours and leave Victoria alone."

Leona dropped her latest travel magazine into her lap and glared at her sister. "If you'd quit thinking I'm being mean and let me finish, you'd know that I only have Victoria's best interests at heart." Then, pointing across the room, Leona took her spot in the limelight. "If Victoria would get eight hours of sleep each night the way I always tell her to, her eyes wouldn't be so dull. And if she'd quit taking on the worries of the world and actually wear the sleep mask I got her for Christmas, she wouldn't have those black circles around her eyes like one of those raccoons who keep getting into the trash can behind the shop—"

"Leona!"

Tori crossed the room to the sofa and sat down. "Debbie, it's okay. Leona is right."

Leona nodded in triumph. "It may have taken you two years, dear, but at least you've finally learned *that* much." Lifting her hand from her lap, Tori's self-appointed life coach took a moment to examine her flawless manicure before focusing on Tori once again. "So which is it, dear? Lack of sleep or failure to cover your eyes?"

"While I'm sure both of those are culprits, I'd say it's the worry most of all," Tori replied as she reached into her tote bag and extracted her sewing box and the pair of pants she'd chosen to hem that evening. "I've spent more time looking at the ceiling, worrying, than I have closing my eyes and actually sleeping these past six nights."

Margaret Louise straightened in the doorway. "Worrying?"

Debbie's brows rose just before she scooted closer to Tori. "What's wrong, Victoria? Is it Milo?"

"No, Milo's fine."

Beatrice paused her needle above the badge she was securing to her charge's Scout vest. "Are you feeling poorly?"

"No. I—"

"Do you think I'd look like this"—Leona gestured toward her salon-softened gray hair, high cheekbones, and perfectly pouty lips—"if I let worry take over?"

Margaret Louise stepped five steps to the right

and plopped into a wooden rocking chair. "Worry? *What* worry? Last time I checked, Twin, you didn't have any roosters to crow."

Dipping her head forward a smidge, Leona pinned her sister atop her glasses. "I have roosters, Margaret Louise."

A chorus of laughter rang around the room, only to be stymied, temporarily, by Leona's foot smacking the floor. "You think it's easy maintaining this?" Again, she pointed to herself. "And don't you forget about Paris. Making sure she's safe from the trigger-happy fingers in this backwoods little town is a full-time job on its own. And if that's not enough, trying to keep Elkin's Antiques and Collectibles afloat in a town that is hardly a vacation destination is difficult at best."

Georgina's head shot up. "Sweet Briar is just *fine,* Leona. We don't need to be a vacation destination."

Leona turned her disapproving gaze in the mayor's direction while addressing Tori's sofa mate. "Debbie? Would the bakery benefit from additional customers?"

"Of course."

"And Victoria? Would the library board keep slashing your budget if there were more people utilizing the library?"

Tori looked from Debbie to Georgina and back again before answering. "I guess not . . ."

"Then I rest my case." Leona grabbed her magazine from her lap and flipped it open. "I have roosters, too."

"No one is going to shoot your bunny, Leona. We have ordinances about that in this town." Georgina held her sewing needle to the light and carefully threaded it with a piece of black thread before pointing it at Leona. "And as for the future of this town, we've been talking to Clyde Montgomery about selling his property out on Fawn Lake for years. But no matter how much those resort companies offer him, he just keeps on saying no. Says he likes his lake and his property just the way it is."

"Just the way it is?" Leona echoed. "You mean stagnant and boring?"

Seeing the fight build behind the mayor's eyes, Tori veered the conversation into different waters. "I'm worried about Dixie."

"Dixie? Why?"

She met Debbie's gaze and shrugged. "The Sweet Briar Public Library was her life. Getting tossed to the curb for a second time has to hurt."

Without taking her eyes off Leona, Georgina addressed Tori. "Dixie will be okay. In fact, I reckon she landed on her feet quite well."

"Landed on her feet?"

Georgina nodded. "She's volunteering for Home Fare. And from what I've heard after just her first few days, she's a hit with the folks on her route."

Tori set her sewing box on the coffee table and ignored the folded trousers on her lap. "Home Fare? You mean the meal delivery program for the elderly?" At Georgina's nod, she continued. "Dixie is volunteering with them?"

"She started on Wednesday."

"Wednesday?" Tori repeated. "But how? The board let her go on Tuesday."

"She was determined to stay standing this time around."

Relief coursed through her body at the news. "That's wonderful, Georgina. I didn't know . . ."

"I think she wanted to surprise you." The mayor laid her needle atop the blouse she was stitching and smiled at Tori. "For someone who was so against you moving here two years ago, Dixie sure has taken a shine to you, Victoria."

"The feeling is mutual." And it was true. Dixie Dunn had taught her the kind of lessons she knew she'd revisit as she aged—lessons about determination and maintaining one's passions in life. "I'm so glad they had some open routes."

Georgina retrieved her needle once again and brought it up and underneath the fabric in her hand. "More like an open client they padded with a few others."

"Open client?" she repeated.

"Clyde Montgomery ran off the third volunteer in as many weeks. The most recent one he belittled and called an incompetent buffoon."

Georgina pulled the thread through the fabric. "So anyway, there I was, explaining our position to his son, Beau, when Dixie showed up looking like something the cat dragged in. She heard what was happening and she volunteered to bring Clyde his afternoon meal every day."

A tsk from across the room brought all eyes back on Leona. "Can you just imagine *that* dinner conversation?" Leona modulated her voice to simulate conversation between an elderly pair. "They stole my job from me! They're trying to steal my land from me! I'll show them! No, I'll show them!"

"Twin, quit!"

Leona waved off Margaret Louise. "Oh, please. You know I'm right."

Beatrice's voice broke the ensuing silence. "Victoria? Do you think being around that kind of negativity will change Dixie back to the way she was before Nina went on bed rest? Especially if Mr. Montgomery can't fancy her, either?"

It was a question Tori, too, couldn't help but entertain. Unfortunately, the answer it demanded was far easier to imagine than she would have liked. "Let's hope not, Beatrice. Because, between all of us, I don't think Dixie could stand another loss."

Chapter 3

Tori glanced at the wall clock and felt the answering slump of her shoulders. All morning long, she'd held out hope that Dixie would breeze through the front door of the library with a stack of picture books and a creative way to tie them all together for the eight or so toddlers now peering up at her from their mothers' laps.

Yet Dixie hadn't materialized.

"Don't worry, I've got this covered." Nina stepped around Tori to claim the one child-size chair amid a sea of toddler-topped carpet squares, a smile lifting her rounded cheeks. "Hi, boys and girls! My name is Miss Nina and I love kitty cats. Do you know what kitty cats say?"

She knew she should be grateful for the chorus of happy meows that erupted around the room, but it was hard. Dixie and toddler story time went together like milk and cookies. To have one without the other just didn't fit.

Slowly, she backed out of the children's room and made her way down the hallway and into the main room. Aside from one patron utilizing a computer, and another, older gentleman, reading a local history book on the other side of the room, all was quiet.

If she was smart, she'd take advantage of the lull and tackle one of the half-dozen or so tasks that had found a spot on her daily to-do list that morning. Yet deep down inside, the notion of shelving, budget tweaking, and event planning fell a distant second to trying Dixie's number one more time.

The likelihood her attempt would go to voice mail was highly probable based on past experience, but still, she had to try. For her own peace of mind, if nothing else.

Lifting the information desk's main phone from its base, she punched in the number she'd committed to memory early on during Nina's leave—a number she'd called every time she needed backup at the library. Only back then, Dixie always answered, her excitement over being needed an instant smile maker.

One ring morphed into two, three, and four rings before Dixie's voice came on the line. But instead of the recorded version Tori was now able to recite by heart, it was live.

"Hello?"

She tightened her grip on the phone, perching on the edge of a nearby stool as she did. "Dixie! I've been trying to reach you all week!"

"I know."

When the woman failed to elaborate, Tori

continued, "I've been worried about you. Are you okay?"

"Actually, I'm on my way out right now. The Home Fare organization has requested my assistance in handling one of their more difficult clients."

Resisting the urge to admit she knew about the volunteer assignment, she, instead, gave the response Dixie craved. "Dixie, that's wonderful. They couldn't have found a better, more creative troubleshooter than you."

The elderly woman's smile was audible over the phone. "Clyde Montgomery ran off three workers in the past three weeks. The first one simply couldn't handle his gruffness. The second one got sick of his demands. And the third walked out after Clyde became convinced he was a spy and an incompetent one at that."

Tori worried her lip as she considered Dixie's words. "You sure you want to get involved with someone like that?"

"Clyde may be old but he's not dumb. He knows when he's being talked *at* and when he's being talked *with*. Accepting meals from strangers is hard enough without being made to feel like you've lost your marbles just because you've got a cane you never thought you'd need propped against your chair and your hands have suddenly decided to start trembling when you eat." Dixie paused long enough to get a handle on the anger Tori heard building in her voice. "But Clyde and me? We get along just fine. I respect him and his need to be seen as a productive member of society, and he respects me and my like-minded pursuit."

"That's wonderful, Dixie."

"Of course I know how distraught the little ones must be in story time right now, Victoria, but Clyde Montgomery really needs his meals and I'm the only one capable of handling him."

The response was typical Dixie. Only this time, the woman's boastful ways didn't make Tori smile or roll her eyes as they had so many times in the past. No, this time they brought her face-to-face with a startling reality: she'd come to rely on Dixie far more than she'd realized—as a sounding board *and* a mentor.

Blinking against the unexpected misting in her eyes, Tori forced her voice to sound upbeat, to deliver the only answer that was right and true even if it pained her to say it. "Then that's where you need to be. Nina and I will just have to make do."

Tori bypassed the peanut butter sandwich she'd made that morning and reached for the leftover brownie at the bottom of her brown paper lunch sack. With any luck, the infusion of chocolate would help offset the doldrums that had rolled in on the heels of her phone call with Dixie.

Part of her felt guilty for being blue. After all, Dixie was her friend. She should feel *happy* that the woman had found a place to feel useful after being unceremoniously kicked to the curb for the second time in as many years.

But it was the other part—the part that was sad—that seemed to be winning in the battle for her mood. Dixie was difficult most days, downright cantankerous on others, yet somehow over the past nine months, the former head librarian had managed to prove herself invaluable in everything from how to handle the board members, to crafting creative ways to cut budgetary corners without affecting the patrons.

Swiveling her chair around, Tori looked out at the library grounds. For two years, the view from her office window had been her saving grace on difficult days. The sight of hundred-year-old moss-draped trees, and the patrons who devoured books beneath them, had become a foolproof way to catch her breath and clear her head.

Dixie's days at the library were over. It wasn't something Tori wanted, nor something Dixie had sought. Nonetheless, it had happened. The least she could do as a friend was help celebrate the woman's new purpose in life.

That's what friends did.

Besides, Dixie wasn't leaving Sweet Briar. Just the library. The former librarian's vast experience and life-based opinions were just a phone call or sewing circle meeting away.

Turning back to her desk, Tori took a bite of brownie and consulted the to-do list she'd managed to ignore for more than half the day. If she cut her lunch short, she could still get most, if not all, of the tasks completed.

Her mind made up, she shoved the rest of the brownie into her mouth and stood, her progress quickly thwarted by the ring of her cell phone. Glancing down at the caller ID screen, she debated letting it go to voice mail. But if she did, she knew she'd be subjected to a lecture on good taste and manners followed by several reminders of her purported offense in the weeks and months to come.

Sighing, she flipped open her phone and held it to her ear. "Good afternoon, Leona, what can I do for you?"

"You can tell me why that gorgeous new police officer ran off on me a few minutes ago."

Resting her head against the back of her chair, she stared up at the ceiling and mentally berated herself for opting out of the lecture. "How would I know that, Leona—"

"He was standing there, outside my shop, admiring my significant assets and working up the courage to ask me out on a date, when that blasted radio they all wear on their shoulders went off. Next thing I knew, he's talking letters and numbers with some masculine-sounding female and he starts running toward his car . . . away from *me!*"

It was hard not to laugh, but she knew if she did, she'd never get off the phone. Instead, she offered the appropriate clucking sound while still trying to keep her friend's feet rooted in some semblance of reality. "Um, maybe he had a police emergency?"

"But I was wearing that white linen dress that hugs my curves!"

"Emergencies trump tight dresses, Leona."

"Not this one, they don't!"

That did it. She laughed. Hard.

"Did I miss something, dear?" Leona fairly growled through the phone, nearly drowning out the staccato beep of an incoming call. "Because the last time I checked, you should be taking notes on the specifics of the dress, not laughing—"

"Leona? Can I put you on hold for a second? I've got a call coming in from"—she pulled the phone from her ear long enough to check the display screen—"Dixie right now and I really should find out what she needs."

"*Dixie?* You want to put me on hold for *Dixie?*"

"I won't be long."

A suffocating pause soon gave way to Leona's infamous martyr voice. "Take all the time you need, dear. *My* trials can certainly wait. It's not like I've had to listen to you drone on about Milo and dead bodies again and again these past two years."

She opened her mouth to protest but it was too late. Leona was gone.

"I'll never hear the end of that one," she mumbled. Then, with the help of a quick and calming inhale, she switched to the other line. "Hi, Dixie! How'd your delivery go today?"

A muffled sniffle on the other end of the line made her sit up straight. "Dixie? Dixie, are you there? Are you okay?"

"N-N-No."

"What's wrong? Did you fall? Are you hurt?"

"I-I'm f-fine. But . . . It's C-Clyde . . . He . . . He's *dead*."

Chapter 4

The sun was already beginning its descent behind the trees when the sound of Dixie's footfalls on the rickety porch steps roused Tori from an unexpected catnap. Pushing the fog from her brain, she rose to her feet and rushed to close the gap.

"Oh, Dixie . . . I'm so sorry you had to find Mr. Montgomery the way that you did." She took the woman's trembling hands in hers and squeezed.

"I'm sorry I couldn't get here sooner, but Nina had to get home to Lyndon and I had to stay and cover the library until closing."

Dixie tugged her left hand from Tori's grasp and brought it to her forehead, rubbing the spot just above her red-rimmed eyes as she did. "Is Lyndon all right?"

She drew back at the croak in Dixie's voice. "Lyndon's fine. Are *you?*"

"I'm old. I'm starved for attention. I'm incapable of having a sane thought in my head." One by one, Dixie ticked off a litany of self-deprecating statements, each addition to the lineup more preposterous than the one before. "And let's not forget the fact I've spent my entire life around books and therefore have an over-active imagination that might lead me to see things that aren't truly there."

At any other place and with any other person, Tori might have laughed at such an attention-seeking self-reflection, but seeing the pain on her friend's face kept that reaction in check. "C'mon, Dixie, what are you talking about? None of those things are true and you know that as well as I do."

"They must be true. Robert Dallas said so."

The mere mention of the Sweet Briar Police Department's top dog made Tori's muscles tighten in response. Too many times over the past two years she'd dealt with the local chief under less than ideal conditions, and each and every time he'd left her wanting to bang her head against a wall. "Let me get this right. Chief Dallas said you're old . . . and starved for attention and . . . incapable of a sane thought . . ." Her words petered off temporarily as her mind worked to fill in the rest of what Dixie had shared. "He really said those things to you?"

"Not in so many words, but the sentiment was there, Victoria." Dixie looked at the ground then gestured toward the front door of her aging home. "I have to go inside. My head is pounding and I'm feeling a bit light-headed."

"When was the last time you ate?" she asked quickly.

"Breakfast, I think."

The woman's body swayed ever so slightly on the way to the door, prompting Tori to grab hold of her upper arm and accompany her into the house. Once inside, she led Dixie to the kitchen and toward one of two vinyl dining chairs. "Sit. Sit. Tell me what you'd like and I'll get it for you."

Then, without waiting, Tori plucked the lone glass that had been left to dry in the drainer and held it under a running faucet. "While I'm making you something to eat, I need you to drink this. Slowly." She carried the glass to the table and set it down in front of a ghostly white Dixie. "If the light-headed feeling doesn't go away, then bend over and put your head between your knees."

Dixie took one sip and then another while Tori moved on to the refrigerator with a plate in hand. "How about a small chicken leg? Or maybe a piece of cheese?"

"Oh Victoria, I can't even fathom eating after . . . after seeing Clyde that way."

She plunked the leftover meat onto the plate and shut the refrigerator, the tremor in her friend's voice pushing worry aside in favor of empathy. "I'm sorry you had to find him like that, Dixie. It must have been awful."

"It was." Dixie leaned back in her seat and stared at the plate Tori placed in front of her. "I knew something was wrong the second I stepped on his porch."

Claiming the chair across from Dixie, Tori leaned forward and patted the woman's arm. "Shhh. It's okay. You don't have to talk about it."

Slowly, Dixie lifted the chicken leg, only to let it drop back to the plate, untouched. "It didn't matter how weak he was, he always greeted me at the door, checking his watch to make sure I arrived during the thirty-minute window Home Fare gives their clients."

"He timed you?" she asked.

"Clyde Montgomery was a regimented man. I suppose that came from his time in the military as a young man, or maybe he was raised that way. I can't really say for sure because we hadn't gotten to that aspect yet."

"Gotten to that aspect?"

Dixie turned the chicken leg over and over on her plate, nodding as she did. "When I showed up on my first day at the exact time I was expected, he invited me to stay and chat while he ate. And since he was the only person on my route that particular day, I accepted. I figured he could use the company as much as I could and it would be a way for me to see that he was eating."

She pulled her gaze from Dixie's hands and fixed it, instead, on her face. "Did you have reports that he wasn't eating?"

"I didn't need a report to tell me that, Victoria. He was as frail as frail can be."

"How old was he?"

"Ninety-one."

"Oh." She filled her cheeks with air, then let them deplete along with a sigh. "Don't you wish we could have a magic wand and wave it over the elderly to stop their bodies from giving out?"

Dixie pushed her plate into the center of the table. "Why is everyone always so quick to point to age as the reason for everything?"

The venom in Dixie's voice caught her by surprise. "I didn't mean anything bad, Dixie, I just—"

"It didn't matter that I'd run that library for forty years. The day I turned sixty-eight, I suddenly became incompetent in the eyes of Winston Hohlbrook and the rest of the board. And Rose?

Everyone is always watching her like she's going to keel over any minute."

"I don't watch Rose like that," she protested.

"You don't follow behind Rose on the way to the dessert table every time we have a sewing circle meeting, Victoria?"

She swallowed. "I don't do that because I think she's going to keel over. I do that because I don't want her to fall."

"Because she's *old*."

She swallowed a second time. "She's more frail now with the arthritis and—"

"And she's old." Dixie warded off Tori's next explanation with raised hands. "I understand, Victoria. I really do. No one wants to see Rose fall any less than I do. But I also know she's aware of everyone hovering and watching all the time and it's defeating."

Defeating.

She hadn't considered that before . . .

"Is that why she didn't come to sewing circle this week? Or the week before?"

Dixie pulled her glass close and stared inside at the water she'd managed to get below the halfway mark. "When you feel as if everyone around you thinks you're incapable of doing things any longer, you start to doubt what you can and can't do, too."

A hint of bile rose in her throat as the enormity of what Dixie was saying hit her with a one-two punch. "Oh, Dixie, I feel *awful*. I never thought of it that—"

"I'm just so tired of age being the scapegoat for everyone else's misperceptions. So I turned sixty-eight? That's not why my ideas for the library became stale. They'd gotten that way from doing the same thing the same way for so long. All I needed was some perspective—a chance to be around new ideas like I was when I filled in for Nina." Dixie wrapped her hands around her glass, only to let it go and push it in the direction of her unwanted dinner. "And Rose? So what if she passed eighty by a few years ago? She might require a little more time to get down the hallway, and she might need a little help with her plate sometimes, but she still needs her dignity and for people just to love her for being who she is instead of always watching her and waiting for her to die."

It was hard not to feel like a puppy getting its nose smacked with a paper as the words poured from Dixie's mouth. She tried to explain the circle's feelings for Rose, but it was no use. Dixie was on a tear.

"And just because Clyde Montgomery was ninety-one doesn't mean his death should just immediately be written off as old age."

She raked a hand through her hair and worked to steady her breath before she spoke, Dixie's emotional state more precarious than she realized. "But you said he was frail, didn't you? And he was obviously housebound or he wouldn't be getting his meals from Home Fare, right?"

"*Rose* gets her meals from Home Fare."

Tori sucked in a breath. "She does?"

Dixie's face drained of all color once again, prompting Tori to nudge the water glass back in the woman's direction. "I wasn't supposed to tell you that," the woman whispered. "I promised her I wouldn't tell."

"But why? Why wouldn't she want us to know that?"

Dixie struggled to her feet and made her way across the kitchen in order to stand by the window that overlooked Tori's shallow side yard. Her back to Tori, she finally answered, "What would you have done if you knew, Victoria?"

"I would have made her some meals myself."

"And?"

"So would Margaret Louise . . . and Debbie . . . and Georgina . . . and . . ."

"And with those meals would have come a host of worry visits, right?" Dixie glanced over her shoulder and pinned Tori with a stare. "Well, am I right?"

"Worry visits?" she repeated. "What's a worry visit?"

Dixie's shoulders hitched up on an inhale then dipped along with the loud exhale that echoed off the tiled walls. "A worry visit is where everyone shows up at your door wanting to know how you are and what they can do, all the while making you feel like some sort of zoo animal."

"But we care about Rose."

"And that's good. You should. We all should. But this is just a low point for her. The arthritis is acting up and she knows it's best to stay close to home, but she also doesn't want a fuss made. She's struggling to hold on to some sort of independence right now. Calling a place like Home Fare and putting herself on the rolls as a temporary client is important for her psyche. So is not letting anyone know."

She'd be lying if she told Dixie she was okay with keeping quiet. Rose held a special place in her heart and had since almost the very beginning. Back then, Tori had just assumed the pull toward Rose was simply a need to be around someone who was about the age her late great-grandmother had been when she'd passed away. But as time went on and she got to know Rose better, she'd come to realize her bond with Rose was unique.

To know her treasured friend was going through a difficult time and didn't want Tori's help was hard to swallow, let alone respect.

"Don't worry, Victoria. I'm keeping tabs." Dixie retraced her steps back to the table and rested a calming hand on Tori's shoulder. "If the situation changes, I will let you know. You have my word on that."

"Can I call her just to say hi? The way I normally would?"

At that, Dixie offered the faintest hint of a smile. "Of course. Normalcy is good. It's why Clyde's son, Beau, showed up with scones every morning at ten sharp. It's why Clyde liked to sit out on his sunporch after their tea and read the classics. It's why he waited at the window when it was time for his dinner to arrive. It's also why he liked to retire to that same porch chair after his meal, looking out at the very lake his daddy and his granddaddy before him admired while they, too, drifted off for a much-needed afternoon nap. Normalcy is a comfort. It makes us feel safe and secure."

"Normalcy," Tori repeated. "I guess I never really thought of it as a comfort but it makes sense."

"It also helps raise a red flag when something is wrong."

She looked up at Dixie. "Raise a red flag? About what?"

"About the truth. Or at least the need to investigate a little further."

"We're talking about Clyde's death again, aren't we?" It was a rhetorical question really, especially in light of the way Dixie's field of vision obviously encompassed a scene beyond the kitchen they both inhabited at that moment.

Dixie nodded, once, twice.

She studied her friend's face closely, her thoughts registering the same take-no-prisoners clearheaded woman she missed terribly at the library. Dixie wasn't about tall tales. Sure, her predecessor could play the martyr routine better than anyone Tori had ever met, but this wasn't about playing a martyr. And if she listened to her gut, she also knew it had nothing to do with proving one's worth, either.

No, Dixie genuinely believed something was amiss about Clyde Montgomery's passing. Maybe it was needless. Maybe it wasn't. But either way, the least she could do for the woman was hear her out.

"Tell me."

Dixie closed her eyes briefly. "Are you going to listen or are you going to write off my ramblings to age? And Clyde's death to the same?"

She patted Dixie's spot at the table. "You think there's more to this man's death, don't you?"

"I do."

"Then there must be a reason, right?"

Dixie nodded again. "There is."

"Then I'd like to hear what you have to say."

Dixie's lower lip trembled ever so slightly before it disappeared behind a well-placed hand. "Chief Dallas thinks I'm crazy."

"At least he doesn't think you're a killer," she quipped.

Shrugging, Dixie dropped into her chair with a thud. "In order for him to think I'm a killer, he'd have to think there was a murder. And he doesn't."

She leaned forward across the table, noting the way Dixie worried her lip and twisted her hands inside one another. She knew those motions, knew them well . . .

"But *you* do, don't you?"

Dixie traced the pattern on the top of her Formica table then stopped, her gaze slowly rising until it mingled with Tori's. "Clyde Montgomery was murdered. And with your help, Victoria, I'm absolutely certain we can prove it."

Chapter 5

Tori had always prided herself on being one of those people who learned lessons the first time, committing to memory whatever knowledge she'd gleaned from a particular situation. But after finding herself searching for clues surrounding one too many dead bodies, she had to consider the very real possibility that she wasn't as smart and savvy as she once thought.

"Are you sure we should be doing this?" she asked as Dixie rooted through an overgrown flowerpot to the left of Clyde Montgomery's front door. "I mean, I'm thinking Chief Dallas wouldn't be too thrilled at the idea of us breaking and entering."

"I imagine you'd be right . . . if we were actually breaking and entering." Dixie pulled her hand from the dirt, brandishing a standard-looking house key in her hand as she did. "But since Clyde told me where to find his key after my second on-time visit, I kind of feel as if I have his permission."

"I'm not sure if permission granted premortem actually extends into postmortem, you know?"

"Well, in the event you're right, I also have Beau's permission. That, alone, certainly covers the gap."

She stepped to her left to afford a glimpse around the northeast corner of the stately plantation-style house and marveled at the view of Fawn Lake, the late afternoon sun sending shoots of light across its surface. It was a view she could get used to if it wasn't for the nagging sense that they shouldn't be there in the first place. "Now who's Beau again?" she asked as she turned to find Dixie brushing potting soil from the key's teeth.

"Clyde's son. I spoke to him on the phone after I found Clyde. He asked me to stay until the body was removed."

"He didn't come when he heard?" she asked.

"He couldn't. He was away on business and the earliest flight he could get has him landing in Charleston sometime tonight. Even if he drove straight here from the airport, it would still be late. So he asked me to lock up." Dixie inserted the key into the lock and turned, a sly smile playing at the corners of her mouth. "Unfortunately, I forgot . . . which is why I have to come back now."

"Dixie, I just heard the lock disengage," she argued.

"You did? Because *I* didn't hear that." Dixie rolled her eyes skyward then pushed the door open, beckoning for Tori to follow as she did.

Ah yes, their breaking and entering that wasn't really breaking and entering . . .

Reluctantly, she followed her friend into the dead man's estate despite the chorus of warning bells sounding in her head. "Dixie? I—I really don't know if this is such a good idea."

"You don't think it's a good idea to call a murder a murder so that a killer can be brought to justice?" Dixie shook her head from side to side, throwing in an unmistakable tsk-tsk for good measure and maximum guilt potential.

She heard the door click behind her as Dixie pushed it shut, the woman's continued tsks and clucks making Tori's cheeks warm in response. "Geez, Dixie, you don't really have to say it that way, do you?"

"I didn't realize there were multiple ways to speak the truth, Victoria."

There was a part of her that wanted to remind her friend of the chief's conviction regarding the elderly man's demise. But to utter such words would be akin to giving the Sweet Briar Police Department's top brass credit for knowing what he was doing.

And she knew better than to make that statement lightly.

"Okay . . . okay." She stayed on Dixie's heels as they traversed the foyer's charmingly scarred wood-planked floors and made their way toward the living room. "So what is it you're hell-bent on showing me?"

Dixie stopped midway across the large room and pinned Tori with the kind of look that had starred in many of her early Dixie Dunn–inspired nightmares. "If you'd quit your yakking, Victoria, and just *follow* me, I'll show you."

Once again, the image of herself with a wet nose and a rapidly approaching newspaper filled her thoughts. Only this time she caught a glimpse of the iron-clad fist holding the paper . . .

"Before you got into the whole library thing, did you ever consider teaching an obedience class?" Tori mumbled as she fell into step behind Dixie.

"No."

"How about something in the criminal justice field?"

"No."

"Drill sergeant?"

"Has anyone ever told you that you talk too much?" Dixie tossed the insult over her shoulder with nary a look back, the woman's singular focus on a floor-to-ceiling bookshelf that ran along the east wall of the room. Like its twin on the opposite side of the room, the built-in unit housed a smattering of books, trinkets, and framed photographs. Grabbing hold of a frame on the fourth shelf from the bottom, Dixie shoved it in Tori's hand. "See? What did I tell you?"

Tori looked down at the image of a man standing alongside a porch railing, gazing out at something beyond the camera's frame, the expression on his face one of complete peace. At first glance, she placed him in his late sixties until a second, more thorough inspection had the previously unnoticed cane in his left hand pushing his age into the early to mid-seventies range instead.

"Is this Clyde's son?" she asked even as her gaze returned, again, to the contentment the man wore with the kind of ease usually afforded a favorite bathrobe or a trusty pair of shoes. It made her wish she could see whatever it was he was seeing.

"That's Clyde."

"Oh." She held the frame aloft and looked from Dixie to the picture and back again. "Wow. The colors are much better than the average twenty-year-old picture."

"That's because it isn't twenty years old. It was taken five weeks ago."

Tori pulled the frame back in front of her and stared down at the image of the man in the khaki-colored pants, off-white collared shirt, and loafers. "I don't think so, Dixie. You told me Clyde was ninety-one." She gave the frame a gentle shake for emphasis. "He can't be more than seventy here."

Dixie closed the gap between them and pointed at the bottom-right corner and the digitalized numbers barely visible beneath the interior edge of the frame. The date shown backed up the woman's words, making Tori gasp in the process.

"But didn't you say he was ninety-one?"

"I did."

She studied the picture yet again, searching for any of the signs one would expect to see in a man of Clyde's advanced age, but there were none. Except, perhaps, the cane. "I don't get it. He doesn't look ninety-one at all."

Without so much as a word, Dixie spun around and retraced her steps back to the handbag she'd dropped on the sofa as they first entered the room, her wrinkled hand disappearing into its cavernous interior only to reappear clutching a small point-and-shoot camera. "Five weeks ago, there was no disputing that. But in the one I took

Friday, he looked every bit his age and then some."

Tori sidled up behind her friend and peered at the illuminated display screen on the back of the camera, a whoosh of air escaping her lips as she did. "C'mon, Dixie"—she glanced down at the frame in her hand and back at the camera with a similar time-date stamp depicted in the corner— "you seriously expect me to buy that these were taken *five weeks* apart?"

"Then *you* do the math, Victoria."

She looked from the corner of one picture to the next, the reality in front of her negating any need for a pen and paper or even a calculator. The pictures were, indeed, taken a little over a month apart. And while the differences between the man in each image were vast, there was no denying the fact that they were the same person, thanks to a dime-sized mole on the left side of his neck.

"What kind of illness made him deteriorate that rapidly?" she finally asked while noting everything from Clyde's extreme weight loss to the ghostly pallor of his skin and the dullness of his eyes.

"I don't know, you tell me."

Unsure of what to say, she stepped away from the camera and focused on the framed photograph in her hand. "Wouldn't you love to know what he's looking at in this picture? He looks so at peace."

"You really want to know?"

She glanced at Dixie. "Wouldn't you?"

Shrugging, Dixie gestured for Tori to follow, leading the way across the room and through an open archway to the left of the bookshelves. A hallway on the other side led to yet another archway—this one bathed in the kind of sunlight capable of chasing away the deepest of chills. "I knew from the first time I stepped in this house last week that this was his favorite room."

Tori walked through the opening and sucked in her breath. For there, on the other side of a bank of windows that ran the entire length and height of the home's western wall, was the most breathtaking view of Fawn Lake she'd ever seen. "Oh my gosh . . . Dixie . . . this is gorgeous! I had no idea the lake was this . . . this big, this *beautiful*."

"That's because all public access to Fawn Lake is on the other side of that island of trees you see over there"—Dixie extended her finger to the right—"and from that vantage point, it doesn't look like a whole lot."

She worked to make sense of her friend's words, the reality they imparted catching her by surprise. "Are you saying he owns all of this access?"

Dixie nodded. "And since the limited public access is such rocky terrain, the uninhibited view you see is about as pristine as it gets. No boats, no crazy teenagers, no noise issues of any kind. Just uncompromised beauty."

Hence the expression the man wore on his face in the framed photograph, the subject's position in the room not much different from where Tori now stood. "Wow. Just . . . wow." It was such a simple response yet it captured the view in front of them perfectly. "No wonder he looked so at peace in that first picture. This is magnificent."

"It was his pride and joy. His heritage."

She scanned the lake from one end to the other as the same kind of peace she'd seen in Clyde Montgomery's face washed over her from head to toe. "How could someone who looked like he did go through so many Home Fare volunteers in the past four weeks?"

Dixie refrained from answering for so long, Tori finally had to pull her attention from the lake and plant it on the white-haired woman perched on the edge of the room's only chair. "Dixie?"

Shaking her head, Dixie released a long, deliberate sigh before launching into one of her long-winded tirades. "It's like I said earlier, Victoria. People have a perception of the elderly. We're all supposed to have thinning hair and sit quietly in a wheelchair drooling all over ourselves. We're supposed to have no opinions about anything anymore, and we're supposed to be content babbling about things that happened in our youth. If we don't make sense to the person listening, we get a reassuring pat on our shoulder or, if we're really lucky, our head."

"C'mon, Dixie, it's not really that bad, is it?"

Dixie hit Tori with her best evil librarian glare and snorted. "From what I gather on the first few drivers assigned to Clyde, he didn't fit the image of a homebound senior. He had opinions on the meal, expectations for delivery, and an appetite for intelligent conversation. Driver number one found his scrutiny of the meals to be offensive. Driver number two had issues with timeliness. And driver number three was insulted by the accusations Clyde hurled at him."

"Accusations?" she echoed.

"Clyde was convinced Randy was a spy. That he was using Clyde's sudden health issues as a way to infiltrate Clyde's home."

"Infiltrate his home? Isn't that a bit extreme?"

Dixie took one last look out at the lake then led the way back down the hallway and into the living room. "If you knew how often that poor man was badgered about selling his land, you'd understand why Randy's potential kinship to several of the town's officials might have upset Clyde."

"What do you mean *potential* kinship?"

"Same last name, no relation. But Clyde didn't care."

"The town really wanted this land that badly?"

"Wouldn't you?" Dixie returned the frame to

its spot on the shelf, then retrieved and hoisted her handbag halfway up her arm. "Either way, everyone thought it was best if I was assigned to Clyde. Which, in hindsight, was probably fate at work."

"I'm sure Home Fare will assign you a new client. Maybe even a list of clients." Tori stood in the center of the room, her heart torn between wanting to return to the sunporch for one last look at the lake and the need to get out of a house they hadn't been invited to enter in the first place.

"That's not the fate I'm talking about, Victoria."

"It's not?"

Once again, Dixie resorted to an exasperated eye roll to convey her feelings. "No. I'm talking about my being assigned to Clyde so I could be the one to raise the red flag over his death."

Tori felt her shoulders slump under the weight of Dixie's conviction—a conviction she still didn't understand. Nothing Dixie had shown her so far gave any credence to the woman's claim that Clyde Montgomery had died of anything other than age.

"You still think he was murdered?" she finally asked.

Dixie's eyes led the way back to the built-in bookcase and the framed photograph of the man she'd found dead earlier that very same day. "Had those two pictures been taken a year apart, I wouldn't think twice about Chief Dallas's findings. I'd merely think old age caught up with him the way it's destined to catch up with all of us. But they *weren't* taken a year apart. They were taken just over a *month* apart. No one deteriorates that rapidly in a month, Victoria. Not even us old people."

Chapter 6

Tori pushed the chocolate frosted brownie around the powder blue plate and did her best to harness the upbeat mood she'd had as recently as that morning. But it was hard. Especially when she couldn't help but feel as if the police chief's unspoken words to Dixie held some semblance of truth.

No, she didn't see Dixie as old. She didn't think the woman's lifelong devotion to books had birthed an overactive imagination. And she most certainly didn't believe the woman was incapable of having a sane thought in her head. Those observations were preposterous.

But the other one? The one about Dixie being starved for attention? Maybe that one wasn't so out of the realm of possibility . . .

"Okay, spill it."

She lifted her gaze from her plate and fixed it, instead, on the part-curious/part-dejected face hovering just over Tori's right shoulder.

"Debbie. I—I didn't realize you were standing there." Pushing her plate to the side, she patted the empty lattice-back stool to her right while simultaneously taking a quick visual tour of the bakery's tiny but heavily utilized dining area. "Do you have a minute to sit and chat?"

"I do unless you're going to tell me I left out a critical ingredient," Debbie murmured before sliding onto the stool and sweeping her flour-coated hands toward Tori's untouched brownie.

"Oh no—no, no, no. It's not the brownie, or anything you did or didn't do. In fact, I'm sure it's as good as it always is." She pulled the plate closer, only to push it away as her stomach sent up the kind of warning bells that shouldn't be ignored. "I—I'm just not very hungry. For anything, apparently."

Debbie flicked the end of her blond ponytail over her shoulder and leaned toward Tori's ear. "Which leads me back to what I just said. Spill it."

She stared at the brownie, willed it to work its usual magic, but to no avail. Instead, she set her elbows on the table and dropped her head into her hands. "I feel like a traitor, Debbie."

Debbie's soft, gentle laugh echoed around them, raising a few curious eyebrows in their direction as it did. "You? A traitor? Yeah, okay. Like I could ever even imagine that tag applying to someone like you."

"It does now," she whispered.

At the forlorn quality in her voice, Debbie's smile disappeared. "What are you talking about, Victoria? How could you possibly see yourself as a traitor?"

How indeed.

Gathering all the courage she could muster, she put words to the guilt ravaging her heart. "Dixie came to me with something yesterday— something she believes with all her heart."

"And . . ."

"I honestly think Chief Dallas is right."

Debbie sat up tall. "Chief Dallas?"

"I think she's so lost right now that she's looking for anything she can find to prove her worth in a community where she's feeling as if she no longer matters."

"Wait. You lost me. Why is Chief Dallas weighing in on anything where Dixie is concerned?"

The bell over the bakery's front door jingled, signaling the arrival of a customer and the end to Debbie's ability to talk. Slipping off her stool, Debbie made her way toward the glass counter and the dozen or so homemade treats chosen to greet the day's patrons.

"Georgina, welcome."

At the sound of their fellow sewing sister's

name, Tori looked toward the door and the statuesque woman sporting a straw hat atop a full head of dark hair. Behind the mayor came three more customers—folks Tori knew by sight but not by name and who were certain to keep Debbie busy for the next ten minutes or so.

Ever mindful of her position in the town, Georgina stepped to the side to allow the other customers to go first while simultaneously canvassing the dining area. When she spotted Tori, she approached the stool left vacant by Debbie's departure and smiled broadly. "Victoria! What a pleasant surprise. How are you?"

"Tired."

In an instant, Georgina's smile was gone, in its place a grimmer set to her generous mouth. "Is something wrong?"

She let her shoulders rise and fall in a non-committal response. Telling Debbie she thought Dixie was attention-starved was bad enough. Repeating the same sentiment to a woman who'd known the former librarian her whole life would be inappropriate and unfair. Instead, she settled on the most basic response she could find. "Did you hear about Dixie's first Home Fare client, Clyde Montgomery?"

Georgina's head bobbed beneath the brim of her hat. "From Robert when it first happened, and then from virtually every business owner in town today. Why?"

"Every business owner in town?" she repeated.

Again, Georgina nodded. "Robert's sharing of the news was done as a matter of course. When someone passes in our town, he lets me know."

"Go on . . ."

"The rest was more of the backyard fence variety with a little bit of celebration thrown in."

"Wait." She permitted herself a brief moment to revisit the mayor's words, equally surprised the second time as she'd been the first. "People were celebrating the man's death?"

Georgina reached across the table, broke a corner off Tori's brownie, and then popped it in her mouth. "I don't mean the kind of celebrating you might see at a party, Victoria. There weren't balloons and cake, of course. But you have to understand that many of our shop owners have been begging and pleading with Clyde to parcel off his land and sell it to any one of the resort companies who have been expressing interest in Fawn Lake for the past five years or so. But he refused."

Instantly, she was back in the man's sunroom, the shoots of sunlight reflecting off the surface of the picturesque lake warming her face all over again as she closed her eyes and gave in to the memory. "Oh, Georgina, the view from his sunroom is spectacular."

"And it's a view that wouldn't have changed if he'd done the right thing and sold off the land to either the north or south of his home," Georgina drawled. "Had he done that, he could have enjoyed his panoramic view the way he always had while helping his fellow residents get closer to their own."

Her eyes flew open. "Why would it matter to anyone else what he did with his land?"

Georgina's mouth gaped open to reveal a hint of brownie in her molars. "Are you kidding me?"

She glanced from side to side before focusing once again on the woman seated at her table. "No . . ."

"Victoria, you saw his property, yes?" At her nod, Georgina continued. "That's the kind of property that attracts the major resort companies. It offers stellar lake views, uninhibited lake access, potential room for future growth, and a quaint little town within easy walking distance. In turn, when the presence of a resort turns a town like Sweet Briar into a destination, it means a significant increase in revenue for its local business owners as well as new job opportunities for its residents. A true win-win all around."

It made sense. It really did. But Tori also knew it was merely one way of looking at things. "Sweet Briar wouldn't be what it is now if it became a destination town."

Georgina waved aside Tori's words. "So we'd have a bit more traffic around the square during certain times of the year. It would certainly be workable."

"You'd have a lot more to worry about than a slight increase in traffic." She eyed the parts of the brownie that remained untouched and found herself breaking off the corner closest to her own chair. Leaving one of Debbie's chocolate frosted brownies to be picked over for scraps really didn't assuage her feelings of guilt where Dixie was concerned. So why let it go to waste? "You'd have more accidents—both on and off the lake, you'd have more crime, you'd have occasional lawsuit-happy tourists to contend with in court, and you'd lose the quiet, close-knit feel that makes Sweet Briar what it is now. And Mr. Montgomery? His view would've never been the same again."

"How do you figure that?" Georgina challenged.

She paused, the final bite of brownie mere inches from her lips as, once again, her thoughts returned to the breathtaking view she'd seen earlier. "Have you ever seen the lake from Mr. Montgomery's home, Georgina? Seen it from the sunroom that runs along the back side of his house?"

"I've seen it a time or two when I've accompanied council members to his home to ask him to consider parceling his land. In fact, I was out there no more than six weeks ago with an offer I still can't believe he turned down. And rather rudely, if I might add."

"It's . . ." She cast about for the best way to articulate the feeling she'd had while staring out at the lake, the same feeling Clyde Montgomery had obviously felt if the look of absolute contentment he wore in the framed photograph was any indication. "It's calming and peaceful. Like you're tucked away from the rest of the world in a place where nothing bad could ever happen."

For a moment, she considered recalling the last sentence, its sentiment rather dramatic in hindsight, but she let it go. Maybe the words had been overly heavy, but the underlying meaning was spot-on.

"Selling land to the north wouldn't have changed that. Not with the way his house was orientated to the shoreline."

She laughed then instantly regretted it when Georgina's eyebrow rose in response. "Georgina, a resort would have brought a marina and rented boats. There would be a swimming area, too, and evening parties on the sand. All of those things would have changed the landscape and feeling of the lake."

"A lake that only Clyde was able to enjoy."

"And why was that anyway?" Tori asked. "I mean, if the council and the business owners really thought a resort on Fawn Lake would have helped everyone so much, why didn't you open up the land around the public access point?"

"Because the public access point is hazardous at best. And the land on either side of it is protected wetlands." Georgina ran her hand through her shoulder-length bob and then repositioned her wide-brimmed hat atop her head. "Until yesterday, Clyde held all the usable cards and he had no intention of dealing anyone else into the game. It didn't matter one iota how nicely we asked, or how many times Councilman Haggarty and Councilman Adams sat in that man's precious sunroom and pled the town's case. It didn't matter how many blasted pies Betty Adams sent along with her husband in the hopes of sweetening their chances. Clyde Montgomery cared about one person and one person only. Himself."

Tori opened her mouth to speak, only to shut it as the theme song from *The Andy Griffith Show* made its way out of Georgina's purse.

The mayor's face paled. "Oh no . . . It's past six, isn't it?" Digging her hand into her purse, Georgina extracted her cell phone from its depths and held it to her ear, struggling to her feet as she did. "I'm on my way. Don't let them start the meeting without me."

And then, just like that, Georgina Hayes was gone, the only remnant of her presence a few scattered brownie crumbs and the lingering scent of her favorite perfume.

"Doesn't that figure?" Debbie reappeared beside Tori's table, shaking her head in mock disgust as she did. "I finally get through that little rush of customers and Georgina takes off."

"I think she had a meeting or something," Tori mumbled around the roar of her thoughts and the memory of Georgina's words.

"Still worried about Dixie trying to prove her worth?"

Until yesterday, Clyde held all the usable cards and he had no intention of dealing anyone else into the game.

Tori sat up tall.

Until yesterday—

"Victoria? Are you okay?"

When Dixie found Clyde's body . . .

Chapter 7

Tori looked up from the mountain of medical books she'd stacked on the table and took note of the time.

Eight fifteen.

Had she simply told Dixie she needed the camera until the morning, she'd be fine right now. Instead, because of her lapse in judgment, she'd promised the woman she'd share her reason for the request within the hour—a feat that was quickly proving itself impossible.

Likewise, had she been able to find what she was looking for in the pages of a mystery novel or inside the cover of a beloved children's book, Tori would be in great shape at the moment. In fact, she'd probably have had the answer she was seeking without having to return to the library as dusk settled over Sweet Briar.

Unfortunately, tales of mischievous teddy bears and the rhyming antics of a rather large cat weren't really conducive for trying to pinpoint possible reasons a seemingly healthy man could deteriorate so rapidly in less than six weeks.

No, that kind of information required medical books.

And a window of time without Dixie's prying eyes and endless questions.

Focusing once again on the display screen of Dixie's camera, Tori zoomed in for a closer look of the man whose inner peace seemed unfazed by the fact his body had finally caught up with his birth certificate.

Skin that had seemed to fit his body like a glove in the framed picture in his home now hung from a frame that had shriveled away to almost nothing. His complexion, which had led her to believe he was twenty years his junior, was now a sickly yellow. And the man who'd stood so proudly looking out over his birthright just five weeks earlier now seemed fatigued while sitting.

It simply didn't fit. At least not in the way age had crept up on her great-grandmother. With her great-grandmother, the aging process had been gradual. A forgotten memory here, a stumble or two there, a steady loss of energy that grew more pronounced with each passing year. Nothing that had happened overnight or in the blink of an eye the way Clyde's had surfaced.

Setting the camera to the side, Tori reached for the leather-bound medical book and skipped to the index, her finger guiding her eyes to the full column of illnesses that claimed rapid weight loss and yellowed skin among their list of symptoms. Chronic liver disease, Wilson's disease, sarcoidosis . . .

She slid her finger back to chronic liver disease and the indicated page number, only to have any page flipping thwarted by the ring of her cell phone. Despite the time crunch she found herself in, Tori couldn't help but smile as she glanced down at the caller ID screen and the backlit name it boasted.

Margaret Louise.

Flipping the phone open, she held it to her ear. "Isn't this a nice surprise? How are you, Margaret Louise?"

"If you don't mind none, Victoria, I'm goin' to put you on speaker so you can repeat what you just said loud enough for my irritatin' sister to hear with her own two ears." She heard the sound

74

of a phone moving, followed by a muffled thump. "Okay, go ahead, Victoria, say it again . . ."

"How are you?" she repeated.

A loud groan echoed in her ear. "Not that part. The other one."

Tori racked her brain to recall the way she'd answered the phone. "You mean the part about this being a nice surprise?"

"*See,* Leona? What did I tell you? It don't matter if it's mornin' or evenin', Victoria always welcomes my calls."

"That's because she doesn't listen to me when I try to tell her how she can spice things up with that handsome fiancé of hers," Leona drawled in the background. "Because if she *did* listen, the last thing she'd want interrupting her in the evening is a call from you, Margaret Louise."

"Harrumph."

Tori looked up at the ceiling and silently counted to ten in the hopes that when she did finally speak, she could do so without laughing. If she couldn't, she risked offending one, if not both, of her friends—something she didn't have the time to deal with at the moment. When she reached the last number, she spoke. "I always like to hear from both of you. And as for Milo, we're not together right now."

Margaret Louise's gasp was quickly drowned out by Leona's distinctive clucking. "I told you this was going to happen one day, Victoria,

75

didn't I? Men like their women to wear form-fitting clothes and to have their hair just so at all times."

"Shut your piehole, would you, Twin? Victoria is hurtin' right now."

She sat up tall. "Hurting? I'm not hurting, Margaret Louise. I . . ." Her words trailed off as her brain finally caught up with the reason behind her friends' reactions. "Wait. When I said Milo and I weren't together, I didn't mean we'd broken up! I just meant he's at his house right now and I'm here. At the library."

"Thank heavens!"

"I wouldn't be thanking the heavens so quickly, Margaret Louise. After all, if Victoria keeps choosing books over that man of hers, there *will* be a breakup," Leona quipped in a voice tinged with a mixture of reproach and relief.

"Oh, shut up, Twin."

Closing her eyes, she increased her count to twenty and then let out the breath she hadn't realized she'd been holding. "I'm not picking a book over Milo, Leona. I'm just trying to see if there's any possibility Dixie could be right."

If it was possible to hear ears perk, Tori heard it times two. "Did you say 'Dixie'?"

She nodded as if Margaret Louise were in the room rather than on the other end of the phone. Then, realizing her mistake, she replaced the gesture with the appropriate word while shifting her gaze back to the specifics of chronic liver disease and its link to alcohol.

"How well did either of you know Clyde Montgomery?" she asked on a whim.

A snort from one was quickly followed by a more reasonable response from the other. "Clyde's been a fixture in this town for as long as I can remember," Margaret Louise explained. "He was always around even if he wasn't."

Tori left her finger at the start of the second paragraph as she focused on her friend's account. "I don't get what you mean."

"That man didn't have to say much or even be around, everyone just always knew he was there."

A pause allowed her to try and make sense of what she was hearing but it was no use. She simply didn't have the background with the people of Sweet Briar the way Margaret Louise did. "I still don't understand . . ."

"People around here looked up to Clyde. He kept to himself, he had a long, healthy marriage to his wife, Deidre, he loved this town, and he wore it all with the air of someone important."

"Deidre?"

"She died 'bout four years ago. But oh, how he adored that woman. She was the envy of every woman in Sweet Briar."

A second, louder snort made its way across the line. "I didn't envy that woman. I pitied her, quite frankly."

"Oh, shush, Twin. Your green is showin'."

"My green?" Leona snapped. "I have no green. For anyone."

She forced herself to remain on topic despite the urge to offer a needling response. "Why did you pity her, Leona?"

"Because she looked at that man like he was the cat's meow, that's why."

"Did you see the way he took care of her? The way he looked at her, Twin? Anyone in Deidre's shoes would have looked at him the same way. Including you."

A third snort was followed by a heavy sigh. "I saw it. Did you?"

"I just said I did, didn't I?" Margaret Louise challenged before Tori could point out the same thing.

"He may have loved her . . . he may have even adored her . . . but that don't mean there wasn't some guilt mixed in—"

"Oh, quit your constant bellyachin' 'bout men, will you? Just because you got blindsided when you were young don't mean every man out there is the same, Twin."

"Why, I never—"

"Was Clyde Montgomery a heavy drinker?" Tori interjected before the brewing fight between the sisters brought an end to a call that could provide some valuable insight into a man she simply hadn't known.

"Clyde? A drinker? Why on earth would you ask that, Victoria?"

She took a deep breath as she glanced, again, at the description beneath her fingertip. "Because I'm wondering if his rapid decline in health could have been a result of alcohol."

"Aside from the fact that Clyde didn't drink, alcohol is a slow killer . . . There ain't nothin' fast 'bout drinkin' yourself into a grave."

Moving her finger from side to side across the page, she realized that Margaret Louise was right.

"So much for that one," she mumbled before flipping back to the index and the next disease on the list. "Do either of you know much about Wilson's disease?"

"Wilson's disease?" Margaret Louise echoed. "What on earth are you doin' over there, Victoria? Trainin' yourself for gettin' a medical degree?"

"No. I'm just—"

Leona's sigh cut through the line. "You're at it again, aren't you, dear?"

"At what?"

Leona ignored her sister's question and continued on. "You just can't ever leave well enough alone, can you?"

"I just—"

"Just because murder is a routine thing in your hometown doesn't mean that's the way it is everywhere else. Because it's not. People *do* simply die from old age around here, dear."

For a moment Tori considered defending the years she'd spent living in Chicago, but opted, instead, to let it go. After all, it didn't matter what she said. Leona's mind had been made up about Chicago long before they'd ever met. No argument she could give would ever erase the heartbreak her friend had endured while living in the lakefront city as a young woman.

"I realize that, Leona. It's just that—"

"Wait a minute. Are you sayin' you think Clyde died of somethin' other than old age?"

Leona groaned. "Welcome to the party, Margaret Louise. Of course that's what she's saying. But the notion is preposterous. He was ninety-something, wasn't he?"

"Ninety-one," Tori supplied. "But he was also in terrific shape until a month ago."

"Of course he was in terrific shape. He was the center of his own universe."

"Ignore my sister, Victoria. She chipped her nail 'bout ten minutes ago and she's still in a tizzy." Then, without more than a moment's pause, the grandmother of eight brought the conversation back to the topic at hand. "I think it's time you switch to some women's fiction, Victoria. Or maybe some romance novels."

She located the page for Wilson's disease and flipped to its entry. "Romance novels? What are you talking about?" she asked as her eyes began scanning the page.

Clumsiness. Difficulty speaking. Difficulty swallowing . . .

"I've been to your house, Victoria. I see what you read at night."

"What does she read?" Leona asked.

Fatigue. Drooling. Involuntary shaking . . .

"Mysteries. Mysteries. And more mysteries. But really, Victoria, just 'cause a chicken has wings don't mean it can fly." Margaret Louise's voice filtered through her thoughts at the same time as she lost interest in yet another disease. "I mean, I enjoy me a good whodunit now and again, too, but no matter how much I love investigatin' with you, Victoria, the likelihood someone in Sweet Briar will be murdered during a magic trick or poisoned with curry is probably 'bout as likely as Leona datin' men her own age."

"And why would I? I need someone who can keep up with me." Leona released the yawn she made no effort to hide. "Curry is dreadful."

This time, Tori had to laugh. It was the only way she could think of to deal with the train wreck the phone call had become. "I have no idea what you're talking about, ladies." She glanced up at the clock and tightened her grip on the phone. Dixie would be calling soon . . .

"You can pretend those books you're readin' aren't seepin' into your subconscious, Victoria, but I know better. Why else would you be thinkin' Clyde died of anything but old age?"

"Because five or six weeks ago, he was fine. Now, he's dead. And in between that time he went from looking like he was twenty years younger to looking like he was twenty years older . . . complete with yellowed and sagging skin, incredible weight loss, and a hollowness to his eyes that was nothing short of haunting."

"Had he been eating curry?"

Margaret Louise's booming laugh brought a second and wider smile to Tori's face. "Good one, Twin!"

"Inside joke between sisters?" she asked. "Or are you going to let me in on why curry is so funny?"

"There ain't no curry joke, Victoria. Leona was just referrin' to what I said earlier. You know, 'bout that mystery novel where the guy is poisoned after eating curry. I think it was arsenic or somethin' like that."

"Arsenic? Hmmm . . . And there we were waiting on the hands of time." Leona's voice grew quiet, only to rebound back to its normal authoritative level. "Oh well, it happened our way anyway."

"What are you babblin' 'bout, Twin?"

"Clyde Montgomery. His time finally came just the way we hoped it would."

"We?" Tori abandoned Wilson's disease once and for all and flipped back to the index and its listing for arsenic poisoning. "Who is *we*, Leona?"

"The members of the Sweet Briar Business Association—the same people Clyde Montgomery hurt every time he chose his precious view over the livelihood of everyone in this town."

She swatted at Leona's words as her focus came to rest on the description of arsenic poisoning. Line by line she read the details of a death that could easily masquerade itself as something other than what it was.

Yellowed skin—check.
Rapid weight loss—check.
General weakness and fatigue—check.

The beep of an incoming call brought her gaze back to the clock.

Dixie.

"Ladies, I'll have to call you back. Dixie is on the other line."

Without waiting for a response, she pressed the green button on her phone. "Dixie? Did Clyde have any sort of rash that you know of?"

"He mentioned something about a rash on his stomach that first day."

She stared down at the book.

Rash on trunk of body—check.

"Any—anything else about his skin?" she whispered.

"No. Not that I can recall. Except, of course, for some bizarre white lines across his nails."

"White lines across . . ." Her words petered off as she skipped ahead two lines.

Mees' Lines (white bands traversing the width of the nail)—check.

She swallowed once, twice.

"So why did you need my camera, Victoria?"

She closed her eyes in time with a deep inhale. She'd asked for an hour, and an hour was all she'd needed.

"I—I just wanted to see if you might be right."

"About what?" Dixie asked.

"Clyde's death."

A long pause gave way to an indignant sniff. "You mean his murder?"

Opening her eyes, she looked down at the book once again and nodded. "Yes, Dixie . . . his murder."

Chapter 8

For as long as she could remember, Tori had always found it fascinating that people traveled far and wide to find solace through difficult times. Mountain retreats were the clarity-seeking destination of choice for some, while lake homes and beach houses fit the bill for others. When travel wasn't an option, long walks, nature sounds, support groups, and when necessary, a therapist's couch became the remedy of choice.

Tori, on the other hand, always headed straight for her desk, a habit that began in her childhood bedroom, stuck with her through her school years, and remained unchanged in adulthood. The desk, of course, had undergone its share of face-lifts over the years, morphing from the typical white lacquer spindle-leg style favored by all females under the age of ten, to the metal and rather nondescript version currently housed in her office. But no matter the color, no matter the style, when it came to working through a problem, her desk was still the ultimate destination.

The only thing that could make it better was the inclusion of her fiancé—whether live and in person, or via modern technology, as was the case at that moment.

"So are you ready?"

She braced the tip of her pen against the desk and slid her fingers down its shaft, flipping it over and repeating the process each time she reached the end. It was a diversion tactic and she knew it, but somehow it still seemed a more alluring use of her time than addressing Milo's question.

No matter how many times she'd run through her thought process with him on the phone the night before, she knew she was facing an uphill battle when it came to sharing those same suspicions with Robert Dallas. In the police chief's eyes, Tori was nothing more than a pesky fly he'd love to smash into oblivion.

In just the two years since she'd moved to Sweet Briar, she'd single-handedly made him look like a fool on a number of occasions and he was just waiting to do the same to her. That's why she had to have her ducks in a row before she showed up on his doorstep with a murder allegation in tow.

"Tori? Are you still there?"

Dropping the pen from her hands, she spun her chair around until she was looking out over the library grounds, her favorite trees guiding her gaze toward the town's main thoroughfare beyond. As was always the case at that time of the morning, the bulk of the people she spied were either jogging or enjoying a leisurely stroll around the town square. She took a moment to breathe in the peaceful setting before giving Milo her full attention. "I'm here, Milo. I just—I don't know . . ." She stared out at the same elderly man who read his paper on the same bench at the same time each and every morning, the routine of it juxtaposed against the roar in her head making her more than a little aware of the lack of sleep she'd gotten during the night.

Stress. It got to her every single time.

"You're worried about how the chief is going to react to your visit today. I get that. But you've done some research, you have some suspicions, and it's worth bringing to his attention if for no other reason than peace of mind for Dixie . . . and for you."

She closed her eyes and inhaled the calming and supportive presence Milo was in her life. It didn't matter what crazy idea or cockamamie worry she shared with him, he listened. He understood when she failed to make headway on a particular wedding plan in favor of taking Rose to a doctor's appointment or pinch-hitting for Margaret Louise with the grandkids. Because when push came to shove, he knew she loved him and she knew he loved her. There were no petty games, no reasons for jealousy, no need to compete against each other's friends.

"You don't think I'm a nut for not telling Dixie

to figure it out herself?" she whispered into the phone. "Especially after our history together?"

"I don't think you're a nut because of *our* history together. I mean, c'mon, Tori. The way you champion your friends is one of the many things I love about you."

She managed a small laugh. "I wasn't talking about our history, silly. I was talking about my history with Dixie . . . specifically the period of time where I was top on her most hated list."

"And here you are, feeling so strongly about something she believes that you're willing to put yourself in the crosshairs of yet another person who misjudged you at the start."

"You say that in the past tense, as if he's changed his tune where I'm concerned." She heard the sudden bitterness in her voice and was ashamed. There was a time and place for self-pity where Chief Dallas's constant scrutiny of her was concerned. Her prized morning phone call with Milo wasn't that place. "You know what? Let's pretend I didn't say that, okay? I think my lack of sleep last night is making me cranky."

A pause gave way to the kind of encouragement she needed at that moment. "You'll be fine. Everything you told me on the phone last night made perfect sense. So lay it all out for the chief the same way. If he thinks there's something there, he'll take it and run with it. And if not . . ."

When he failed to continue his sentence, she tightened her grip on the phone. "Why'd you stop?"

"I don't know, I just did."

An unfamiliar briskness to his voice made her sit up tall. "Milo? What were you going to say? Tell me. Please."

Silence filled the space between them, making her doubt whether he was going to acquiesce, but in the end, he finally did, his words sending an unfamiliar shiver down her spine. "If Chief Dallas thinks there's something there, he'll take it and run with it. And if not, you fly solo."

She pulled her gaze from the man with his newspaper and spun back toward her desk, her hand instinctively reaching for the pen. "If he doesn't think there's anything to my suspicions, I'll let it go."

"No you won't."

For the first time since he'd come into her life, Tori heard a resignation that sounded far more tired than playfully supportive. "Milo?"

She imagined him walking down the sidewalk on the way to the elementary school, the day's lesson plans and hands-on activities housed in the dark brown satchel that served as his school bag. It was a picture she imagined every morning as they wished each other well for the day. This time, though, the smile she always saw and heard wasn't there, in its place an expression and a demeanor that were as alien to Milo Wentworth as cuddling babies was to Leona.

"I'm sorry, Tori. I don't mean to get weird on you. Ignore me, okay?"

"Talk to me, Milo."

After several false starts, he finally answered, his words and their meaning dousing her with a healthy measure of guilt. "I always thought your delayed response to my proposal was because of fear. I mean, who *wouldn't* be afraid to get married after being engaged to a jerk like Jeff? He had no clue how good he had it with you. But then you said yes and I figured we were good."

She swallowed against the lump that began to form in the base of her throat. "And we are."

"Then why haven't we talked about the meal for the reception? Why haven't you taken my mom up on her offer to help you look for a dress? Why don't you ever seem to want to talk about honeymoon possibilities when I ask for your thoughts? The wedding is in six months, Tori."

Before she could answer, he continued, his trademark optimism noticeably missing from his tone. "I guess I can't help but wonder if maybe it wasn't fear that kept you from saying yes but, rather, disinterest in marrying *me*."

She sucked in a breath. "No! That's not it at all."

"Then what is it? Why are you ducking all talk of our wedding?"

She opened her mouth to protest his description of her actions—or lack thereof—but closed it as he changed direction with a hollow laugh. "You know what, now isn't the time to do this. I've got a classroom of third graders waiting to see if our eggs have hatched yet, and you have your detective work to do."

"I have a detective to *talk* to. There's a difference."

"Right now that might be true, but when he shrugs you off, it won't be."

An ache coursed through her body like one she'd never felt before, the hint of resignation that accompanied his forced cheeriness, only making her feel worse.

"Milo, I'm just taking the possibility of arsenic poisoning to the chief. What he does with it is on him, not me. I have a wedding to plan and a honeymoon to dream about."

Her breath hitched at the audible smile she heard on the other end, the temporary reprieve it gave her guilt only shoring up her need to focus on what mattered most. Milo Wentworth was her future. It was time to start treating him—and their upcoming nuptials—as such.

"You have no idea how much I needed to hear that, baby. Thank you." Milo's voice deepened as they got to the point of their conversation where he was, undoubtedly, at the steps of the school and ready to sign off for the workday.

"So what do you say about coming over tonight for dinner and then looking at some of the brochures I've been collecting the past few months."

"Brochures?" she echoed.

"Yeah. For potential honeymoon spots."

"How come you haven't shown them to me if you've been collecting them for months?" she teased.

A momentary silence soon reignited the guilt she'd managed to shove to the side. "Well, you were busy with the holiday book festival . . . and Margaret Louise's hurt feelings over the Christmas committee . . . and then the welcome-back-to-work party for Nina . . . and the stress over what was going to happen to Dixie with Nina coming back . . . and then Dixie was let go and you were upset about that . . . and—"

"Okay. I get it," she whispered. "I've been an awful fiancée."

"Not awful. Just preoccupied. But that's over now, right?"

"Absolutely." A knock on her office door made her look up to find a not-so-smiling Leona and a nose-twitching Paris. "You have a great day, okay? And I'll see you this evening."

"I'll see you tonight. I love you, Tori."

She couldn't help but smile as she pulled the phone from the side of her face and snapped it closed inside her hand. Life was good. She had a job she loved, a fiancé who was second to none, and friends who—

Her gaze snapped back to the door and her rabbit-holding friend. "Leona, what a nice surprise."

"Ahhh, yes, your standard run-of-the-mill greeting." Leona clutched Paris to her bosom as she made a show of looking up and down the hallway before scouring Tori's office from beneath a raised eyebrow. "Which, if past experience suggests, will soon be followed by an extremely rude click in my ear."

"Click in your ear?"

"Yes, dear, a click. Like the one Margaret Louise and I were treated to last night." Leona sashayed herself across the office to the empty chair on the far side of Tori's desk. "And like the one I was treated to the other day when it was just you and me on the phone together."

"I—"

"And *why* did I have to hear that? Because you preferred to hobnob with someone who kept a diary on ways to get rid of you up until seven, maybe eight months ago."

And then she knew.

Twice in as many days, Tori had prematurely ended a telephone conversation with Leona . . . in favor of Dixie.

She retrieved her pen from the top of the desk and slowly twirled it between her fingers. "Look, about that, I needed to talk to Dixie because . . ." Her words trailed off as part of what Leona said looped its way back through Tori's thoughts.

Because you preferred to hobnob with someone who kept a diary on ways to get rid of you up until seven, maybe eight months ago.

Her mouth gaped open as she met Leona's pointed stare. "Wait. Dixie wanted to get rid of me?"

Leona looked down at the newly manicured fingers on her left hand and nodded, a slow yet satisfied smile making its way across her collagen-enhanced lips. "Like yesterday's trash, dear."

She considered her friend's words. "What kind of ways?"

Waving Tori's question aside, Leona scooted to the edge of the chair and crossed her ankles delicately to the side. "Oh . . . you know . . . a few well-timed accidents, a few tainted treats, a few trips and falls, nothing out of the ordinary, dear."

"Tainted treats?" she repeated in disbelief. "Trips and falls? You can't be serious."

Leona turned her gaze back on Tori. "You don't believe me, dear? Then perhaps you should inquire about such facts with someone you find more truthful. Like maybe, Mayor Georgina . . . or Beatrice, the sainted Mary Poppins . . . or, I don't know, perhaps the ancient yet always perfect-in-your-eyes Rose Winters."

She gasped. "Rose knows about this diary?"

"*Everyone* knows, dear." Then, before she could respond, Leona released a cluck that echoed around the room. "And you're going to unceremoniously hang up on *me* in order to talk to *her?*"

Tori cast about for something to say while simultaneously processing everything she was hearing. "I—I—"

"For someone who has stood by while I've been admonished for supposed loyalty issues, you might want to take a long hard look at yourself in the mirror when you get home today. And if you do, perhaps you might also take the time to notice that you're still applying your eyeliner much too lightly. You need to darken it up, dear, so your eyes will *pop.*"

She stilled her fingers around the pen. "You're onto my eyes now?"

"Of course. What kind of friend would I be if I didn't tell you that you look like"—Leona leaned forward a hairbreadth—"*death,* dear."

Death.

In an instant, her thoughts were right back where they'd been when Milo and then Leona derailed them from the path they'd been on since Dixie first uttered the word *murder.* Inhaling deeply, she took command of the conversation and hoped it was enough to smooth Leona's ruffled feathers.

"Dixie thinks Clyde Montgomery was murdered."

"I'm not surprised."

She dropped her pen and focused, entirely, on the woman seated across from her. "About which part? That Dixie thinks it? Or that Clyde was murdered?"

Leona stood and wandered around the room, her sudden geographical change bringing a flurry of nose twitching from the floor. "When was the last time you came down to the town square, Victoria?"

Leaning back in her chair, she followed Leona around the room with her eyes. "I don't know, last weekend maybe? When I picked you up for dinner."

Margaret Louise's twin sister wound her way around Nina's empty desk and double backed to Tori's. "No, I mean, when was the last time you came down to the square and walked through the shops?"

"I don't know. A couple of months. Christmastime probably."

"Christmastime," Leona repeated. "I imagine that's the answer most everyone in this town would give if asked the same question."

"What are you getting at, Leona?"

"They're struggling. *We're* struggling."

She studied her friend closely, only to be surprised at the appearance of lines around the woman's eyes that weren't normally there. Or if they were, they tended to be covered with the kind of artful expertise befitting the likes of Michelangelo or Monet. "I don't understand."

Leona's false lashes mingled together momentarily before parting to reveal the kind of worry that normally bypassed the carefree sixty-something. "Do you know how many people have even walked through my antique store in the past four months? Maybe ten. And do you know how many of those ten actually made a purchase? Zero."

"Zero?"

"And do you know why they didn't make a purchase?" Leona drawled without so much as pausing to allow for an answer. "Because they've been through my store a million times and they've already purchased whatever it is they wanted to purchase."

"Okay . . ."

"I can handle that. Elkin Antiques and Collectibles exists to give me something to do. But Bruce Waters over at Waters Hardware? And Lana Morris at Southern Style Gifts? They need customers so they can eat and so they can pay the mortgage on their shops *and* their homes. So, too, does Caleb Zackary and Joe Neidham and everyone else who owns a shop on the square."

Tori tried to think of something to say, something to ease the rare show of compassion for mankind now etched across Leona's face, but she was at a loss. Her thoughts were still centered on Clyde and how her friend had gotten so off topic.

"That man's selfishness was hurting a lot of good people, Victoria."

Her ears perked. "That man? You mean, Clyde Montgomery?"

Leona's head bobbed once, twice. "He was more concerned with being the envy of everyone in Sweet Briar with his picturesque piece of property than he was with the fact that many of those same people were struggling to make it through another day."

And then it clicked. Suddenly what seemed like sidebar babbling was providing an answer to a question Tori had posed as rhetorical more than anything else.

"So you think there's a chance Dixie is right? That Clyde's death may have actually been *murder?*"

"While I'm not one who enjoys giving someone like Dixie Dunn credit for anything besides being mean-spirited and holier than thou on more subjects than I care to count, on this particular subject, I have to grudgingly consider that she's absolutely right."

Stunned, Tori leaned forward against her desk and dropped her head into her hands, the enormity of what she was hearing giving her the added punch she needed when she finally sat down with Robert Dallas to make her case for an autopsy. But even as her mind began to swirl around the words she'd say to the police chief, a question formed in the foreground that made her sit straight up.

"Anyone in particular you'd finger as the culprit?"

"Can I borrow some of yours, dear?"

She felt her brows furrow. "Borrow some of my what?"

Leona pointed at Tori's hand. "Your fingers. I don't have enough to point at everyone who wanted Clyde dead."

Chapter 9

Talking to Sweet Briar Police Chief Robert Dallas was like walking through a minefield, each word she spoke, each inflection she used, one step closer to setting the man off on a veritable tirade. When he'd finally explode, though, was the real question.

Tori pushed the medical book across the man's desk, tapping the section on arsenic poisoning as she did. "It's all right here, Chief. The rapid decline in his weight, the yellowish color to his skin, the lines across his nails . . ." She took a deep breath, released it slowly. "It makes a lot more sense than old age."

Chief Dallas leaned back in his high-backed leather chair and tented his fingers beneath his chin. "He was ninety-one, Miss Sinclair. Old age makes all the sense in the world."

She pulled her hand back toward her lap and resisted the urge to scream. In the two years since she'd had her first run-in with the chief, she'd come to realize one irrefutable fact about the man. Robert Dallas liked face value. It afforded him time to fish, hunt, camp, and do whatever else it was he did when he hightailed it out of town virtually every Friday afternoon and for multiple weeks throughout the year.

Still, she of all people knew how dangerous face value could be. In fact, face value would have had her rotting behind bars with half the sewing circle as her cell mates. She met his tented fingers with a desk lean and a raised eyebrow. "I might be more apt to agree with you if he'd exhibited signs of this purported old age for longer than five or six weeks. Pets tend to deteriorate rapidly, not people."

The chief's eyes narrowed on her face as a ripple of irritation made its way across his own. "So because Clyde's health went south quicker than you saw fit, you think I need to lock someone up?"

She took a second, deeper breath and held it for a moment as she tried to settle on a tone that wouldn't be such a giveaway to her thoughts. After all, treating the chief like the buffoon he was could slow the truth-seeking process.

"No, but I think, perhaps, an autopsy might be a smart idea. Especially when so much of his decline matches that of someone who was being poisoned."

For a moment, he pulled his gaze from hers and fixed it, instead, on the section she'd indicated by her finger, the side-to-side movement of his eyes evidence he was at least reading. When he was done, he went back to the top and read it again, the passive set to his jaw making it difficult to decipher what, if anything, he was thinking.

"I know it sounds crazy, I really do, but when you take that possibility and hold it alongside the fact that he'd irritated a good number of people in this town—"

"Like whom?" the chief barked.

Startled, she drew back, her mind racing to output even two or three of the names Leona had mentioned not more than an hour earlier. "I—uh . . . well, basically anyone and everyone who owns a shop along the square—or at least—a *struggling* shop along the square."

A blanket of silence cloaked the chief's office as he seemed to consider her words before looking, again, at the open book in front of him.

"You mean because he wouldn't sell his land to those resort places?"

She nodded.

"It was mighty selfish of him not to think of how a sale like that could have benefited so many others."

"It was *his* land, Chief."

He held up his hands. "Trust me, I know. He had no interest in letting anyone use that land to access the lake to fish, or his woods to hunt. Not even the chief of police."

"So what did you do?" she asked.

Dropping his hands to the desk, he cocked his head as he studied her. "What do you mean, what did I do?"

"I mean, if he wouldn't let you onto the lake via his property, how did you fish?"

"I drove twenty miles to the south and fished on a different lake."

She glanced at the book then back at the chief. "And to hunt?"

He waved aside her question. "I prefer to head up into the mountains for that anyway. More peace and quiet that way."

"But what happens if you couldn't drive to another lake or into the mountains. Then what?"

A pause was quickly followed by a grudging tone and the words she was waiting for. "I guess I'd be a lot more angry at Clyde Montgomery."

"Packing up a struggling shop and moving it to

another town when your roots are in Sweet Briar would be sort of like not being able to drive to another lake to fish, don't you think?"

There. She'd said it. Now all she could do was hope the chief would dispense with his take-the-easy-route default button and at least consider the merits of her concern.

When the chief didn't respond, she stilled her trembling hands inside one another and made one final attempt. "I'm not saying I can't be wrong, because I certainly could be. But I think there are too many question marks about this man's death to be able to write it off as old age. And if you do write it off as old age and it wasn't, Clyde's murderer could very well walk past this building on a daily basis. Free as a bird and laughing at the perfect crime he pulled off right under your nose."

It had taken every ounce of restraint she had to get up, collect her purse, and bid farewell to the chief before learning his verdict, but sometimes it was best just to make your case and go. Less chance of saying or doing something that might end up being counterproductive. At least that's what she'd told herself as she made her way down the hallway of the police department and out into the brilliant spring sunshine.

Now that she was outside sans a definitive answer, though, she wasn't sure she'd made the smartest move. She liked answers. If she didn't, she wouldn't forgo so many hours of sleep each night racing to see how the latest book she'd chosen to devour actually ended. If she didn't, she'd be bringing baked treats to her friends in a jail cell rather than at a weekly sewing circle meeting. It was the way she was. The way she'd always been.

Her cell phone vibrated inside her blazer pocket and she pulled it out, Dixie's name on the display screen only making things worse.

"Hi, Dixie."

"Well? Is Robert going to have Clyde's body tested or not?"

She turned east when she hit the sidewalk and headed toward the library, her promise to be back in time to cover Nina's lunch break quickening her steps. "I don't know."

"You don't know? How could you not know, Victoria? You *did* talk to him, didn't you?"

"Yes. But I didn't press him for an answer."

An exasperated sigh echoed its way through the phone and into Tori's ear. "Why on earth not?"

"Because I didn't think I should. I made our case, underscored it as carefully as I could, and then left him to make the decision on his own." A second and more insistent sigh matched the one Tori managed to nibble back. "But if I had to take a guess, his wheels were definitely turning when I left."

"His wheels were definitely turning," Dixie mimicked. "Well, stop the presses! Robert's wheels were turning!"

She did her best to ignore her friend's sarcasm, choosing instead to remain calm. "It's in his hands now, Dixie. If he thinks there's a chance we might be right, he'll order an autopsy. If he doesn't, he won't."

"If he doesn't, he won't? You'd be okay with that?"

When Tori reached the edge of the library grounds, she veered right and headed toward the picnic table that served as a lunch spot for her and Nina, as well as the occasional patron craving a little afternoon sun. She dropped onto one of the built-in benches and stared up at the branches of the moss-draped tree that tempered the sun with a healthy dose of shade. "I'll have to be okay with that. And so will you, Dixie."

"You don't *have* to be okay with anything, Victoria."

She leaned her back against the edge of the table and tightened her grip on the phone. "What's that supposed to mean?"

"Do you think Clyde died of old age?"

She thought back over everything she'd learned during the past sixteen hours or so and gave the only answer she could. "No."

"So you're telling me that if Chief Dallas decides not to autopsy the body, you can just put that belief aside and move on as if everything is okay?"

"I have a wedding to plan, Dixie. A honeymoon location to decide on with Milo. I can't keep playing detective all the time."

When Dixie didn't respond, she pulled the phone from her ear long enough to see if they were still connected.

They were.

"Dixie? Are you still there?"

"I'm still here. I guess I'm just surprised that you could push aside one of your convictions. Shocked, actually."

Tori sat up tall. "If he lets it go, it doesn't mean I won't always wonder."

"Which means you won't be enjoying all those plans like you should, Victoria."

"Huh?"

"Wouldn't you rather make wedding and honeymoon plans with a clear head rather than one filled with nagging should-haves and could-haves?"

It was her turn to sigh. "So what am I supposed to do?"

"Don't give up until we know the truth."

She let Dixie's words settle in her thoughts, their pull more than a little surprising. "But Chief Dallas will figure out what's true if the autopsy comes back the way we think it will."

"*If* he autopsies."

Dixie was right and she knew it. There were simply too many factors that pointed to foul play where Clyde's death was concerned. And even if the chief did decide to pursue her claims, his investigation skills weren't exactly fine-tuned. Especially when spring brought new opportunities for weekend fishing trips.

"What are you proposing?" she finally asked.

"We investigate."

There was no denying it, Dixie's words stirred up a healthy blend of hesitation and excitement inside her chest, with excitement winning out in the end. "By . . ." she prompted.

"By getting together and making a list of all the people who may have had both motive and access to kill Clyde."

Motive and access. The two key ingredients to just about any murder investigation.

Once again, she pulled the phone from her ear long enough to check the display screen, this time narrowing in on the clock feature in the bottom-right-hand corner. "Okay. I can probably be out of here as early as five thirty. Where do you want to meet?"

Chapter 10

Dixie was waiting for her in the back booth of Johnson's Diner, a pair of brand-new notebooks carefully positioned on the wide Formica-topped table. Beside each notebook was a ballpoint pen and a glass of sweet tea.

Scooting onto the empty bench across from Dixie, Tori nudged her chin in the direction of the supplies. "What are those for?"

"Notes." Dixie plucked two menus from the silver holder at the end of the table, passing one of them across to Tori.

She caught herself mid–eye roll. "What kind of notes?"

"Possible suspects. Possible motives. Possible means." Dixie paused long enough to run her finger down the senior dinner specials listed on the right side of the menu, her entrée choice coming halfway down the laminated page. "Basically a blueprint of sorts for how we'll be spending our next few weeks."

Before she could respond, Carter Johnson, the diner's owner, appeared beside their table, a hint of irritation evident around his eyes and mouth. "What can I get for you ladies this evening?"

Dixie peered around the man's waist, her wide eyes taking in their immediate surroundings before coming to rest, once again, on Carter. "What happened to your waitress?"

"She called in not more than ten minutes ago. After my lunch shift had already left," Carter groused. "So I've got your table and three others until we can get a hold of someone else to come in and cover."

With a flick of her wrist, Dixie pitched her body forward against the edge of the table. "Carter? Were you a Clyde Montgomery hater, too?"

Tori felt her mouth gape at the question and knew the shock on Carter's face was mirrored on her own. "Dixie!" she hissed from between clenched teeth. "This isn't the time."

"Of course this is the time." Dixie turned an expectant gaze on Carter, drumming her squat fingers on the table as she did. "Well? Were you?"

A cloud of something Tori couldn't readily identify flashed across the man's eyes. "I can't say I was much of a fan."

"Then what *can* you say?"

Tori readied her mouth around yet another protest, only to have it die on her lips as the tips of Carter's ears turned crimson. There were no two ways about it—Dixie's tenacious scrutiny was having a noticeable effect on the man. The throat clearing and fidgeting that followed were merely the icing on the cake.

"Look. Ladies. I'd love to stay and gossip with you, but I've got tables to attend to and coverage to track down." Whipping a pencil out of his shirt pocket, he tapped it against the order pad in his hand. "So, if I could just get your order right now, that would be great. There'll be time for chitchat some other day."

"How about tomorrow?"

He eyed Dixie over the pad. "Tomorrow?"

"Yes. Will you have time to answer my question tomorrow?"

Aware of the tension building around their table, Tori gestured toward the menu and selected the first item she saw. "I—I'll take the meatloaf special, please."

"Red sauce, okay?" he asked.

"Red sauce is fine." She nodded at Dixie. "You were looking at the pot roast, weren't you, Dixie?"

At Dixie's nod, Carter took off for the kitchen, leaving Tori to incur the full wrath of the woman seated across the table. "Don't you know that in order to get answers, we need to ask questions, Victoria?"

"Yes, but Carter Johnson? Why on earth would you ask him a question like that?" Tori glanced to her left and right for any sign of eavesdroppers. "I mean, c'mon, Dixie, it was almost as if you were accusing him of Clyde's murder."

"If the shoe fits, Victoria . . ." Dixie took a sip

of her sweet tea and then pointed a finger over Tori's shoulder. "Before we leave, I suggest we stop at Lana Morris's table over there by the door. I'm rather curious as to how she'll answer the same question."

Pulling her elbows inward, Tori teed her hands in the air. "Oh no. You're not going to start randomly pulling people to the side and asking them if they hated Clyde. You just can't do that, Dixie."

"And why not? We *are* trying to find the truth, aren't we?"

"Of course we are. But those kinds of questions put people on the defensive or make them run in the other direction. Either way, that'll only make our job tougher."

Dixie's eyes widened momentarily, only to narrow to near slits as a smile broke out across her face. "So it's official then, yes?"

Tori drew back. "What is?"

"You're going to help me catch Clyde's killer."

She stared at Dixie. "Help you catch—wait. I didn't say that. I just—"

"Just now. You said *our* job."

She opened her mouth to protest, only to let it close around the futile attempt. Dixie was right. And not just because of Tori's choice in pronouns. Something about Clyde's death felt off.

In fact, deep down inside, she didn't need the results of any autopsy to tell her the man had been murdered. The physical clues pointed in that direction all on their own. The extensive list of people who stood to benefit from his rapid demise merely served to tie the whole theory up with a neat little bow.

The problem was, she was incapable of leaving the package wrapped. Bows were meant to be pulled, suspects were meant to be analyzed, justice was meant to be served, and all stories were designed to have an ending. It was the way it was supposed to be. In Tori's world anyway.

Reaching out, she raked a notebook in her direction and flipped it open to the first page. "So who do you think belongs on our list?"

"Our killer list?"

She pinned Dixie with a glare. "First up, we don't know Clyde was murdered—at least not officially anyway. Secondly, if he was, you need to realize that just because a person might have motive doesn't mean he did it."

Dixie opened her own notebook and wrote *Killers* across the top of the first page. "I think it's a bit premature to assume the killer was male, don't you think? Poison could just as easily be administered by a female as a male. Heck, I think a woman could do it even easier than a man."

Feeling her head begin to spin, Tori grabbed hold of her own pen and pointed it at Dixie. "You think *I'm* being premature?" She lowered her finger to encompass the bold heading scrawled across the woman's notepad. "The correct word, Dixie, is *suspect*. As in *possibility,* not tried and convicted."

A string of unintelligible words, whispered between impatient snorts, made its way out from between Dixie's lips as the woman crossed out the offending word and replaced it with Tori's. "When did you become so literal, Victoria?"

Ignoring the woman's comment, she found herself replaying something Dixie had said— something that actually made sense. "Why did you say that thing about females and poison?"

Dixie looked up, the flash of irritation suddenly gone. "Because it makes sense, that's why."

"Then help me understand your thinking."

A waitress from the other side of the diner appeared beside their table with their dinner plates. "Who's got the pot roast?"

Dixie shoved her notebook to the side to open up the spot directly in front of her body. "I do."

"Then the meatloaf must be yours . . ." The middle-aged waitress backed up a step and motioned to their table. "Anything else I can get you?" At their collective head shake, the brunette headed back toward her own section.

"We've got him running scared, don't we?" Dixie mused before swapping her pen for a fork and taking the inaugural bite. "Mmmm. Pretty good . . ."

Tori blinked once, twice, her focus torn

between the sauce-drenched meat on her own plate and her companion's cryptic words. "Him? Who?"

Dixie moved on to her rice, sampling it quickly. "Why, Carter, of course."

"What are you talking about?"

Dixie looked up from the carrot she'd just pierced. "Are you going to tell me you haven't noticed that Carter brought orders to all of the tables around us except ours?"

She held her first bite of meatloaf just shy of her mouth and quickly scanned their surroundings. "I hadn't noticed."

After a long pause that included a few bites of vegetable and a few bites of pot roast, Dixie finally laid down her fork. "Oh, I get it. All of this is just a big joke to you, isn't it, Victoria? You're here because you still feel bad that Winston cut my meager hours from the library budget." Pulling her napkin off her lap, Dixie brushed it across her mouth and then tossed it onto the table. "If that's the case, I don't need you. I can find the truth on my own."

Stunned, Tori found herself scrambling to keep Dixie from leaving the table. "Wait. I'm not here out of guilt. I'm here because you asked for my help. Though, in all honesty, I'm still trying to figure out why you're so deter- mined to investigate regardless of what the chief decides to do."

For a moment, Tori wasn't sure whether the woman was going to say something or simply collect her newly purchased notebook and leave. Eventually, though, Dixie spoke, her words, her tone providing a bird's-eye view of the pain buried not so far beneath the surface. "I spent my life building the library into what it was when you came along. It didn't have the children's room and all the buzz that you've garnered with that, but I held my own. I kept the shelves stocked with the classics and the best-sellers. I learned the ins and outs of computers so I could help my patrons transition into the world of technology. I knew the parameters of the board's new budget each year and operated accordingly.

"Then, one day, they decided I was too old and too boring to do what I'd done for more years than you've been alive. Bam, I was out on my ear with a pat on my back and a wooden plaque for my years of service. And it hurt, Victoria. It hurt more deeply than I can even begin to explain."

Tori leaned back in her bench seat, the rising lump in her throat making it difficult to breathe. So many times over the past two years, Dixie had slung her share of biting barbs over the fact that Tori's dream job had come at her expense. But now, at that moment, there was no over-the-top martyrdom, no hint of guilt, no evidence of anger in Dixie's words. Just pain. Raw pain.

"I—I'm sorry the board did that to you, Dixie."

It was such a simple response, yet no less true. She *was* sorry.

Dixie slowly spread the napkin across her lap once again, her gaze cast downward as she shook her head ever so slightly. "I've had a chance to see what you've done at the library since you arrived and I can see that they made the right decision. You've livened things up. You've brought in younger readers. You've made the library a fun place to be.

"Being able to work beside you during Nina's maternity leave was exciting. It brought a new purpose to my days and, in some ways, made me feel young and alive . . . in a way I haven't for far longer than I realized."

When Dixie's hands returned to the table, Tori reached over and gave them a gentle squeeze. "Having you there was invaluable. To me and our patrons."

Dixie's lips trembled upward into a shy smile. "Thank you for saying that, Victoria. It means a lot. It really does. But when the board sent me packing again last week, I felt empty. Like I no longer had any use."

"Dixie! That's not true."

Dixie pulled her hands out from underneath Tori's. "But then I overheard Georgina talking about Home Fare's issues with Clyde and I felt like I could do something. Like maybe I could make a difference all on my own. Like I used to. And even though I only delivered out to his house four times, I felt like I made a connection with him."

Before Tori could respond, Dixie continued on, her eyes sparkling as she spoke. "Because I'm new and only have another client or two, I could stay and chat rather than just hand him a meal and walk away. We talked about books. We talked about food. We talked about our lives. He showed me pictures, told me about his land, complained about the previous folks who'd delivered his meals, and the day before he died, he shared with me his frustration over the sudden downward spiral his health was taking."

"I'm sure you were a blessing to him, Dixie."

"As he was to me by giving me a reason to get dressed and leave the house."

And there it was. The reason behind Dixie's desire to see justice served.

She picked her fork up off her plate and pointed it at Dixie. "Then we need to eat, my friend. Playing detective can be very hard work and more than a little stressful at times. We need to keep up our strength."

"Agreed."

Tori scooped up a bite of meatloaf and slid it into her mouth, the flavor-filled meal eliciting a tiny groan of pleasure. "This is so, so good."

"Let's just hope it's not laced with arsenic."

Pushing her plate forward, Tori grabbed her water glass and took a large mouth-swishing gulp. When she was done, she met Dixie's gaze head-on. "Okay. Walk me through your theories. I'm all ears."

Undaunted by her own words, Dixie took yet another bite of pot roast and chewed it slowly, deliberately. When she finished, she leaned back in her seat like a queen holding court. "Clyde deteriorated over a five- . . . maybe six-week time period, right?" At Tori's nod, Dixie continued. "According to the research I did on my own computer after we spoke last night, he was most likely poisoned slowly—a little here, a little there throughout that time period."

"Okay . . ."

"Food was given to him all the time, Victoria."

"By the Home Fare organization," she reminded.

"And by council members and business owners who thought they could sweet-talk their way into making Clyde change his mind about selling his land to a resort company. Even before I started delivering his meals last week, I always knew Clyde loved food. Why, he didn't care about any of the games or rides at the various festivals throughout the years. He didn't go for the chitchat or the gossip. He went for the food and the food only."

Her meatloaf special now forgotten, Tori found herself staring at Dixie as another sewing circle member's voice began to play in her head . . .

It didn't matter one iota how nicely we asked, or how many times Councilman Haggarty and

Councilman Adams sat in that man's precious sunroom and pled the town's case. It didn't matter how many blasted pies Betty Adams sent along with her husband in the hopes of sweetening their chances.

"In fact, I think he may well have been one of Margaret Louise's taste testers for her sweet potato pie recipe a year or so back. Probably even lent a tongue for all those cookbook concoctions she's been trying out on us the past six months."

Clyde Montgomery cared about one person and one person only. Himself.

"Victoria? Have you heard a thing I've said?"

Had she ever.

Suddenly, it all made sense. The pleas of Sweet Briar's business owners and town officials may have fallen on deaf ears when it came to asking Clyde to sell some of his property. But there were other ways to reach their goal.

Pulling her gaze from Dixie's exasperated face, Tori retrieved her pen from its resting place atop her still-clean notebook and began to write.

*Sweet Briar Business Association—find out who is on its roster.
*Councilman Adams/wife Betty.
*Track down all food deliveries—what/from whom.
*Compare all to the start of Clyde's visual decline.

119

When she reached the end of her list, she glanced up to find Dixie now staring at her.

"What kind of list is that?" Dixie snapped.

She took in her notes and shrugged. "It's a to-do list, of sorts."

"I thought we were supposed to be drafting a list of suspects."

"We are. This to-do list will help us do that." She spun her notebook around to face Dixie then watched as the woman took in each and every entry. "We find out these things, we just might be able to narrow our list of suspects down to the right one."

Dixie's finger tapped Tori's second line. "Why do you have Betty Adams on here?"

"She apparently sent along some home-baked treats when her husband would try to plead the town's case."

"I went to high school with Betty's older sister. I don't think she'd be party to something like murder."

Murder.

That's what all of this talk came back to . . .

"Dixie, if we're going to consider the possibility that Clyde was murdered, we're going to have to accept the reality that someone did it. That someone could be *anyone*. Even the sister of an old high school chum."

Chapter 11

Tori propped herself up on her pillows and carefully studied the names who'd made their way into her notebook before she and Dixie had parted ways.

Many, like Carter Johnson and Lana Morris, were longtime business owners who stood to gain immeasurably if a resort opened up on the outskirts of Sweet Briar. Carter's diner—one of the only restaurants in town, and Lana's gift shop—chock-full of the sorts of souvenirs that tourists craved, stood to reap the kind of rewards most small business owners could only dream about.

Bruce Waters at Waters' Hardware had proven a harder sale for the list as vacationers had little to no reason to shop in his store.

No, the stores that stood to truly benefit from the sale of Clyde's lakeside property were the ones that would appeal to those who flocked to Sweet Briar for a little rest and relaxation. Places like Elkin Antiques and Collectibles, Calamity Books, Shelby's Sweet Shoppe, and Bud's Brew Shack all fit that bill, just as their respective owners claimed a spot on the list she and Dixie had drafted.

She'd wanted to cross out Leona's name the second Dixie added it, but left it for appearance purposes. Leona was, indeed, a local shop owner. The possibility the sixty-something had anything to do with Clyde's accelerated demise, though, was virtually nonexistent.

Then, there were the council members most closely aligned with the businesses along the town square. They, too, stood to gain from a resort by way of votes from grateful constituents in the next election. Travis Haggarty and Granville Adams made that portion of the list as did Granville's bribe-baking wife, Betty.

Stifling a yawn behind her hand, Tori turned her head and took in the clock on her nightstand, the digital numbers on its face shoring up what her subconscious seemed to know without the visual confirmation . . .

Ten o'clock had come and gone without Milo's nightly phone call.

Unease washed over her as she retrieved her cell phone from its spot beside the clock and flipped it open to check the time. Sure enough, her clock radio was right. And sure enough, there wasn't a missed call indicator anywhere to be found.

Positioning her finger over the speed dial number she'd assigned to her fiancé, she took a deep breath and pushed, the near-instant ringing in her ears difficult to hear over the sudden pounding in her chest. Milo's ten o'clock call was a given. In fact, it had become as much a part of her bedtime routine as brushing her teeth and scrubbing her face. For him not to call meant something was amiss.

He answered on the fourth ring with a simple "Hey."

"Hey, yourself." She tried to make her voice sound as carefree as possible but she knew her effort wasn't totally successful. "Is everything okay with Rita?"

"Mom's fine. Talked to her a little while ago."

"Did you fall asleep?" she asked.

"Nope."

She cast about for something else to explain the sudden break in their nightly routine. "Get lost in a TV show?"

"Nope."

"Phone call?"

"Nope."

Suddenly wary, she decided to change topics completely in the hopes of getting more than a one-word reply. "So Dixie and I compiled a list this evening."

"Oh?"

She nibbled her lip inward. "Uh-huh. We figured we need a starting place. You know, people to start looking at more closely while we wait to hear whether Chief Dallas will even order the autopsy."

123

Silence filled the space between them, magnifying Tori's tension tenfold. "That way, if he autopsies the body and it's determined we're right, we'll have a jump on finding the person responsible."

"And if he doesn't?"

Finally, a real response . . .

Scooting lower on her pillows, she gazed up at the ceiling as she did every night when they talked, the sound of Milo's voice a comfort she not only counted on but needed, as well. "What do you mean?"

"All this list making . . . won't it be a waste if he *doesn't do the right thing,* as you say."

She rolled onto her side and stared at the framed photograph of her and Milo on a picnic shortly after they started dating. One of many pictorial souvenirs of their ever-deepening relationship, this particular one was her favorite as his smile was both captivating and contagious. Even eighteen months later it still stirred up the parade of butterflies in her stomach that were normally reserved for their face-to-face encounters. "I thought that, too. But after talking to Dixie, I have to agree that someone took this man's life. And if we hit a brick wall in one place, we need to back up and take another route to the truth."

"The truth . . ." he echoed.

Nodding, she willed herself to hear the unfamiliar edge to his voice as end-of-the-day exhaustion rather than the anger it most resembled. "And we've got some really good places to start. People who will stand to gain tremendously should Clyde's land be sold to Nirvana Resorts & Spas or any of the other companies who have tried and failed to open up shop out on Fawn Lake."

She glanced at her notebook and began reading off names, pausing to give a reason why each had been added and then waiting to see if he'd weigh in with a comment or disagreement. When he said nothing, she'd move onto the next name. All too soon, though, she reached the end of the list and the reality of the silence in her ear. "Of course this isn't an exclusive list. More names will be added as we go along, but at least it's a start."

"Well, that'll certainly keep you busy."

"It sure will. It'll also have me navigating some tough waters when you consider the fact that I'm acquainted—and *even friends*—with some of the names on the list. If I don't find a delicate way to get the information I need, I could very well turn back into Tori Sinclair the Yankee, rather than Tori Sinclair the Yankee-Librarian-with-the-Sweet-Briar-Seal-of-Approval."

"It could certainly get a little dicey."

When his comment wasn't followed up with his usual offer to help, she rolled onto her back and stared at the ceiling for a second time, her thoughts running in a million different directions. Something was wrong.

"Um, so how was work today?" she finally asked.

"Good."

"Any funny stories to share?" She closed her eyes and waited for the normal onslaught of tales that left her both laughing at the ways in which third graders saw the world and wishing she'd had a teacher like Milo when she was nine.

"Gibson Jenner licked the basketball pole on the playground to see what would happen to his tongue if it touched warm metal."

"Warm metal?"

"Apparently he'd gotten into some of the Christmas movies his father had been late to pack up. Gibson was intrigued by the kid's tongue getting stuck to the cold pole. Said he wanted to see what happened if it was warm."

"And?"

"He didn't see the mosquito guts until it was too late."

She savored the welcome release her laugh afforded until she realized she was laughing alone. "Anything else?"

"Nope."

"Any impromptu staff meetings after the kids left?"

"Nope."

So they were back to "nope" again . . .

"So tell me about the rest of your day. Did you do anything after work?"

"I did."

She waited for him to respond, but when he didn't, she inquired further. "O-kay . . . What did you do?"

"I stopped at Debbie's and had her box up your favorite dessert. Then I came home, picked out a movie, and made dinner. While it was cooking, I culled through all the brochures for the best ones. I lit the candle in the center of the table. And then I sat out on the front porch and waited."

Bolting upright, she made a halfhearted attempt to grab the notebook before it slipped off her bed and onto the floor, but it was too late. "W-W-Waited?" she stammered even as reality reared its ugly head from the pit of her stomach.

"For you, Tori. I waited for *you*."

Chapter 12

Tori wasn't entirely sure how long she had laid there with the still-open cell phone pressed to her ear and tears rolling down her cheeks at the mess she'd made with Milo. But it didn't really matter.

In some ways, she wished he'd yelled and

screamed at her for her forgetfulness. At least then they could have cleared the air. Instead, he'd merely said he was tired and needed to go to sleep, his normally cheery farewell heartbreaking in its simplicity.

How could she have been so thoughtless? How could she have forgotten an evening she'd committed to not more than twelve hours earlier? Especially when it meant so much to Milo?

Yet even as the questions lined up, one behind the other, she was well aware of the matching answer for each one.

She was trying to be there for Dixie, trying to heed the woman's pleas for help. Plain and simple.

Or was it plain and simple? Was she really just trying to help Dixie or was she—as Milo implied earlier in the day—seizing on just about anything she could find in order to dodge the subject of their approaching nuptials?

Unsure of what to do, Tori snapped the phone closed inside her free hand and jumped when it vibrated in response. But as quickly as hope rushed in at the thought of a second chance phone call, it rushed back out via the ID screen and the name it boasted.

For a moment, she contemplated letting the call go to voice mail, the self-chastising she'd undergone since hanging up with Milo not completely done. Then again, if she didn't pick up, she ran the risk of a frosty shoulder at the next sewing circle meeting.

Sighing, she flipped the phone open and held it against her damp cheek. "Hi, Leona."

"Victoria? Are you okay?"

On some level she knew she should be surprised Leona's antennae had risen so fast. After all, the sixty-something's main focus in life was almost always on one of three things— herself, her beloved Paris, and whatever hot young male had crossed her path that particular day. But just as sure as those three things were, Tori also knew that beneath Leona's all-about-me exterior was a sensitive soul.

She closed her eyes against the instinct to pour out all her fears and, instead, found herself pushing everything aside for a moment or two of normalcy. "I'm fine. Just a busy day, I guess."

A slight hesitation gave way to the sound of the phone being moved as Leona addressed her faithful, long-eared sidekick. "Our dear sweet Victoria is upset about something, Paris. But she doesn't want to talk about it right now. So we're going to play along for a little while and pretend like everything is okay."

Before Tori could form a response, Leona moved on, the gradual change in volume indicating the woman's full and undivided attention was back on Tori once again. "Anyway, I was thinking about what you said this morning.

And I think I have a way that you can see all of your suspects in the same place at the same time."

Tori sat up, pulling her knees to her chest as she did. "What are you talking about?"

"I'm talking about all of the people who are beside themselves at the news of Clyde Montgomery's passing, dear."

"Tell me," she urged.

Obviously aware of the coveted information she possessed, Leona's voice took on an almost singsong quality. "Once a month, the Sweet Briar Business Association holds a breakfast meeting at the diner. Carter Johnson, bless his heart, cordons off that back room he has and tries to pretend he's doing all of us a great favor by setting out a few breakfast platters and inviting us to eat. But as my sister will tell you, Carter's eggs are runny and *shoe leather* has more flavor than his bacon."

She felt the smile as it crept across her lips and was grateful for the momentary break in her mood. "Bacon? I thought you said bacon wasn't good for a woman's figure, Leona."

"It's not."

"Then how would you know what Carter Johnson's bacon tastes like?"

The hesitation was back, this time a bit longer than the first as, once again, it coincided with the sound of the phone being held to the side. "Paris, dear? Aunt Victoria is trying to bait your mama, but Mama is above such nonsense, isn't she?"

Then, to Tori, she said, "I listen when people talk, dear . . . which is yet *another* life lesson you could learn from me if you'd pay attention."

Stifling the urge to laugh out loud, Tori took a deep breath instead. "I'm sorry, Leona. Please. Go on. About this breakfast meeting . . ."

A dramatic breath was followed by a second, and then a third. "Everyone who owns a business in town is there most months, unless someone is sick. The purpose of the meeting is supposed to be about brainstorming—you know, coming up with ways to entice people into our shops. Or to talk about some of the things storefront owners in other places are doing to reach new customers."

"Makes sense. I do something similar online with a few dozen librarians across the country."

"For every six meetings we have, maybe one actually births a good idea. Something we can do around the town square that helps us all. But most of the time, the hour is comprised of Bud sharing stories from the bar, and Carter and Bruce talking about their latest fishing trip with Robert."

Tori couldn't help but cringe at the conflict of interest that could come about if the police chief took her request seriously. Because if he did, and the autopsy determined Clyde had indeed been poisoned, two of the suspects on her list were the man's fishing buddies. "So why do you go, Leona, if the food is so bad and nothing's really accomplished in the first place?"

"Habit, I suppose." Leona took what sounded like a sip of something and then released a dreamy sigh. "Did I mention that John Peter attends the meetings, as well?"

John Peter Hendricks owned Calamity Books, a small bookshop specializing in hard-to-find first editions of some of the literary world's finest offerings. Like Leona, he ran his shop more out of a passion for his inventory than a need to bolster his financial standing. The man was a rabid reader, an interesting conversationalist, and approximately the same age as Leona . . .

"Wait. Since when have you ever been attracted to someone your own age, Leona?"

"Did I say I was attracted to him, dear?"

"Well, no, but I can hear it in your voice."

"*He's* attracted to *me*. Why else would those delightful dimples of his make an appearance every time I walk into a meeting?"

Delightful dimples?

"And why else would he make a point of sitting next to me every month? Especially when that puts him next to Shelby Jenkins, as well?" A series of tsks resonated in Tori's ear. "Bless her heart, that poor woman actually brings him *candy* from her sweet shop like some pathetic waif."

"Maybe she's just trying to be nice."

"Oh Victoria, tell me you're not really that naïve. Women who bring little offerings to a man are looking for one thing and one thing only."

She was almost afraid to ask but did anyway. "And what one thing is that, Leona?"

"To be noticed."

"So what did you bring John Peter to make him seek you out each month?"

A gasp of horror zipped across the line, making Tori pull the phone from her face until the volume was more tolerable. "I don't have to bring *anything* to get a man's attention, Victoria. All a man has to do is look at me."

She was grateful for the presence of the phone as it gave her a safety net when she rolled her eyes. Leona was a piece of work—a confident, if not completely full of herself, piece of work.

Then again, anyone capable of seeing two feet in front of their face knew reality backed up everything her friend was saying. Men of all ages *did* notice Leona. The woman could walk past a group of men on a street and, with a simple nod of her head, make them all turn in her direction.

It was a gift Tori didn't possess.

Fortunately, the lack of whatever Leona possessed hadn't mattered where Milo was concerned.

Milo.

She released her knees and let them drop back to the bed, the welcome reprieve that had been Leona's call disintegrating right before her eyes.

"You can see for yourself if you come on Monday morning."

"Monday?" she echoed.

"That's the next business association meeting. It starts at seven o'clock."

"But I can't just waltz in there . . ."

"If it were a normal meeting, I'd have to agree. But since this appears as if it will be taking on more of a celebratory feel, I think it will be fine. Especially if you're there as my guest."

"What will they be celebrating?"

"You know those buzzards Margaret Louise is always referring to when something happens in this town?"

At the mere mention of Leona's sister, Tori's smile returned. "Yeah . . ."

"They've stopped circling and they're coming in to eat."

"Excuse me?"

"Clyde's death, dear. It's cause for celebration for many of my fellow shop owners. In fact, Shelby is even bringing a box of truffles for the occasion."

She felt her stomach flip-flop. "You can't be serious."

"Oh I can and I am."

"Leona, that's awful!"

"I suppose." Leona's voice grew hushed as she, once again, addressed the garden variety bunny who was surely twitching her nose from the safety of her owner's lap. "I think we've played along with Victoria's little game long enough now, don't you, Paris?"

"Little game? What little—"

"Something happened with Milo before I called, didn't it?"

She considered protesting, considered telling Leona she was off base, but it was no use. To do so would be an exercise in futility. Leona knew her. Knew her voice, knew her inflections, knew her better than she even knew herself at times.

"Yes."

"He's grown tired of you playing detective, hasn't he?"

She swallowed. "Yes."

"I could be the kind of friend who says, I told you so. I could be the kind of friend who reminds you of all the times I warned you this would happen. But I'm not that kind of friend, Victoria."

"Gee, thanks, Leona."

"I will also choose to be the kind of friend who ignores your sarcasm, dear, because you're in pain. But it's not a becoming quality. Not at all."

"Sorry," she mumbled as she stared back up at the ceiling.

"The most logical piece of advice I can offer is this: leave the Clyde Montgomery thing alone."

"I can't."

"Because of Dixie?"

She considered her answer, shaping and tweaking it as reality saw fit. "Partly. But mostly because everything about his death adds up to murder in my book. How can I walk away from that?"

"Have you explained it that way to Milo?"

Had she?

"I think so." But, deep down inside, she knew their issue was about more than just her interest in Clyde's death. It was about their relationship and whether she truly wanted to marry him. She said as much to Leona.

"Well? Do you?"

"Do I what?" she asked.

"Do you want to marry Milo?"

Closing her eyes against the prick of tears that threatened to make a delayed encore, she searched for the steadiest voice she could find. "More than anything, Leona."

Chapter 13

Tori maneuvered the grocery bags onto the kitchen table and got straight to work making sandwiches, baking brownies, and washing fruit. It had been a long time since she and Milo had indulged in a picnic and she hoped the surprise would be a welcome one. They needed time together—time to talk, to laugh, to dream about their future, and to mend fences.

His fences.

Talking with Leona into the wee hours of the morning had made her realize something she'd failed to see prior to their talk. She'd been a lousy girlfriend as of late, her focus on everything but her relationship with Milo. It was important to be a good friend and a hard worker, but if she couldn't find time for the man she was about to marry, he had every right to question her commitment.

All she could do now was hope she hadn't pushed the envelope too far. She wanted to marry Milo, of that she had absolutely no doubt. But her actions, or lack thereof, could certainly give the opposite impression.

She hoped the surprise picnic she was putting together would be the first step in letting him know how she felt. And if it worked as she planned, she'd have Leona to thank for the notion of a peace offering, even if their respective definitions of that word couldn't have been more different.

For Tori, a picnic was the perfect peace offering. For Leona, the perfect peace offering involved a very different kind of blanket and absolutely no food items except for those that came in a spray can.

"Victoria?"

She pulled her hand from the cabinet above the stove and spun around, her initial surprise morphing into happiness at the sight of Leona's twin sister standing just inside the back door.

"Margaret Louise! I didn't hear you come in. How are you?"

"I s'pose that's why you jumped clear out of your skin, huh?" Margaret Louise made her way across the kitchen and peered into the mixing bowl on the counter. "Everyone loves the deer 'til it eats from the garden."

"Excuse me?"

Hooking a finger over her shoulder, Margaret Louise shrugged. "Can't count how many times you've told me I should just walk right in. But when I do, you jump like a nervous chicken."

She laughed. "Do chickens really jump?"

The woman pointed her pudgy hand at the box of brownie mix to the side of the empty bowl. "If you needed some brownies, Victoria, all you had to do was ask. I'd have made 'em for you lickety-split."

"And they'd probably taste a million times better than mine. But I want to make these ones by myself."

"These ones?" Margaret Louise slowly turned atop her sensible Keds, her ever-present smile widening as the picnic basket Tori had commandeered from the crawl space came into view. "Ooooh, someone's goin' on a picnic."

"That's right. I'm surprising Milo with a picnic once I get all of this together."

"Can I help?"

"I was, um, kinda wanting to put all of this together myself." She finished pouring the required oil into a measuring cup, grateful for the diversion the task provided from having to see any disappointment on Margaret Louise's face. "I've been kind of neglecting Milo lately and, well, it's time to make things right."

When the liquid reached the desired line on the cup, she transferred it to the bowl along with the mix from the box. "I want to be able to tell him that I put all of this together on my own . . . for him." Once the egg was added along with the correct amount of water, she turned around and swept her hand toward the kitchen table. "But I'd love for you to stay and keep me company while I bake these. Seems like forever since we've had any real time together."

Margaret Louise grinned and claimed a chair alongside the grocery bags Tori had yet to fully unpack. "There ain't no flies on you, Victoria. Never is, if you ask me."

She searched the utensil drawer for her favorite mixing spoon and began to stir the mix, the ingredients growing darker with each rotation of her hand. "Being busy isn't an excuse for neglecting the people I love."

"You ain't been neglectin' Dixie . . ."

She stopped stirring long enough to look a question in Margaret Louise's direction.

"Don't matter none, really. Lots of people love you, Victoria, and I understand that I can't be the only one playin' Ned to your Nancy, or Nora to your Nick."

"Ned to my Nancy?"

Margaret Louise nodded, her gaze firmly planted on the mixing bowl. "Ned. Nancy Drew's friend. Why, that boy was like a vault when it came to the things she told him. And Nora, why, she was funny and smart and helped her husband find the truth in *The Thin Man*."

Tori spooned the batter into the waiting brownie pan and made sure to spread it around evenly. "No, I know who Ned and Nora are in relation to their respective sleuths, but I don't understand why you brought them up."

"Because you're usin' a different Nora." Margaret Louise pointed at the cabinet above Tori's head. "You got any white chocolate on your bakin' shelf, Victoria?"

"Uh . . ." She forced herself to shift conversational direction even though her thoughts were still on her friend's nod to some of Tori's favorite mysteries. "I think so. Why?"

"Makes a nice drizzle on top of brownies when they first come out of the oven."

"I'll keep that in mind. Sounds like something Milo would love." She opened the oven door and slid the pan into the preheated oven. When the door was shut, she set the timer for thirty minutes. "I'm still lost on the other part, though. The part about Ned and Nora."

"Don't mind me none, Victoria. Even Melissa thinks I'm bein' overly sensitive."

She reached into the grocery bag, only to pull her empty hand out just as quickly. "Margaret Louise, I don't have any idea what you're talking about."

"Your new case. The one you're workin' on with Dixie." Margaret Louise reached into the bag, plucked out the apples and grapes, and handed them to Tori. "I believe you were lookin' for these."

Tori nodded.

"Why, I must admit, I was a little surprised when Leona told me Dixie was ridin' shotgun this time, but I s'pose we need to take turns with these sorts of things." Then, leaning forward, Margaret Louise lowered her voice. "But, Victoria? Dixie ain't always quiet. Sometimes, when you least expect it, all them beans she insists on eatin' every night show back up at the worst times."

Holding the grapes in her left hand and the apple bag in her right, Tori stepped backward, the image her friend had created in her mind making her laugh out loud. "That was probably more information about Dixie than I really needed, but thanks."

"Seems that might be somethin' you need to

know if you're goin' to be sneakin' 'round tryin' to catch a killer with Dixie by your side."

Ahhhh . . .

"I didn't choose Dixie as my accomplice in this whole Clyde Montgomery thing. *She* picked *me*."

Relief sagged Margaret Louise's shoulders. "I should've known you can't tell the size of the turnips by lookin' at their tops."

Tori set the fruit beside the sink, set a colander in its base, and turned on the faucet. Apple by apple and grape bunch by grape bunch, she washed her way through both bags. When she was done, she set them aside to air dry before housing them in the large cooler she'd soon fill with ice packs from the freezer. "Dixie asked for my help. At first, I thought she was wrong. Clyde was ninety-one. But then I changed my mind. I think there's a strong chance his death was helped along."

"Helped along by what?"

"Arsenic."

If Margaret Louise was surprised, she didn't let on. Instead, she jumped on board with Tori's theory as if it was not only plausible but probable. "Lots of ways someone can get that into their system."

"Which is why my list of potential suspects is as long as it is," Tori mused. "There's an awful lot of people in this town who had motive to want to see Clyde dead."

"Leona told me she's takin' you to the business meetin' with her on Monday."

Retracing her steps back to the table, she reached into the last remaining grocery bag and pulled out the sandwich rolls. "From what Leona says, all my suspects should be there."

"You might want to double-check some of those suspects with Kate. She might have a little insight beyond anything my sister may have offered."

She set the bag of rolls down and met Margaret Louise's expectant gaze. "Who's Kate?"

"That's the sweet thing that's been helpin' taste test some of my recipes for the cookbook. Why, she loves food every bit as much as Clyde did."

Tori froze. "Clyde?"

"Yes, Clyde. And don't you go lookin' all surprised on me. I told you months ago that Clyde was one of my taste testers. Why, he was such a help back when I was makin' my sweet potato pie. Seemed only right to have him help me with my cookbook. Kate was an unexpected bonus."

"But who is this Kate person and what does she have to do with Clyde?" she repeated.

"Kate Loggins. She's just a little bit older than me, I think. Maybe a little more. Anyway, I reckon she was friendly with Clyde on account of them both bein' creative types. Why, when I'd come by with my next recipe in the mornin', I'd find them both sittin' on that sunporch of Clyde's—him paintin' and her writin' in some

143

journal he gave her. Guess the view of Fawn Lake made her as happy as it did Clyde."

"Was she his girlfriend or something?"

Margaret Louise made a face. "Even though Clyde lost his beloved Deidre to cancer 'bout four years ago, he wasn't lookin' to move on. Besides, Kate was a good twenty years his junior."

Tori tucked the information aside and carried the rolls to the cutting board, where she proceeded to slice them in preparation for the meat and cheese she'd soon be adding. "I wonder why Dixie didn't mention her."

"Clyde was very regimented with his days. He painted in the mornin', which was when Kate was most often there. Then he had tea with his son, Beau. Clyde treasured that time because it gave him someone to talk 'bout Deidre with. Then he'd read until it was time for lunch. That's also the time he took visits from whoever was tryin' to convince him to sell his land on that particular day. He told me the tactics they used gave Kate fodder for her stories. As soon as he'd kick them out, as he always did, he'd make his lunch.

"Once he started feelin' poorly 'bout a month or so ago, Home Fare started bringin' his lunch—which, between you and me, he must've hated on account of how much he valued his indepen-dence. After lunch he took his nap in the same chair he used for paintin' and enjoyin' his view."

"It sounds like you saw him a lot."

"Nah. Not really. Tried to stop by once a week with whatever recipes I'd perfected at that time. Didn't matter what day I chose, his schedule was always the same."

"When was the last time you used him as a taste tester?" she asked.

"Just before the Home Fare folks got involved. In fact, I didn't know anything 'bout that until Georgina told me about his death. Had I known, I'd have made all his meals myself."

Tori glanced at the timer on the brownies and moved on to the basket she'd readied with napkins, plastic cups, and wine goblets. "So how would I go about finding this Kate person?"

"You ask me."

"Okay," she teased. "Can you help me find Kate?"

"Does that mean I'm part of the investigatin'?"

She had to laugh. "Do you want to be?"

"That's a fool thing to ask, Victoria. Of course, I do." Margaret Louise struggled to a stand and then pointed out Tori's back door just as the oven timer chimed. "You could bring along a bundle of those daffodils you've got bloomin' in your backyard. They'd make a mighty pretty center-piece on your picnic blanket."

Yet another good suggestion and one that Tori would implement as she was carrying the picnic basket out to her car. Reaching for the oven mitt that hung on a hook above the stove, she opened the door and inhaled the sweet aroma. "Mmmm . . . These smell so good, Margaret Louise."

"Now remember the white chocolate. You'll thank me after the picnic, Victoria."

Tori set the piping hot brownie pan on the top of the stove and reached for the box of white chocolate baking squares. One by one she unwrapped each square then dropped them into the double boiler Margaret Louise had quietly set on the front left burner. "So is there anyone you think we should be looking at extra closely? Anyone with a really strong motive?"

Margaret Louise turned back to Tori, a triumphant smile working its way across her rounded face at the sight of the melting chocolate. "You mean besides Shelby Jenkins?"

Tori stopped stirring, only to resume the motion at Margaret Louise's insistence. "You stop stirrin', it's going to get lumpy. It needs to be smooth in order to drizzle."

She slowed the pace of her hand and looked up at her friend. "Why would Shelby Jenkins have a strong motive for killing Clyde? I mean, her sweetshop does a good business already, even without the presence of a big resort."

"True. But when her daddy is some big shot at Nirvana Resorts, you can't help but wonder if she was workin' some sort of inside track. Especially when Clyde loved her chocolate-covered cherries the way he did."

This time the spoon slid into the chocolate when she stepped back. "Chocolate-covered cherries?"

Margaret Louise stepped around Tori, expertly fishing the spoon from the melted chocolate with the help of a pair of tongs from the utensil drawer. "This is ready to drizzle on the brownies now, Victoria."

When Tori didn't move, Margaret Louise took over, drizzling white chocolate across the top of the brownies with an expert hand.

She tried to focus on the drizzling process so she could duplicate the lattice-like effect on her own in the future, but she couldn't. Not really anyway. "How often did Clyde eat these chocolate-covered cherries?"

Margaret Louise's broad shoulders rose and fell with the woman's shrug. "Once a week, maybe. And they had to be made by her . . . not one of her employees. He said she was the best at makin' them the way his grandmother used to make 'em when he was a little boy."

Tori swirled the information around in her head as Margaret Louise continued. "Clyde Montgomery was a sucker for tradition. He liked the recipes that reminded him of his childhood. He liked his days to follow the same schedule. He liked to look through old photo albums in his chair before he'd drift off for his daily nap. And it's why he refused to sell even so much as an acre of his land no matter how much money was waved in front of his face."

"I imagine they offered him a lot of money, no?"

"Probably more than you or I could ever dream 'bout." Margaret Louise placed the empty saucepan into the sink and filled it with soapy water. "Have you ever seen Clyde's place?"

"Dixie took me the other day."

"Then you saw the view he had from that sunporch of his, yes?"

She closed her eyes at the memory, the sense of peace afforded by that view washing over her once again. "Yes."

"Well, it wasn't just the view that Clyde was desperate to hang on to."

Her eyes flew open. "It wasn't?"

"No. Why, it was more the fact that his daddy looked out at that same lake every day. So, too, did his granddaddy, and his granddaddy before him."

"So it was the tradition," she whispered. "He didn't want to give up his link to the past."

"That 'bout sums it up."

Tori looked around at the various picnic foods now stretched across virtually every square inch of available counter space, her mind working overtime on everything she was hearing. "It's kind of ironic, don't you think?"

"What is, Victoria?"

"That Clyde was fighting to preserve his past and the memories he held dear, while the folks at tomorrow's meeting were fighting to change the very essence of this town forever."

A hush fell across the kitchen as both women became lost in thought, the fixings for Tori and Milo's picnic untouched around them. Eventually, though, Margaret Louise spoke, her simple response sending a chill down Tori's spine.

"Sure seems the meetin' folks won, now don't it, Victoria?"

Chapter 14

Tori was waiting atop the rocky ledge that served as the public access to Fawn Lake when she heard his car approaching, the excitement she wanted to feel over his arrival counterbalanced by the apprehension that came with the unknown.

Would Milo still be angry over being stood up? Would the hurt over her lackadaisical attitude about their wedding still be as pervasive as it was on the phone the previous night?

The questions themselves were silly, of course, especially in light of the fact that a yes was not only a given but more than warranted. She'd been selfish the past few months, her thoughts and her energy on everything and everyone except Milo.

But that was about to change. She owed her future husband that much.

Taking one final peek at the red-checked blanket and the daffodils that graced its center, Tori took a deep breath and let it out slowly. There was no reason to be nervous. Milo loved her every bit as much as she loved him. They just needed time. Time to be together, to focus on their future as man and wife.

When he cut the engine, she walked to the top of the ledge and waited for him to step out of his car, the detailed drawing Margaret Louise had walked her through clutched tightly in his hand.

"You found the place, I see," she called out, the tremor in her voice failing to mask the nervousness her mental pep talk had been unable to vanquish.

Milo lifted his chin until he pinpointed her location, the less than enthusiastic smile on his face increasing the moisture in her hands. "What's going on? Why did you need me to meet you here?"

"Come on up and see for yourself." She knew she was being cryptic, but there was a part of her that was afraid he'd get back into his car if she told him it was a picnic lunch. After all, she'd hurt him terribly, and the mere mention of a picnic really didn't go far in smoothing that kind of emotion. She had to hope that the climb up to the top of the ledge and the reality of what she'd set up for them would have more impact than simple words.

After a momentary hesitation, he tucked the drawing into his back pocket and began the slow climb up the side of the ledge, the huffing and puffing that had accompanied her effort next to nil with his. "So, what is this all about . . ." His question disappeared into the air as he reached the top and took in the blanket, flowers, and nearby basket.

"Ta da!" Tori flung her arms out to the side and did a little turn on the edge of the blanket. "So? What do you think?"

He looked from the blanket to Tori and back again, the faintest hint of a smile tugging at the edges of his mouth. "How did you get all of that up here on your own?"

She pointed to the opposite side of the ledge and the more forgiving grade it boasted. "I came that way, though I'm sure I was quite the sight struggling to get the basket around that tree over there. Step to the side too much and you're lucky if you don't fall all the way down the hill."

"You're nuts, you know that?" he finally said as his gaze met and held hers.

"Nuts about you, yes." She put one trembling hand inside the other as she took yet another calming breath. "I went to the store this morning and tried to think of all the things you might like. Then I went back to the house and baked up a batch of brownies and got everything together."

"And the map?" he asked, reaching into his pocket and retrieving the drawing she'd done with the handful of crayons Margaret Louise had supplied.

She felt her face warm under his scrutiny and looked away. "Margaret Louise helped me with that. I—I'd never been here before."

"So what's in the basket besides brownies?"

Careful not to get too excited by the inquiry, she plopped down beside the basket and considered the responses she could give, opting to go the route Leona would take in a similar situation. "How about you sit down next to me and find out?"

His laugh warmed her from the inside out, allowing her to finally relax. "Don't mind if I do."

As soon as he sat, she reached for the basket, her hands still shaking despite the positive signs. "To start us off, I figured we could have a little—"

He reached across the blanket and pulled her close, the feel of his arms around her midsection finally permitting a real smile. "You can show me what's in there in a minute. After I get to hold you for a while."

She snuggled against his chest, the smell and

the nearness of the man lifting the stress of the last fifteen hours or so off her shoulders. "Oh, Milo. I'm so very sorry I forgot about last night. I—I have no explanation beyond stupidity. It certainly wasn't a case of not wanting to see you. Please believe that."

A momentary pause gave way to the kind of kiss that let her know everything was going to be just fine. Wrapping her arms around his neck, she took comfort in the reassurance his lips offered. When the kiss finally broke, she tapped his nose with the tip of her finger. "I love you, Milo."

"I love you, too, Tori. It's why October can't come fast enough for me," he said by way of a huskier than normal tone. "I want to be your husband. I want to come home to you every night and wake up with you every morning. And I want to know you feel the same way."

"I do. It's just that . . . well"—she pulled her hands into her lap and searched for the best way to explain how they'd gotten to that point—"I guess I needed the library events during the holidays to go well . . . and then the stuff with Charlotte Devereaux came up and I couldn't walk away from figuring out what happened to her husband and . . ." She let the words disappear as she saw them for what they were—excuses.

He reached out, tilting her chin upward until their eyes met. "I'm not questioning any of that, Tori. I'm really not. I just want to know that our

wedding is important, too. Because if it's not . . .
I mean, if you're not ready yet . . . we can wait.
Or if I'm not the right guy—"

She covered his mouth with her index finger
and shook her head. "Trust me, Milo, you're the
right guy. The *only* guy that's right for me. I just
need to give myself permission to focus on my
own life for a while instead of everyone else's."

At his nod of agreement and the tender tilt to
his head, she scooted backward and pulled the
picnic basket into the now empty space between
them. "Today is our day. Just you and me. Time
for us to catch up on everything we've missed in
the busy-ness lately."

Finally, the smile she'd come to draw on for
strength over the past two years reached into his
eyes and made them twinkle. "Sounds good to
me."

Over the next two hours they ate their way
through the food she'd prepared, their progress
hampered only by snuggle breaks, kiss-athons,
and endless laughter about everything from the
latest jokes making the rounds of the third graders
at Sweet Briar Elementary, to details of the
ongoing war of words between Rose and Leona.

"Think those two will ever get along?" Milo
asked as he fit the last bite of brownie into his
mouth and then flopped onto his back to peer up
at the clouds as they marched across the spring
sky.

Tori gathered up the last of the food and put it in the basket before claiming a spot beside him. "Who? Rose and Leona?"

At Milo's nod, she laughed. "Don't be fooled by their antics. Underneath Leona calling Rose an old goat, and Rose taking potshots at Leona's prissiness, they care about each other immensely. If they didn't, Leona never would have given one of Paris's babies to Rose, and Rose never would have teamed up with Leona to get rid of Sweet Briar's very own Grinch back in December."

"I suppose you're right." He pointed to the sky, drawing her attention to an oddly shaped cloud as he did. "See that one right there? Looks sort of like a kayak, don't you think?"

She squinted against the late afternoon rays, trying her best to see Milo's vision. Unfortunately, all she saw was a long cloud. "Do you like to kayak?"

"I love it. Would love to give it a go in the ocean one day."

Rolling onto her side, she studied the curve of his cheek as he continued to search for shapes in the sky. "We could go ocean kayaking on our honeymoon . . ."

He turned his head, his gaze mingling with hers as she offered a playful wink. "We could, I suppose. Heck, there are lots of things we could try depending on where we go."

"Like?"

"Like zip-lining if we did a mountain/woodsy kind of trip. White-water rafting if our location offered a river. Ocean kayaking if we gravitate toward a coast."

The animation in his eyes nearly took her breath away, and she found herself hoping the next six months would fly by just so they could live out some of the things he mentioned. "That all sounds wonderful, Milo."

He, too, rolled onto his side, his hand reaching out across the space between them to tuck an errant strand of light brown hair behind her ear. "Then again, there's a part of me that just wants to hole up in front of a fireplace, holding you all day. Or wrap my arms around you as we jump waves together."

"Both of those sound great, too." And they did. Basically anything and everything sounded great so long as they experienced it together.

"We need to pick something soon. So I can make the reservations and so we can start looking forward to it."

"Then let's pick."

He stared into her eyes for a moment then rolled onto his back and got to his feet. "Wait right here. I'll be back in a minute."

She felt her smile disappear as he headed in the opposite direction. "Wait. Where are you going?"

"To get the brochures."

"You brought them?" she called after him.

He stopped just before he headed down the side of the ledge and grinned back at her over his shoulder. "I guess I was hoping that wherever that map was taking me would give us a chance to look through the stuff from the travel agent and finally pick our honeymoon spot."

"Then hurry up, will you? I can't wait to see what you got." Then, while he headed toward the car, she collected the last napkin or two from the picnic blanket and tossed it into the basket. When the blanket was clear, she pulled the closed basket into the middle once again so they could use its lid as a place to set the brochures.

Five minutes later, Milo was back, a burgeoning manila envelope in his hands and an ultrawide smile on his face. "Here we go." He set the packet on the top of the basket and lowered himself to the blanket beside Tori. Then, reaching inside the envelope, he extracted two distinct bundles. "This bundle"—he held up the stack in his left hand—"has mountain-y kinds of places—with cabins and lakes and rivers. And this other stack is more about beaches. Popular touristy ones and more secluded ones, too."

"If we go beach, I think I'd prefer secluded."

He placed both stacks on the lid and then slid his left arm around her waist. "I couldn't agree more. And by its very nature, a cabin in the mountains would give us that secluded kind of feel, too."

She couldn't help but smile as she imagined cuddling up with Milo in front of a fireplace after a day spent hiking or rafting or simply sitting on a dock tossing bread crumbs to the fish. Just the simple notion of a date that didn't have to be rushed because of work or other commitments was fun to imagine.

"What are you thinking about right now?" he asked as he nuzzled her cheek with his chin. "You look so happy."

She pulled back just enough to run her hands through the burnished brown hair he kept short on the sides, yet longish on top. "I am happy. Because I'm here with you."

He tilted his head into the sun, the dwindling rays picking out the amber flecks in his warm brown eyes. "No, I meant at that moment . . . while you were looking down at the stack of brochures. Your smile came from deep inside. It was beautiful."

She glanced down at the brochures and shrugged. "Oh, that. I guess I was just imagining being alone with you in a cabin somewhere with no worries or cares except the two of us. For an *entire week*."

The dimples that usually unleashed the butterflies in her stomach lived up to their reputation as his smile stretched wide across his face. "Aww, Tori, you have no idea how much I needed to hear you say that."

"But that was easy. It's how I feel." She pointed at the stacks. "So? What are you leaning toward? Mountain or beach?"

His gaze dropped to the stacks just before his hands did. "I'm torn. I've got two favorites in each category and I'm just not sure which would be best."

"Well, whatever we don't pick we can go back and do on our first, fifth, tenth, twenty-fifth, and fiftieth anniversaries." Feeling the warmth of his gaze directed back on her, she pointed again at the brochures. "So show me what you've narrowed it down to."

He shook his head. "I can't do that. Maybe something that speaks to you will be outside the four I've found."

"Trust me, I know enough about you at this point to know that if you've narrowed it to four, they'd probably be the same four I'd have zeroed in on, too."

A quick and thorough search of her face resulted in an endearing shrug. Then, with careful hands, he unleashed the stacks from their rubber bands and liberated the top two from each pile. "First, the mountain ones. This one"—he handed her the top one—"is for a place in Tennessee. The Smoky Mountains, to be exact. It's got lots of hiking, rafting, and kayaking opportunities. And the cabins are pretty awesome, too. This second one is up north in Vermont. Same basic stuff with the possibility of seeing some moose added into the mix. The cabins look good but don't have the romantic feel of the place in Tennessee."

She flipped through both brochures, her excitement over their looming honeymoon accelerating rapidly. Each pamphlet held its own intrigue, but the cabin company in Tennessee gripped her interest more. She said as much to Milo as she set that one aside and pointed toward the two beach selections he'd made. "Okay, and now for the beach?"

He handed the first of the tropical brochures to her, adding some commentary as he did. "This one is for a resort on the Gulf Coast of Florida. It has everything you could want to do—snorkeling trips, ocean kayaking, swimming, nightlife, et cetera. That all looks great, but I'm not sure how well it would hold up in the private-time category."

She glanced through the pictures depicted in the flyer and then back up at Milo. "I definitely want some private time no matter where we go."

"Me, too." He took the brochure back and dropped it onto the stack that didn't make the final cut. "And then there's this one. It's here in South Carolina but down at the very edge. It has lots of stuff to do if we want, yet they also do a really good job of making you feel like you can be alone regardless of how full the resort might be at any given time."

The brochure itself was more like a small book with each page devoted to a different aspect. There was a page for water activities, a page for resort activities, a page for on-site restaurants, a page highlighting favorite sightseeing spots in the local town, and finally, a page that boasted the specific amenities offered in each guest room.

"Wow, this place really outdid itself, didn't it?" She reclined back against Milo's chest and made her way through the entire brochure a second time, the pictures the company had selected for the advertisement making it easy for Tori not only to imagine being there, but also to motivate her into putting it on her personal vacation bucket list. "I like it. And I want to go here with you sometime soon. But honestly? I have to say the cabin in the Smoky Mountains feels more honeymoon-ish to me."

His arms tightened around her waist as he released a happy sigh. "We really are a good fit, aren't we?"

She peered up at him, surprised. "You were leaning toward that one, too?"

"It was top on the stack for a reason." He met and held her gaze with the kind of look that got the just-settled butterflies on the move once again. "So it's settled then? I can call and make the reservations?"

She nodded then looked back down at the booklet in her hand, the pull of the South

Carolina beach resort refusing to go lightly. "But we can check this place out one day, too, right?"

"Sure. Why not?" Milo continued talking, his thoughts, his energy now entirely focused on the trip they'd be taking in conjunction with their autumn wedding.

She heard some of what he said, even processed a little bit, too. But somewhere between talk of white-water rafting and the fire he'd build in their cabin's fireplace each night, she found herself looking at the resort brochure in her lap. There was something about the look and feel of the vacation destination that sucked you in. She supposed some of it was the pictures themselves—after all, who could resist the image of walking hand in hand with your special someone along the ocean's edge or the thought of sitting on a porch swing reading away the hours while cuddled up in someone's arms?

There was no doubt the resort held immense appeal. Or at the very least, the company had a top-notch marketing team . . .

Slowly, she turned the brochure over to the last page, her finger guiding her eyes down to the bold yet tastefully written name centered across the bottom: Nirvana Resorts & Spas.

"Nirvana Resorts . . ." she whispered.

"What was that, baby?"

She raised the brochure into the air and gave it

a little shake. "Nirvana Resorts. This is one of their places."

"You lost me."

Leaning forward, she pulled her back from its resting spot against his chest and scooted around to face him. "Nirvana Resorts. That's one of the companies who was trying so hard to purchase Clyde Montgomery's land on the other side of this very lake."

When he didn't respond, she continued, the excitement she felt over the unexpected connection bringing her suspect list back into the forefront of her mind. "Apparently, from what Margaret Louise said, Shelby Jenkins's father is some bigwig at Nirvana Resorts. Toss in the fact that she made hand-dipped chocolate-covered cherries for Clyde on a weekly basis and, well, she not only has a possible motive, she also had the means with which to poison him over time."

Silence fell around them as he stuffed all but the Nirvana brochure back into the manila envelope and then tucked it under his arm, pushing off the blanket as he did. "Well, it appears as if the real world has come knocking once again, huh?"

She looked up from the brochure. "I'm sorry, what?"

He waved off her question with a flick of his hand and then held it out to her as she, too, rose to her feet. "Never mind. It doesn't matter." Then, as she stood where he indicated, he shook out the blanket and folded it into fourths, tucking it under his arm alongside the envelope.

"Hey . . . what about this one?" she asked as she held the Nirvana Resort brochure in his direction. "Don't you want to keep this with all the rest?"

"Nah, you keep it. Seems that's where your focus is these days anyway."

Chapter 15

It was five minutes to seven when Tori pulled into the parking lot and cut the engine outside of Johnson's Diner, Leona and Paris holding court in her passenger seat like the royalty they knew themselves to be.

"When I get my cable show, that woman will be featured often." Leona's chin pointed toward the pleasantly plump woman making her way toward the diner. "In fact, between you and me, *she's* one of the reasons I've decided to include a ten-minute segment entirely devoted to such fashion faux pas."

Her mouth agape, Tori took a moment to study the totality of Shelby Jenkins's attire.

"You'd think such things would be part of every little girl's upbringing, especially here in the south, but it isn't." Leona lifted Paris from her towel-draped lap and held her at eye level. "Mama has taught *you*, though, hasn't she, my precious little angel?"

Tori reined in her bottom lip, only to have it fall back down as she made a mental note of Shelby's clothes—the attractive lavender pantsuit, the simple yet tasteful white blouse—and came up empty in the aforementioned faux pas category.

"Ahhh, yes. And now we see the reason for her failed attempt at fashion . . ."

Shifting her gaze to the left, Tori watched as John Peter Hendricks, the owner of Calamity Books, stepped from a white convertible coupe parked beneath a tree on the far side of the parking lot and made his way toward the diner. Like his car, which looked to be in pristine condition, John Peter was flawless in his appearance. His lightly salted hair, still thick enough to sport a stylish flair, shimmered in the early morning sun while his freshly pressed khaki trousers and collared black dress shirt solicited a gentle sigh from Leona.

"One look at that man and you can just tell he's not from Sweet Briar. The grooming alone speaks to a sense of cultural superiority that certainly isn't native to a place where flannel and beer bellies are the norm." Leona handed Paris to Tori, removed the towel from her lap, and then ran a quick hand down the front and sides of her dusty rose pencil skirt. "He, of all people, will take one look at Shelby and know that women do not wear white pumps before Memorial Day. It simply isn't done."

"Well, that answered one of my questions," she murmured between pets of the nose-twitching animal now nestled in her unprotected lap.

Leona gasped. "Victoria! Please tell me you know the proper time to wear white!"

At her ensuing silence, Leona plucked Paris from Tori's lap and opened the car door, the exasperation and disappointment on the woman's face unmistakable. "Do you know how disheartening it is to give so much of yourself and your expertise to someone, only to find out everything you've worked so hard to teach them has fallen on deaf ears, Victoria?"

Tori pushed open her own door and stepped onto the asphalt parking lot, the sudden burst of sun on her face doing little to rival the shame-induced warmth she felt in her cheeks as she turned to face Leona over the roof of her car. "Wow. You're good. Really, really good."

Leona's momentary surprise gave way to a look of intense satisfaction. "You're just now realizing that, dear?"

Shaking her head, Tori came around the front of her car and fell into step with Leona as they made their way toward the diner. There were so many things she wanted to know from the people she'd see inside. She knew it was naïve to think the killer would impale himself on one of the seemingly innocent questions she'd prepared in her head when she should have been sleeping, but still, she hoped.

"You never said how the picnic went," Leona said, stopping midway to the door. "It didn't go well, did it?"

Oh, how she wanted to correct Leona, to tell her that everything went exactly as Tori had hoped. But she couldn't. Because it hadn't.

"Can we just not do this right now? Please?" Tori continued past Leona onto the sidewalk, her kitten heels making a soft yet hurried staccato sound against the concrete. "If we don't get inside, we might miss something."

"The only thing you'll miss this early in the meeting is Carter's runny eggs and Shelby's ridiculous smile when she thinks John Peter has chosen his chair because of *her*."

"That's okay . . . it sounds fun." She cringed at the almost singsong quality of her voice and knew Leona saw through it as the diversion tactic it was, but it would have to do. If she gave words to the way she'd messed up her time with Milo, they'd never make it inside. And while there was certainly a part of her that wanted to leave the whole question of Clyde's untimely demise to someone other than herself, the curious side of her couldn't walk away.

Not yet anyway.

Not before she had the answers Dixie needed.

When she reached the front door, Tori glanced over her shoulder in her friend's direction. "Leona, *please*. I can't go into this meeting as your guest if you're not there, too."

After a long hesitation that included a nearly lethal stare down, Leona finally closed the remaining gap, the string of muttered words emanating from between her recently plumped lips drawing a smile from Tori. "Thank you, Leona."

"Don't think I'm done with my questions, dear. They're simply on hold until you're done playing Nancy Drew."

"Fair enough." She tugged the glass door open and stepped to the side for Leona to pass. "Now, why am I here with you again?" she whispered.

"So you can figure out which one of my fellow shopkeepers poisoned Clyde Montgomery." Leona hoisted Paris to eye level. "I don't know how Auntie Victoria ever functioned without me."

Resisting the urge to give Leona a dose of her own medicine in the lethal stare department, Tori gestured toward the back of the restaurant and the half-dozen or so faces she recognized from around town. "What's the reason we're telling everyone that I'm here . . . at a meeting I have no business being at?"

"Oh. That." Leona tapped her chin with her

fingertip, narrowing her eyes in thought as she did. "I think the most believable thing would be to say you're shadowing me this week."

"Shadowing you?" Tori parroted.

"Yes. To see how I live on a daily basis. Since, of course, you aspire to be just like me before it's too late."

She closed her eyes and did a mental count to ten. "Okay, and let's suppose I did"—she studied her friend through parted lashes—"*aspire to be you,* Leona . . . why would this meeting help me do that?"

Leona glanced at the ceiling as she considered Tori's words. "Well, it would allow you to see how I conduct myself in a public forum. And it would allow you a bird's-eye view of how I interact with men in a way that doesn't insult my intelligence yet has them all looking at me and imagining what it would be like to be seen with me."

It took every ounce of restraint Tori could muster not to laugh out loud, but somehow, she managed. Barely. Nonetheless, there was something in her reaction—perhaps the flinch or the rapid swallow—that brought Leona's narrowed eyes back on her.

"Is there something wrong with what I said, dear?"

Uh-oh.

She swallowed again. "Shadowing, that sounds

good to me, Leona. Only maybe we could refrain from giving the reasons."

Leona paused before offering a quick nod. "Perhaps that's best. We wouldn't want word getting back to Milo prematurely."

"Word?"

"That you're working on your personal appeal in case you're unsuccessful at saving your engagement."

This time when Tori closed her eyes, it wasn't about counting or finding patience. No, this time it was in reaction to the jolt Leona's words sent through her body.

Was Leona right? Was her engagement to Milo really in jeopardy? She shuddered at the thought.

"Leona, can we just get to the meeting now, please?"

Lifting her chin a hairbreadth, Leona led the way toward the diner's back corner and the handful of business owners it hosted.

Sure enough, just as Leona had predicted, Shelby Jenkins and her stylish white pumps were positioned beside John Peter Hendricks at the makeshift buffet table Carter Johnson had set up for the occasion. On the other side of the table, helping himself to a generous serving of eggs, was Travis Haggarty, one of the two councilmen who represented Sweet Briar's business district.

"Victoria!"

A glance to her right delivered the face that

went with the familiar voice. "Georgina . . . hi." Breaking stride with Leona, Tori hurried over to the table and bent down long enough to offer the mayor a warm hug. "I guess I should have realized you'd be here this morning but I didn't connect the dots. How are you?"

Georgina pulled her napkin from her lap and laid it beside her breakfast plate. "Well, just fine. So what brings you here"—the mayor gestured down the table at the smattering of business owners already seated, enjoying their coffee and breakfast—"to a business owners' meeting?"

She shifted her weight from foot to foot and hoped her voice was steady, her words believable. "I'm . . . um . . . shadowing Leona today and this is her first stop."

Georgina's brows arched. "Shadowing Leona? Why?"

Why indeed . . .

"Well, I—I'm thinking of doing an adult book club and . . . she seems to think I, um, could recruit members here."

Georgina's gaze flitted toward the buffet table, where Leona had managed to wink and blink her way to the front of the line, before pinning Tori once again. "Don't you think a simple flyer would have sufficed?"

A swipe at the sides of her skirt did little to erase the sudden clamminess in her hands as she cast about for a response that sounded less dumb.

"I—I thought that, too. But Leona insisted. She said the likelihood of people responding to a flyer wasn't as promising as a direct invitation."

She followed Georgina's focus back to Leona, using the momentary reprieve from her friend's scrutiny to breathe.

An adult book club? Where on earth had that come from?

"She's probably right. People do get busy."

"They do."

"Well, count me in then."

Confused, she turned back to Georgina. "Count you in?" she repeated.

"That's right. Count me in."

She worked to make sense of the mayor's words but came up empty. "I'm sorry, Georgina, I think I must have zoned out or something. Count you in for what?"

"Your new book club."

"My new book—" She stopped and took another, longer breath, this one accompanied by a fair amount of mental chastising for straying from the truth in the first place.

Her new book club . . .

Feeling the weight of Georgina's stare, she scrambled for a way to extricate herself from the quicksand beneath her feet. "Since my being here is really just to see whether there might be any interest, I'll have to get back to you with details. If we have interest, I'll proceed ahead with definitive plans. If there's not, I'll let it go. Sound good?"

"No."

The single word, spoken clearly and succinctly, hovered in the air between them, sending a skitter of unease through Tori's thoughts. "Do—do you have a better suggestion? Something you think will work better?" she whispered.

Georgina's nod was followed by an invitation from the woman's index finger to move closer. "It doesn't matter how many rocks you turn over, Victoria. When all is said and done, the man is still dead. So let it go. *Now*."

Chapter 16

The monthly meeting of the Sweet Briar Business Association was like every other meeting Tori had ever been to, save, of course, for the lack of glazed eyes and the cake that showed up in the center of the table just as the formal portion of the meeting was drawing to a close.

"I ordered the cake from Debbie's Bakery last night and she had it ready for me at six thirty this morning." Carter positioned a stack of small plates next to the cake and topped them off with a handful of forks. "Debbie was sorry she couldn't make it today but Colby has some sort of publicity event in Columbia and he wanted her to go along."

Lana Morris flipped to the back of her leather-bound day planner and tapped a finger to the lined page. "According to my notes, we don't have any birthdays in the group this month."

Carter made a long cut down the cake, stopping when he reached the edge. "It's not a birthday cake."

"It's a celebration cake," Bruce Waters said by way of explanation. "And that's why I want my piece to be a whole lot bigger than that one you just cut, Johnson."

Pulling the top plate from the stack, Carter set two pieces on it and passed it to the hardware store owner. "Take two. You've earned it."

Tori leaned to her left, bringing her mouth in line with Leona's ear as she did. "What are they talking about?"

Leona's shrug was cut short by a throaty laugh from the opposite side of the table. Sure enough, all eight of Bud Aikin's teeth were on display inside a smile that stretched from one end of the bar owner's face to the other. "If all goes well, we'll be eatin' one of them cakes at every meetin' once the cash finally starts flowin' through all our registers. Heck, maybe you can even buy you some gold plates, Carter."

Shelby Jenkins paused, a bite of cake midway

to her lips. "We're all still assuming the son's gonna do the right thing, yes?"

"Beau Montgomery is a lot less pigheaded than his old man." Granville Adams waved off the cake Carter tried to pass in his direction, and focused, instead, on the faces of the business owners assembled around the table. "And with Clyde finally gone, I don't really see any reason Beau would stick around in Sweet Briar. Why would he?"

Call her slow but the meaning behind the cake and the conversation finally hit home for Tori, their collective landing making it difficult to breathe let alone think. Leona was right. The men and women who made up Sweet Briar's business district were happy about Clyde's death. Ecstatic, even.

Swallowing against the lump reality served up inside her throat, Tori allowed her gaze to travel to the end of the table and the woman she'd silently vowed to avoid for the remainder of the meeting. For as much as she wanted to see Georgina abstaining from the cake and the party-like chatter responsible for Tori's unease, she also needed to consider adding the mayor's name to the list she and Dixie had drafted.

"I'll admit, Victoria," Leona whispered in her ear, "I like a party as much as the next gal, but not this way. This is . . . this is just—"

"Weird? Disturbing? Highly inappropriate?"

she interjected via a mumble as she studied Georgina's relaxed pose and quiet demeanor with a mixture of curiosity and disgust. "Trust me, Leona, I feel exactly the same way."

"Don't get me wrong, dear, I'd like to see people flocking to Sweet Briar just as much as anyone else seated at this table. More people mean more shoppers. More shoppers mean more money for all of us. More money—at least for me—means more opportunities to travel and to meet new and exciting people."

"You mean, *men*." Under other circumstances, Tori would have followed the reflexive barb with more extensive teasing, but considering the atmosphere around them, it felt wrong. Very, very wrong. "You know something, Leona? I didn't know Clyde Montgomery. I never saw him, never knew his house and that view existed. But sitting here, in this room, I can't help but ache a little for his son and for Clyde himself. I mean, he was a person, Leona. A person just like you and me and everyone else in this room. Yet *these* people are"—she stopped, swallowed, and continued on—"*celebrating* the fact that he's dead."

"Cake?"

An elbow jab to her side stole her focus from Georgina and placed it squarely on the meeting's host. She looked from Carter to the cake and back again, her stomach roiling at the sight of the decadent treat. "Um, no, that's okay . . . I think I'll pass—"

"Hey . . . Granville." Bud Aikin, owner of Bud's Brew Shack, leaned back in his chair with a smug smile. "Any chance now that Betty ain't havin' to send all her pies off to work with you that maybe I can land one sometime? Especially if it's got some pecans in it?"

Granville Adams lifted his cake fork into the air. "I have to tell you, Betty's the first person I called after the news came in. Figured she'd be relieved to know I wouldn't be pestering her for baked bribes anymore."

"You sure you want Betty baking you a pie, Bud?" The smack of Bruce's hand on Bud's wide back echoed around the restaurant. " 'Cause it seems to me you might want to stick around awhile and actually get to hold some of that money we've been waiting to see for so long."

The councilman popped his last bite of cake into his mouth, glanced at his watch, and then rose to his feet. "Now, Bruce, you keep talking like that and I'll have to consider assessing that doghouse your wife keeps sending you to every time you get home late from one of your fishing trips."

"Eh, I don't mean no harm, Granville, you know that." Bruce tossed his napkin onto the table and pushed back his own chair. "I know Betty's pies are the least of Bud's problems."

"Hardy, har, har." Councilman Adams stopped beside Shelby Jenkins and placed a gentle hand on her shoulder. "If you find yourself craving sweets, Bud, Shelby has a lot more time on her hands these days now that she doesn't have to spend her Fridays trying to satisfy that old codger's sweet tooth."

"At least he was a loyal customer," Shelby drawled while batting her lashes at the handsome bookstore owner to her right.

"Trust me, Shelby, you'll make a lot more on the folks your daddy is going to bring into this town in the course of three months than you would have in three years of hand dipping cherries for Montgomery."

"Bruce is right," Councilman Adams said as he lifted his hand into the air, signaling his impending departure. "Y'all take a few moments over the next few days to really enjoy this victory, you hear? It's not every day your plans fall into place the way they did this past week."

She tried to smile and be polite as the various members of the business association began to push back their chairs and head toward the door, but it was hard. Clyde Montgomery was dead. And while Tori had never really met Dixie's Home Fare client, she couldn't ignore the sudden connection she felt to the man who'd valued things like routine and tradition.

Maybe he truly didn't need all the land he had.

Maybe a resort on Fawn Lake really would help the residents and business owners of Sweet Briar. But the fact was, it was Clyde's land. He'd grown up in that same house, looking out at that lake each day of his life just as his father and his father before him had done. Some people had no problem turning their back on that kind of tradition in the interest of cold hard cash. Clyde Montgomery just hadn't been one of them.

Unfortunately, his preference for tradition stood in the way of cash for just about everyone else, or so it seemed.

"I'll be honest, Victoria, I thought this whole thing with Dixie was merely a way for her to get attention. But now I'm not so sure." Reaching down, Leona retrieved Paris from beneath the table and tucked the garden-variety bunny into the crook of her arm. "In fact, the way I see it, figuring out who *didn't* kill Clyde might be every bit as hard as figuring out who *did*."

She wished she could argue, but she couldn't. Leona was right. Virtually every single person around the table that morning stood to benefit from the elderly landowner's demise. The question was how far they went—either singularly or as a group—to achieve that end.

Slowly, she rose to her feet beside Leona and headed toward the door, her thoughts whirling with everything she'd seen and heard since walking into the diner some sixty minutes earlier.

179

She'd come hoping to get a better look at some of the suspects on her list. She was leaving knowing that every name on that list not only belonged there but also demanded far more of her time and energy than any breakfast meeting could ever afford.

Chapter 17

Tori was just setting the pitcher of sweet tea on the dining room table when she heard the first knock. A quick check of her watch as she made her way to the door confirmed what she already knew—it was seven o'clock, the official start time for the weekly Sweet Briar Ladies Society Sewing Circle meeting. And with the official start time came the arrival of the Queen of Punctuality . . .

"Dixie, hi! Welcome." She stepped back to allow the woman access to her cottage, sweeping her hand toward the living room as she did. "Somehow, I managed to get everything wrapped up at work in time to get home and actually straighten up a little."

Dixie took two steps inside, pressed her covered dessert dish into Tori's free hand, and hoisted her sewing tote farther onto her shoulder.

"So? How'd it go? Did you figure out who did it?"

"Are you talking about the business owners' meeting?" she asked as she made her way around Dixie to add the latest dessert to the display of brownies she'd already set out. "Because it was okay, I guess. No one person jumped out at me in terms of Clyde."

Dixie's shoulders sank. "No one?"

"No, I mean there were lots of people who gave me pause." She gestured Dixie toward the various chairs she'd grouped around the room yet remained standing herself in anticipation of the next knock. "But most of the time I was just sad."

"Oh?" Dixie settled into the rocking chair to the left of the couch. "Did something happen?"

She shrugged, her words whisking her thoughts back to the breakfast meeting that had left her more than a little unsettled throughout the workday. "It was like they were happy a man had died. Like all that mattered was the fact that a hotel can now be built on his land . . . assuming, of course, his son doesn't feel as strongly about heritage as Clyde obviously did."

"Young people don't care about tradition anymore," Dixie groused before pulling her sewing bag onto her lap and retrieving a piece of rectangular fabric from its depths. "I'm going to propose a new project for the group this evening. Something that'll make—"

"Hello? Anyone here?" Margaret Louise herded her mother through the door then followed closely in the ninety-something's steps. "I brought a pie, and Mama brought some chocolate chip cookies."

Tori closed the gap between the living room and the new arrivals with several easy strides, planting a kiss on each woman's forehead before securing the covered plates from their hands. "Annabelle, it is so good to see you. I was hoping you'd be here with all of us tonight."

Annabelle grinned in response, the clarity in her eyes no doubt responsible for the lighthearted twinkle in Margaret Louise's.

"I stopped by Leona's on the way here and she asked me to bring Mama with me. Said she needed to swing by the spa first."

"Does that sister of yours ever do anything besides have her nails done?" Dixie laid the rectangular fabric across her thighs then reached into her bag for her box of colored thread.

"This time it wasn't for her." Margaret Louise tucked her hand through Annabelle's and gently escorted her mother to the end of the couch that was bathed in the most light. "It was for Paris."

"Paris?" Tori and Dixie said in unison.

Once Annabelle was settled in a comfy corner, Margaret Louise claimed one of the folding chairs Tori had set up next to the couch and lowered herself onto it with only a few quiet grunts and groans. "I tell you, that bunny lives better than I do. Why, do you know when I last had my nails done? Never. That's right—never. Ain't never had the time or the inclination to have someone messin' with my fingers like that. Specially not when I spend most my days playin' in the dirt with one of them grandbabies of mine."

Tori cast a sideways glance in Dixie's direction to see if she'd heard their friend correctly. The gaped mouth she saw on her predecessor's face brought a smile to her own. "Wait. Are you telling us that *Paris* got her nails done?"

"That's what I'm sayin'. Clipped and polished if you can believe it."

Dixie opened her mouth to speak but could only manage a sputter.

"Clipped and polished?" Tori echoed on her behalf. "Are you serious?"

Margaret Louise nodded once, twice. "Seems that vet that opened up shop halfway between here and Lawry is offerin' a spa for animals— washin', shampooin', and nail clippin'. So my twin asked 'bout nail paintin', too. From what she told me, they didn't even blink. They just told Leona to bring Paris over and they'd pamper her for the afternoon."

Again, Dixie tried to speak. Again, she sputtered. Only this time Tori didn't have to offer a translation thanks to the arrival of three more of their sewing circle sisters. Jumping up from the

183

corner of the chair she'd briefly inhabited while Margaret Louise regaled them with stories of bunny manicures, Tori greeted Debbie and Beatrice with a smile while simultaneously slipping her hand beneath Rose's upper arm and helping the group's matriarch to the open spot on the couch beside Annabelle.

"Rose, it is so good to see you. We missed you at the last meeting." Then in an effort to keep from fussing too much, she gestured toward the rest of the group. "Well, we're almost a full house tonight. All we're waiting on now is *Leona* and"—she glanced at Margaret Louise for confirmation—"*Melissa* . . . and . . . Georgina."

She was grateful when Margaret Louise chimed in with Melissa's baby-related no-show and hoped the distraction would cover for the tone shift in her own voice at the mention of the mayor. It didn't matter what vibe Georgina had given off that morning or even that the elected official was out of line when she told Tori to leave Clyde's death alone. The only thing that mattered inside the confines of their sewing circle was loyalty to one another.

Georgina was one of them and had been since long before Tori ever dreamed of living in Sweet Briar. To share her disappointment about Georgina's behavior with the women assembled around her would be a recipe for disaster.

Inhaling deeply, Tori took advantage of

Margaret Louise's update on grandchild number eight to claim a chair of her own and get her own sewing items situated within easy reach. When she was done, she looked up to find Rose watching her closely. "Georgina isn't coming this evening, either."

Margaret Louise sent her latest photo of Melissa's new son around the circle then turned to address Rose's proclamation with its appropriate due. "She have some sort of town meetin' tonight?"

Rose pulled the flaps of her cotton sweater closer against her body and shook her head.

"She bein' treated to dinner by someone lookin' for a favor?"

Rose shook her head a second time, her gaze never leaving Tori's.

"She visitin' that rascal ex-husband of hers in the pokey?"

A chorus of moans rang up around the room, negating any need for Rose to shake her head a third time.

"I know . . . I know," Margaret Louise said around her belly laugh. "Georgina would no more visit that man than my sister would shop for clothes at a secondhand store."

"Then why did you ask?" Rose groused.

"Just bein' funny, I guess." Margaret Louise reached across the divide that separated her folding chair from the corner of the couch where her mother sat and gently patted the woman's leg. "So why ain't she comin'? Does anyone know?"

"She's angry at Victoria, that's why."

Heads turned toward the front hallway and the stylishly clad woman who'd managed to let herself into the room without anyone noticing. Rising to her feet, Tori shot a glare to end all glares at Leona.

"Don't look at me like that, dear," Leona admonished over the top of her stylish glasses. "You know it's true. Pretending otherwise is a waste of time and effort."

Without waiting for a reply, Leona crossed the living room in her dusty rose stilettos and eased herself into the armchair Tori had purchased shortly after moving to Sweet Briar. The chair itself was as cozy as it was pretty and had become Leona's official spot anytime she came to visit. The fact that Tori made sure to put Paris's travel bed at its base prior to those visits only helped to underscore Leona's claim to the chair.

"When I stopped at the spa just now, everyone just went on and on about how wonderful Paris was for all her procedures."

"Her procedures?" Beatrice looked up from the Easter outfit she was making for her charge, her brows furrowed.

Leona turned Paris so everyone could see the bunny's bright pink bow and matching nail tips. "They washed and groomed her, and gave her her very first official manicure. Doesn't she look precious?"

A quick glance around the circle revealed more than a few open mouths and raised eyebrows. But only Rose had the courage to speak.

"Has one of those lip-plumping shots you take gone to your brain, Leona?"

Instantly, Leona's head dipped forward, affording her eyes an uninhibited view of Rose from atop her glasses. "I don't use anything artificial to enhance my looks, you old goat."

A soft laugh escaped Rose's own thinning lips, the sound soliciting a smile from everyone in the room except Leona. "Do you honestly think I was born yesterday, Leona?"

Seconds turned to minutes as Leona continued to stare at Rose before finally breaking eye contact and setting Paris in her bed. "I'm well aware of the date you were born, Rose. In fact, I believe your birthday predates dirt."

A collective gasp echoed around the room, only to disappear with a wave of Rose's arthritic hand. "Ladies, please. Gasps like that should be saved for surprises. Leona's classless comments no longer qualify."

Leona's hand flew to the base of her neck in horror as a second, louder round of gasping circulated the room. "Did you say *classless?*"

"If the shoe fits," grumbled Rose. Then, turning her head a hairbreadth to the right, the elderly woman focused on Tori. "So why is Georgina upset with you? What did you do?"

A sudden surge of warmth crept its way into Tori's cheeks as all eyes left the Leona-Rose battlefield and focused squarely on her. "I, um, I'm not sure exactly."

"Oh, Victoria, quit your hemming and hawing as my sister likes to say." Leona opened her latest travel magazine and lifted it up to reading level. "You know very well why Georgina is cross with you. She made it perfectly clear over breakfast this morning, dear."

Like an active Ping-Pong match, all eyes left Leona and returned to Tori, waiting.

"Victoria?"

She looked from the floor to Rose and swallowed, the concern on the matriarch's face warming her own all over again. "Dixie has asked me to help her figure out what happened to Clyde Montgomery."

Dixie's needle-holding hand stilled mere inches above the rectangular fabric on her lap. "Clyde was murdered, you know."

"You're still hanging on to that one with both gums, Dixie?" Rose scooted forward on the sofa to take a closer look at Dixie's project.

"I am. And so is Victoria."

Her attention still on Dixie's lap, Rose addressed Tori once again. "Victoria? Is that true?"

She took a deep breath, her answer forming

before she'd completed a full exhale. "Something doesn't add up about his death, Rose. I mean, I get that he was ninety-one, but I'm having a hard time accepting the speed with which he deteriorated over the past month. Especially in light of the fact that virtually every business owner in this town was livid over his decision to hold on to his land in spite of their ongoing campaign to make him change his mind."

"Y-You actually think someone wanted that resort so badly they'd kill a man to see it happen?" Debbie stammered.

A few days ago, Tori had still felt some of the same incredulousness she heard in Debbie's voice, but now, after everything she'd seen and learned that day, she couldn't help but see Dixie's suspicions in a whole new light. "I think it's very possible."

"Why?"

The simple question, posed without a shred of sarcasm or second-guessing, allowed her to not only take another breath but to actually relish it this time. When she was ready to answer, she gave Rose her full attention. "I went with Leona to a business owners' meeting at Johnson's Diner today and virtually every single person in that room was happy about Clyde's death . . . *happy* that his passing will now pave the way for some big resort company to set up shop here in Sweet Briar.

"They even had a cake to celebrate his death, Rose. *A cake*."

"Cake?" Debbie parroted. "You mean the one I made?"

At Tori's nod, the bakery owner leapt to her feet and began pacing around the living room. "Carter asked me to make a cake for the meeting. He told me not to write 'Happy Birthday' on it the way I usually do, but he never said what it was for . . ."

Rose cleared her throat, pulling her sweater still tighter against her body in an attempt to ward off a chill only she felt. "Go on, Victoria . . ."

"Anyway, it bothered me, really bothered me. I mean, I can't say I knew Clyde because I really didn't, but he was a person, Rose. A person who loved his land because of the connection it provided to his past. How was that wrong?"

When no one answered, she continued, the anger she felt at the diner rising to the surface all over again. "So when I got to the library, I decided to do a little checking. During lulls in patron traffic I began researching towns like Sweet Briar who have turned to tourism as the main source of income. And, Rose? The kind of money a resort like Nirvana can generate for a town is absolutely unbelievable. Stores that were once struggling are now more successful than their owners ever thought possible. Restaurants that were on the verge of closing down are now opening second and third locations. Even the schools in these towns have benefited from the increased tax dollars . . . allowing them to offer bigger and better after-school programs. I mean, it's been an absolute windfall for these places."

"And the negative side to these resorts?" Rose countered.

"Not big enough to offset the good." It was a simple reply but accurate nonetheless.

"And Georgina is mad 'cause why?"

Tori took a moment to consider Margaret Louise's question, knowing the answer had her walking through a potential minefield. "Because she loves this town and everyone in it. Accusing one of its residents of a crime that was committed for the express purpose of benefiting the town probably hits a little too close to home."

"If you ask me, my money is on Shelby Jenkins." Leona lowered her magazine long enough to inspect her own French manicure. "She had motive, she had means, and she's got to do something to please the only man who'll ever think she's pretty."

Debbie looked up from her own box of colored thread and made a face. "Shelby Jenkins? You can't be serious, Leona. She's as sweet as the candy she makes."

"And if she poisoned some of that candy, would it still be sweet?"

"I—"

With a nod of satisfaction at the job her

manicurist had done, Leona turned her attention squarely on the bakery shop owner. "When you hand dip the same candy for the same man each week, it certainly provides a clever way to administer poison on an ongoing basis. Watch any one of those detective shows on TV and you'll see I'm right."

Tori rewound Leona's initial statement in her head, hitting pause when she reached the part that made her internal radar ping. "What did you mean by having to please the only man who'll ever think she's pretty?"

Leona slid forward on the armchair and perched primly at its edge, her moment in the spotlight demanding a straight back and crossed ankles. "You saw her this morning, dear. How she batted her lashes and fairly drooled all over herself every time John Peter Hendricks so much as sneezed in her vicinity . . . but it didn't work. She's too needy, too obvious. That's why she spends her evenings alone."

"Okay . . ."

"Her father, from what I hear, thinks the sun rises and sets on darling Shelby. He purchased that shop for her, helped her get her business off the ground, and pays all the expenses so she can stay busy doing what she wants. Therefore, it stands to reason she'd try to help him out in return."

"You mean because her father is a bigwig at

Nirvana Resorts?" It had taken a moment, but she'd finally picked up Leona's line of thought.

"Precisely."

"Her father's connection to the big picture is certainly noteworthy, but there are an awful lot of people in town whose quality of life would improve significantly with that kind of tourism revenue," Tori reminded her.

"Like who?" Beatrice asked.

"Essentially anyone who owns a shop in the town square, for starters."

"Hmmm." Rose lifted her chin and pinned Leona with a stare. "That would certainly include *you,* Leona, wouldn't it?"

"If I needed my antique shop to survive, you old goat, I'd be a suspect, too. But since I don't, you can just wipe that smug look off your face."

"I imagine Georgina is fit to be tied right 'bout now," Margaret Louise summarized. "Specially when she's up for reelection this fall."

"But murder is murder," Beatrice whispered. "If that poor man was killed, surely Georgina would want the bloke responsible to be punished . . ."

"You'd certainly think so, wouldn't you? But either way, Victoria and I will find the truth. I owe that to Clyde for inspiring me to write again."

Debbie lowered herself back to her chair. "You write, Dixie?"

The former librarian's broad shoulders rose and

fell beneath her flowered housedress. "I used to, as a young girl. Clyde encouraged me to start back up. He said it would be a way to work through the library board's betrayal in a creative way."

"Did Clyde write?" Tori asked.

"No, he painted. But he said it was that kind of thing—writing, painting, drawing—that allowed a person to be happy in a way money and possessions never could." Dixie retrieved the fabric from the armrest and held it up for all to see. "That's why I want us to make these . . . as a way to help people like Clyde. People who might need a little help from time to time yet still have passion and dreams deep down inside."

Leona lowered her magazine. "Looks like a placemat to me."

"It is." Dixie turned it around to show the back side of the fabric then once again to display the front. "If I hadn't agreed to deliver Clyde's midday meal with Home Fare, I'd still be sulking around the house plotting against Winston Hohlbrook and the rest of the library board. But because I did, I'm spending my days writing stories that make me happy . . . just like Clyde spent his days painting pictures that made him happy."

"But why a placemat?"

"Because I brought one to Clyde that first day and he said it made him feel special, like he wasn't just getting some doggy bag dropped at his door." Dixie passed the placemat to Annabelle first then watched as it made its way from one sewing circle member to the next. "When he inquired about it, I told him I'd made it just for him. That's when he invited me to stay and talk. The next thing I knew, I was telling him about what happened at the library and he was encouraging me to find an outlet.

"When I finally left that afternoon, I felt like a very different person than I'd been when I arrived on his doorstep."

Just like that, Dixie's drive to find the truth made sense. Not only had Dixie given Clyde someone to talk to when she delivered his meals, but Clyde had helped Dixie find purpose in her days again. Her need to help him—even postmortem—was only natural.

Margaret Louise turned the placemat over in her hands, studying the simple stitches before handing it to Rose. "It wouldn't take us long to make a hundred or so of these."

"Seems to me we could round the edges on some, leave the others rectangular, like this," Rose said. "And if we know something about each person receiving the meal, maybe we could pick a fabric specific to them. Lord knows, I've accumulated enough remnants over the years to make a *thousand* of these placemats if we wanted."

"Is that a yes?" Dixie leaned forward, looking from face to face as she did. "Can we consider our next group project to be placemats for Home Fare?"

"I say we do it." Giving voice to the wave of nods around them, Margaret Louise slipped her hand across the gap between her chair and the couch and squeezed Annabelle's hand. "You'll help us, won't you, Mama?"

Chapter 18

Armed with a peanut butter sandwich in one hand and a napkin in the other, Tori swiveled her desk chair until she was looking out at the grounds. Everywhere she looked she saw flowers thanks to the hard work and dedication of the Friends of the Library group. Yet even as pretty as the daffodils and hyacinths were, they couldn't maintain her focus for long.

The sewing circle she'd hosted the night before had been a success. The group had unanimously agreed to make placemats for Home Fare, the gossip batted about had been relatively innocent, and the new brownie recipe she'd tried out had been a smash hit.

In fact, by the time the last straggler had left,

she'd been more than ready to curl up on her bed and share the evening's highlights with Milo. But her phone never rang.

The little voice that had made it nearly impossible to sleep kept saying the same thing—leave the Clyde Montgomery thing to the police. If she listened, she could concentrate all of her energy on Milo and their upcoming wedding.

Unfortunately, every time she'd start to think the little voice was right, another louder voice would push its way to the foreground—reminding her of the countless ways in which Dixie had gone above and beyond to help Tori during Nina's maternity leave. Besides, the notion that a man had been killed and the perpetrator might never be held accountable wasn't one she could accept.

Her cell phone vibrated against the top of her desk, bringing a momentary end to her latest bout of soul searching. She laid her napkin on her lap and reached for the device.

"Hello?"

"Good afternoon, Victoria. Mama and I had a mighty fine time at your house last evenin'. Thank you."

She smiled in spite of the headache brewing above her right eye. "I'm so glad Annabelle came. She looked really good, Margaret Louise. Very clear."

"It was a good night. Haven't talked to Leona

yet this mornin' to know whether Mama woke up that way, too. I reckon I'll hear 'bout it if she don't. But I didn't call to talk 'bout Mama. I called to talk 'bout you and that big black cloud that followed you 'round the house last night."

"There wasn't any cloud," she protested. "I was fine. It was great to see everyone just like always."

"When are you goin' to quit actin' like I was born yesterday, Victoria? That sister of mine might like to pretend she's younger than she is, but I don't. Livin' life makes you smarter. It makes you wiser to things happenin' below the surface. And I know there was a lot more goin' on underneath your surface last night than sewin' some placemats and waitin' for proper gushin' 'bout those brownies of yours . . . which, I have to say, were outstandin'."

Lifting her sandwich to her mouth, Tori took a bite, the act of eating giving her something to do while she mulled over her friend's words. There was a part of her that wanted to unload all her troubles on the woman in the hopes of gaining clarity where the little voices were concerned. But then there was the other part that needed the lighthearted warmth Margaret Louise provided on a normal basis—the kind of simplicity that came with tales of grandbabies and tried-for-the-first-time recipes.

"The picnic didn't go the way you hoped, did it?"

Tori paused mid-chew and closed her eyes. So much for simplicity . . .

"How did you know?" she finally asked as she lowered the sandwich and turned back to the window. "Did you see Milo? Did he say something?"

A long-held sigh filled the line. "So I was right. Why, I knew it the second I saw you last night. You tried to be chipper when Mama and I arrived, but I saw it plain as day."

Oh, how she wished she could tell Margaret Louise that everything was fine. That plans for the wedding and the honeymoon were all sewn up. That she and Milo were counting down the days until they could start their life together. But she couldn't. Not with the kind of conviction she should be able to anyway.

"Milo is feeling neglected," she finally said, staring out, unseeingly, at the library grounds. "But it's not intentional. I *want* to marry him. I *want* to go on our honeymoon, I *want* to move in together."

"Have you found your dress yet?"

"No."

"Have you decided where the reception is goin' to be?"

"Not exactly."

"Music?"

She shook her head.

"Victoria?"

Realizing her mistake, she put the action into words. "No. But that doesn't mean I don't want to get married."

A beat of silence on the other end of the phone made her sit up tall. "Margaret Louise, I love Milo. With all my heart."

"I know that, Victoria. But you have to know that plannin' a weddin' is usually all any new bride can think 'bout. The fact that yours is six months away and you ain't doin' much plannin' has to have Milo wonderin'."

"We have the church. We've picked the cake with Debbie, and secured the menu with you. It's not like I haven't done anything, because I have." But even as the words left her mouth, she knew Margaret Louise was right. She also knew her failure to check all the boxes on her wedding to-do list had everything to do with her schedule as of late and nothing, whatsoever, to do with her feelings for Milo. "Oh, Margaret Louise, how do I fix this? I mean, I know the easiest way would be to drop everything and give Milo and our wedding my undivided attention. But how can I do that when I truly believe Dixie is right about Clyde's death? Especially when I know better than anyone else how ineffective Chief Dallas can be when it comes to doing the work necessary to find the truth—particularly when some of his fishing buddies are on the list of suspects?"

"You let me help."

She closed her eyes against the sudden mist in her eyes. "Help? How?"

"I could go with you to find your dress. I could make some calls about the reception—Georgina's backyard would make a lovely spot to celebrate your weddin'."

"Georgina wouldn't even come to last night's sewing circle meeting because of me. You really think she'd want to offer up her yard for my wedding reception?"

"Now don't you fuss none 'bout Georgina. The only way someone in this town will be held accountable for Clyde's death is if they're guilty. And if that happens, she can't hold that 'gainst you. Wrong is wrong no matter who's doin' the wrong." Margaret Louise's sigh tickled the inside of Tori's ear. "I could even talk to Milo if you think that'd help."

Her eyes flew open at the image. "No!"

"I wouldn't say anything bad, Victoria."

She worked to soften her tone, bring it in line with the spirit in which the offer had been made. "I need to handle this thing with Milo myself. I'm just not sure how, short of telling Dixie she's on her own with her suspicions."

"Like I said the other day, I could help with that, too." The sudden smile on Margaret Louise's face was audible through the phone line. "You know I like investigatin' with you, Victoria. Why, we've made quite a team in the past with this sort of thing and I'd be willin' to help again."

"Willing?" she teased, grateful for the sudden lighthearted escape to the conversation. "Is that what it's called these days?"

Margaret Louise's answering belly laugh said it all. "I *do* know the folks in this town, Victoria. And my cookin' has a way of gettin' all sorts of answers outta people."

"Oh?"

"You just watch and see." A hushed thump in the background was followed by the sound of a drawer slamming. "Okay, I got me a piece of paper and a pen. Now who's on the list besides Shelby Jenkins?"

"Basically everyone who was celebrating Clyde's death at Leona's meeting yesterday morning—Lana Morris, Bud Aikin, Carter Johnson, Bruce Waters. Oh, and Councilman Adams, too."

"I never have liked Granville Adams. Why, when he was up for election 'bout two years ago, he was runnin' 'gainst a friend of my Jake's— Carlton Wiperly. Carlton was in the lead on account of most people in this town havin' watched him grow up."

"So what happened? Why didn't he win the council seat?"

"Granville uncovered a shopliftin' incident in Carlton's past. Didn't matter the boy was only six when it happened. Granville pointed to it again and again as a reason to doubt Carlton's integrity, his upbringin'."

"And people fell for that?"

"Granville won, didn't he?"

A flash of movement in Tori's peripheral vision hooked her focus onto the sidewalk in front of the town hall. Georgina stood underneath a tree talking to two men—one of whom Tori recognized instantly as the police chief. She leaned forward, bobbing her head to the side to afford a better view of the second man she still didn't recognize.

"Um, Margaret Louise? Would you mind if we table this conversation until later? I think I need to use the rest of my lunchtime for a walk."

"You're goin' to snoop, ain't you?"

At any other time, she knew she'd have laughed at Margaret Louise's perceptiveness, but she didn't want to lose the opportunity to find out what was behind the impromptu soiree. "The chief and Georgina are having some sort of deep discussion outside town hall. There's another man, too—one I don't recognize. And from what I can tell sitting here in my office, Georgina doesn't look too terribly excited."

"You go snoop and I'll get cookin'. From what I remember, Bud Aikin likes my sweet potato pie . . ."

She let the woman's words wash over her, the

meaning behind them chasing the last of her doldrums away. "Margaret Louise, I don't know what I'd do without you."

"I'm sure you'd think of somethin'," Margaret Louise quipped. "But before you go, I need to know if you still want Kate's number."

"Kate?"

"You know, Clyde's friend. The one from my church."

And then she remembered. Looking from the trio beneath the tree to the wooden pencil holder on her desk, Tori plucked out a pen and readied her hand to write. "Go ahead, I'll take it now."

She took great pains to make her stride seem as natural as possible as she rounded the back side of the library and headed toward the threesome on the sidewalk. It didn't take a rocket scientist to know the mayor and the police chief were discussing something important. Georgina's erect posture and clenched hands were as much a giveaway to that fact as was the chief's widened stance and occasional hand motion. The second man, while unfamiliar to Tori, stared up at the branches above them as if he wanted to be anywhere else at that moment.

Something was going on, something she had a feeling she'd want to know . . .

Swiping the back of her hand across her brow,

Tori slowed her pace as she approached the trio. "Hi, Georgina, Chief Dallas. Beautiful day we're having, isn't it?"

The chief nodded. Georgina merely shrugged.

She cast about for something to say, something that might get her invited into the conversation or give her a reason to linger if even for just an extra minute or two. Finally, she thrust her hand in the direction of the tall man with the salt-and-pepper hair and offered her best smile. "Hi, I'm Tori Sinclair."

"I'm Beau Montgomery."

"Beau—" She looked from Georgina to the chief and back again, the mayor's wooden pose and the chief's obvious resignation only serving to shore up the connection being made in her thoughts. "You mean, Clyde's son?" At his nod, she allowed her shake to morph into a squeeze. "I'm so sorry to learn of your dad's passing."

"Thank you. He was a good man and lived a good, long life."

Breaking eye contact with the mayor, Robert gestured a hand in Tori's direction. "Tori, here, is the one who first alerted me to the fact your father's death might be more than it seemed."

Surprise snapped Beau's head backward. "How did you know my dad?"

"I didn't. My friend Dixie did."

"My father was ninety-one, Miss Sinclair."

She nodded. "He was. He was also in amazing

physical shape as recently as six weeks ago. Animals age quickly, people do not."

Before Beau could respond, Georgina spoke, the mayor's voice weary at best. "Robert tells me an autopsy was conducted on Clyde's body yesterday morning. A rush has been put on the findings. If he was poisoned the way you suspect, we'll know before week's end."

She glanced at the chief, felt the relief as it coursed through her body at his nod of confirmation. "Thank you, Chief."

"I'm not doing this for you, Victoria. I heard what you said in my office the other day and I decided to do my own checking. The best way to know for sure was to autopsy the body."

It was the best scenario she could have hoped for and she said as much to the group. "You're doing the right thing, Chief. If nothing shows up, suspicions are put to rest once and for all. If something *does* show up, then we can find the person responsible for Clyde's death and see that he—*or she*—is brought to justice."

Chapter 19

Tori tilted her cheek to the swath of sunlight creeping across the information desk and smiled in the general direction of the front door, the momentary reminder of the day's perfect weather warming her from the inside out.

"Welcome to the Sweet Briar Public Library. If there's anything I can help you find, please don't hesitate to ask." She waited for her eyes to adjust to the rapid change in lighting as the door swung closed and returned the room to its normal fluorescent glow.

"Miss Sinclair, right?"

"Yes, I'm Victoria." She bobbed her head to the left and instantly recognized the salt-and-pepper hair and taller-than-average stature of Beau Montgomery. "Oh, Mr. Montgomery, it's nice to see you again."

"Call me Beau." He closed the gap between the front door and the information desk with several long strides, a tentative smile rounding his otherwise narrow jawline. "I was hoping you'd still be here."

"I'm still here," she said, gesturing toward the computer in front of her stool. "Next month is a big month for new releases, and if I don't make sure to order a few copies *now,* my patrons will have my head."

A flash of amusement ignited behind Beau's blue eyes, paving the way for a warm, easygoing laugh. "I didn't know being a librarian could be such a dangerous profession."

"Believe me, it is." Reaching forward, she minimized the order screen and pivoted on the stool until she was facing the man. "So, what can I do for you?"

In an instant, the sparkle she'd seen in his eyes only moments earlier was gone, in its place the dullness of someone in mourning. "I—I was hoping to ask you a few questions about this whole thing with my father. Chief Dallas told me you're the one who came to him with the possibility Dad had been . . . *poisoned?*"

Glancing toward the bank of computers in the right-hand corner of the main room, Tori did a quick mental head count—one, two, three. Everyone currently in the library was accounted for and otherwise occupied. She released a soft sigh of relief and tugged her stool closer to the man. "I didn't know your father, Beau. But my friend Dixie did."

"Dixie," he repeated softly. "I believe that's the woman who called to tell me he was dead."

Tori nodded. "She was asked to deliver meals to your dad for Home Fare and had been doing so for a few days. From what I can tell, they became fast friends. Anyway, when she found him that last day, she was understandably upset."

He closed his eyes briefly, only to open them again with a sigh. "I'll have to make sure to call her and thank her. The thought he might have been there for some time before I got back from my business trip makes me shudder."

She allowed him a moment and then continued on, her words addressing his original question. "When Dixie heard that his death was being blamed on his age, she got upset. And that's when she came to me with her suspicions."

"But *poisoned?*"

After a second glance toward the computer bank, she slid off her stool and led him toward a table on the opposite side of the room. When they were both seated, she did her best to take him through the steps that had landed her in Chief Dallas's office with the autopsy request. "Dixie never said he was poisoned. She just questioned his rapid decline in health. I mean, you saw him fairly regularly, didn't you?"

"Every chance I got. When my mother was alive, she and Dad used to have tea every morning. He'd make the tea and she'd make scones or muffins or whatever she felt like making that particular morning. After she passed a few years ago, Dad told me that was one of the things he missed most about Mom—that time to talk. So, whenever possible, I came by and we had tea. Dad used to joke I wasn't as pretty as Mom, and I used to tell him it was comments like that that would put a stop to my previsit bakery runs. To which, of course, he'd say the scones I brought were never as good as Mom's. But it was all in good fun."

"That sounds wonderful," she mused. "I bet that kept you two very close."

He shrugged. "I guess. My dad was kind of opinionated and awfully close-minded at times. Made it hard to talk to him about much of anything besides his art . . . and Mom. And if I was having trouble with the business, he had a way of pooh-poohing it like it wasn't important. But we both knew he had the benefit of being retired and set for life . . . I didn't." He traced a faint pen mark along the tabletop in front of him, shaking his head when he reached the end. "But I'd listen to his pontificating all over again if it meant I could have him back."

Reaching across the table, she patted his listless hand until it stilled beneath hers. "I'm sure you would."

"So how did you get to the idea of poison?" he finally asked.

"Pieces just started to fall into place. I did a little research here at the library one evening and discovered that a rapid decline in health, such as the one your father exhibited, could be indicative of arsenic poisoning. I wouldn't have thought much about that if it wasn't called to my attention just how many people were upset with your dad . . . people who had access to him via food. The fact that those same people would benefit greatly from his death made it difficult to write off as a possibility."

Beau drew back, his eyes wide. "Benefit from his death? What are you talking about?"

She pulled her hand into her lap and stared at the man. "You knew that resort companies were trying to get hold of your dad's land, didn't you?"

"Of course. But what does that have to do with . . ." His words trailed off as the image Tori was creating became crystal clear. "Wait. You think someone from one of the resort companies killed him off? But—but how could that be? They didn't have access to Dad. He wouldn't even take their calls after the initial round of offers."

"But he took visits from people who wanted a resort to happen every bit as much as the resort companies themselves."

His brows furrowed as his gaze bore into hers. "Again, what are you talking about?"

"Shopkeepers in Sweet Briar. Their businesses would take off with the kind of traffic these resorts could bring." Lifting her index finger into the air, she pushed her chair back and scurried over to the information desk and the folder she'd put together during the weekend.

Lowering her voice to a near whisper, she returned to the table and handed the folder to Beau. "I did a little research on the kind of money one of those resorts could mean for a town like Sweet Briar. The figures are really quite staggering."

He looked from the folder to Tori and back again before setting it on the table and flipping it open, his gaze skipping down the notes she'd taken and the calculations she'd made. When he reached the last page, he pushed the folder into the center of the table, his shoulders slumped. "Wow. I had no idea."

At a loss for what else to say, she merely nodded and waited, the man's hushed voice making its way through clenched lips. "So what you're telling me is that I'm going to reward my father's killer?"

"Only if you sell," she pointed out.

Raking a hand down his face, he exhaled a burst of air. "What else am I supposed to do? I don't need that kind of land. I'm a single man—"

"As was your father," she reminded him gently.

"With a job that has me traveling extensively."

"You need a place to call your home base."

He slouched back in his chair and stared at the folder, the sadness in his eyes heartbreaking. "Staying here in Sweet Briar would be too hard. Everywhere I look in that house I see my mom— the kitchen where she baked her scones, the bed she tucked me into each night as a child, the chair we shared while she read with me . . . all of it. Some people find comfort in that kind of tangible reminder. I'm not one of them."

She closed her hand atop his once again and gave a gentle squeeze. "You don't have to decide anything like that right now. But no matter what you choose to do, autopsying your dad's body was a smart move. If he was murdered, we don't want the killer to benefit from the crime."

A beat of silence fell between them before Beau pushed the folder back toward Tori and stood. "My dad used to get hand-dipped chocolate cherries from a sweetshop in town. Requested the owner make them herself each and every time. Think arsenic could find its way into something like that even if she'd been delivering them for months?"

"Shelby Jenkins. And she's on my list should the autopsy back up my belief."

He took a step toward the door and stopped, snapping his finger in the air as he turned back to Tori. "Come to think of it, I remember eating some leftover pie one morning when I didn't make it to the bakery for scones. Dad said the councilman's wife made it for him as a bribe. And Dad said it just like that . . . as a bribe."

"Granville Adams and his wife, Betty," she supplied. "They're also on my list."

"But how will we know if those items had

poison in them if they're gone now? An autopsy can't tie the poison to something he ate a week ago, can it?"

"I don't know. I don't think so. But all of that will certainly give us a place to start if this turns into a murder investigation." It was the best reassurance she could give under the circumstances. "If your dad was murdered, Beau, I'll figure out which one of them did it. I promise you that."

He studied her closely, his gaze taking in every aspect of her face before moving slowly down to the feet on which she was now standing. When he reached the floor, he returned his focus to their starting place, the dullness in his eyes tempered by something else. "My dad always said that there are good people everywhere. People who come into our lives to help . . . or to listen . . . or even to get us where we need to go more easily than we could ever do alone. It's a shame he never got to know you."

Her cheeks warmed at his praise and she did her best to wave the moment off. "I don't know what's going to come of any of this, but either way, we'll find the answers we need."

At the door, he turned and smiled. "When I was a kid, the librarian I knew read stories and helped me find books. Now I wonder what else she did."

"Wait. You grew up here in Sweet Briar, right?" At his nod, she continued. "Then that librarian who read to you was Dixie Dunn, the woman who found your father."

A glimmer of surprise passed across his face before disappearing behind the same sparkle she'd seen when he first entered the library. "See? I always thought being a librarian was a fairly mundane job. But now, in the time span of what—twenty minutes, maybe—I've learned that your profession is not only dangerous but also provides a cover for detective types."

She laughed. "Don't tell anyone, okay? We kind of like the whole incognito part."

Chapter 20

Tori dropped the library's master key ring into her purse and glanced at her watch, the seven o'clock hour affording a host of possibilities for a quiet evening with Milo. There was the tried-and-true popcorn-and-movie-on-the-couch idea, the sit-on-Milo's-front-porch-swing-and-cuddle idea, and the ever-popular long walk, all of which would give them what they desperately needed— time together.

The movie idea would allow them a chance to be together without necessarily having to address the issues responsible for the current strain between them. Then again, it was the not having time to talk and plan that was upsetting Milo most.

Her mind made up, Tori slipped her hand into her purse and pulled out her cell phone, its vibration against her skin catching her by surprise. She glanced at the display screen then flipped the phone open and held it to her ear.

"Margaret Louise?"

"Phew. I thought I was 'bout to hear that voice mail message of yours. Always makes me think it's you, but then it's not."

She crossed the parking lot and stopped beside her car. "Is everything okay? You sound kind of winded."

"I'm fine, Victoria, don't you worry your head none," Margaret Louise said. "But before I get to the reason for my call, tell me 'bout the snoopin'. Did you get somethin' good?"

"Snooping? What snooping—" And then she remembered. "Oh. Good news. Clyde's body was autopsied yesterday. We should know if we're right in the next day or so."

"That don't mean we have to wait for our investigatin', does it?"

She smiled at the disappointment in Margaret Louise's voice. "Do you think it should?"

"No siree. I reckon we should get a jump on things so we don't waste time when the report comes back in."

"And if it's not murder?" she asked as she unlocked the car door and sat down.

"My bones say it's murder, Victoria."

If anyone else had made such a statement, she'd dismiss it as the ranting of an overly confident person. But two-plus years of knowing Margaret Louise had taught her many things, not the least of which was the psychic-like ability of the woman's bones. If they said it was murder, who was Tori to argue?

"I met Clyde's son, Beau, today."

"And?"

"He's a nice man. Still reeling from the idea that his father may have been murdered." She ran her right hand along the steering wheel and stared through the windshield at the line of bushes that separated the library's parking lot from the back side of Leeson's Market. "Anyway, so what's up?"

"I did some checkin' of my own."

"Oh?"

"Bud's too dumb and Lana wasn't a huge fan of the resort idea. She knew it would bring in money and customers, but she loves Sweet Briar for the peace and quiet."

"So your gut on the two of them?"

"Take 'em off the list."

Considering what she knew about Margaret Louise and the woman's antennae, that was endorsement enough in Tori's book. "Anything else?"

"Whatcha doin' right now?"

She held the phone closer to her ear to counter-act the sudden muffling of the voice on the other end. "I just locked up for the night and I'm in my car. Why?"

"Any chance you might think 'bout swingin' out to church for a few minutes? I'm out here usin' the kitchen for some of my cookbook recipes."

Tori's stomach grumbled at the thought of Margaret Louise's cooking. "As tempting as that sounds, I was thinking maybe I'd stop by—"

"Kate is here."

Kate.

Clyde's friend.

"She's there?"

"She sure is. She's in a Bible study right now but that should be wrappin' up 'bout the time you get here. You won't miss her 'cause she's comin' in to do a little taste testin' for me when she's done."

Tori knew she should decline, stick with her original plan and call Milo, but the opportunity to talk to one of the dead man's friends was simply too good to pass up. Maybe something Kate had witnessed or overheard could shed light on who was responsible for Clyde's death.

Then again, if the autopsy came back clean, she'd have wasted her evening . . .

"Come on by, Victoria. Kate's real nice. You can talk to her for a few minutes and be on your way before you know it. Between the two of us, we might think of a few questions she can answer that'll help set us on the right path where Clyde's killer is concerned."

Twenty minutes later, Tori walked through the side entrance of Sweet Briar's most picturesque church and turned right, her nose guiding her feet in the direction she needed to go. The hint of cinnamon, combined with the smell of cooking beef, led her down one hallway and then the next, her feet moving in tandem with her nose.

"Are you trying to torture me, Margaret Louise?" she asked as she rounded the corner and stepped into the first open doorway she found. "That smell is absolutely amazing."

"And it doesn't hold a candle to the way it tastes." A statuesque woman with a neat bob of graying hair slipped a fork from between her lips then used it to gesture toward the plate in front of her.

A beaming Margaret Louise emerged from behind a row of cabinets, her gaze ricocheting between Tori and the woman seated at the counter. "Kate, this is Victoria. Victoria, this is Kate. And no, I didn't give her so much as a dollar to say such things about my food."

"If you did, I'd give it back," Kate joked. "People should be paying to eat your food, not getting paid to eat it."

Tori sidled up to the counter and stared down at the plate. "Um, Margaret Louise? How about a second taste tester? After all, I have a keen sense for spices." Then, turning to Kate, she extended her hand. "Hi, Kate. It's nice to meet you."

Margaret Louise wiped her hands on her apron then pointed to a second stool wedged beneath the counter's overhang. "Why don't you sit there next to Kate and get acquainted while I dish up another serving of my latest concoction."

Kate pushed the now empty plate across the counter to Margaret Louise and pouted her lip. "You know, come to think of it, I sure could use another taste or five, myself. Just to be sure, of course."

The look of pride on Margaret Louise's face brought an instant misting to Tori's eyes. There was so much to love about Leona's twin sister— boundless energy, limitless loyalty, true kindness, and humility. So when there was a chance to see something special going back in the woman's direction, it did Tori's heart good.

"I think I can find a little bit more for you, Kate." Margaret Louise made her way around the stove with Kate's plate in one hand and a clean plate for Tori in the other. "It's nice to see Kate smiling, Victoria. She's had a rough week."

Tori settled onto her stool and glanced between the women. "Oh?"

"Clyde Montgomery and Kate were friends."

She opened her mouth to remind Margaret Louise she knew about the connection but closed it when she realized the intentional genius behind her cohort's words. Instead, she turned to the woman on her right and reached for her hand once again. "Kate, I'm so sorry. From everything I've heard, Clyde was a good man."

Kate's face crumpled, deepening the lines around her eyes and leading Tori to guess her age to be in her late sixties, possibly early seventies. "Clyde was the best."

"How did the two of you meet?" she asked.

Propping her elbow on the counter, Kate lowered her chin into her hand. "I used to see Clyde here at church when I was a little girl. He was the man who always had a lollipop in his pocket and I was the little girl who was always more than happy to accept it." A wistful quality tinged the edges of the woman's voice as she continued. "I'd see him at the occasional potluck and he'd always come outside and pitch the ball to us when we were playing baseball, or come see whatever bug one of us had found.

"When times were tough for me and my mother, he'd see to it we got what we needed, whether it was groceries for the week or new shoes for school. Then, when I was in high school and all upset because no one had asked me to the prom, he told me I was better than all the boys in my grade and sent me and a few of my friends who didn't have dates to the theater in Lawry."

Tori nodded along, filing away everything she was hearing for further inspection at a later date. "So he was like a father figure of sorts?"

Kate's long lashes mingled together as she worked to catch her breath. "I always kind of thought that, though I never really voiced it out loud. I mean, he was nice to everyone. But then, when my mother died about fifteen years ago, he showed up at the funeral in a show of support. I guess he knew I'd never married and that I didn't have any siblings to stand next to in my grief."

"Did you see him often?" she asked, knowing the answer to the question but wanting to hear it from Kate's own mouth.

"When his wife died a few years ago, I felt it was time to repay the favor. I knew he was hurting and that he was lonely. I'd just retired from the shoe store and didn't have all that much to do with my days, so I started to visit Clyde."

"What would you do during your visits?" She peered in the direction of the stove to find Margaret Louise standing perfectly still, her lack of noise and movement an obvious attempt to help Tori learn as much as she could about Clyde's life the past month or so.

"On days that Beau wasn't there, I'd make him his tea and we'd read. On other days, after he'd had his tea and scones with Beau, we'd take long walks if he was up to it, or simply sit inside and talk. No matter what we did, though, we invariably ended up in his sunroom with him and his easel, and me working on my latest story."

Tori's ears perked. "Are you a writer?"

"I am. Nothing huge yet, but Clyde always said I'd get there. When I was at home by myself, the doubts would kick in. But when I was at the house, looking out at the lake and walking the shoreline with Clyde, I actually believed it would happen one day. Clyde and the magic of that house made me think anything was possible."

"Magic?" Margaret Louise chimed in from her spot beside the stove. "How was the house magic?"

"There's something about the woods, the lake, the view, the history of that house that made you feel so hopeful and happy. Like its very essence wrapped you in a hug one minute and gave your wings a puff of air the next." Kate brushed a strand of hair off her forehead and released a pent-up sigh. "I remember the day I finally said that to Clyde. I'd been wanting to tell him for a long time but figured he'd think I was nuts."

"Did he?" Tori asked.

"Quite the contrary. He told me that's exactly how he felt about his house and his land and that hearing me say the same thing convinced him it was time to tell . . . eh, it doesn't matter." Kate drummed her fingers atop the counter and shrugged. "He turned down millions of dollars to keep that land. He said you couldn't put a price on peace and tranquility and I couldn't agree more. I've scrimped and saved all my life for the things I've wanted—a certain car, a particular vacation destination, a favorite purse or dress. But no matter how special they were when I first got them or first experienced them, their effects on my happiness were essentially superficial. The peace I felt whenever I was out at Clyde's was a constant. It's why I did my best writing there, and where I had the most faith in myself."

Tori swallowed against the sudden lump in her throat, Kate's words affecting her on a level she hadn't expected. A glance in Margaret Louise's direction told her she wasn't alone.

"Losing Clyde was hard enough. Losing that place and what it did for my soul is something I can't even fathom right now. For me or for Clyde."

Chapter 21

"We did it, Victoria!"

Tori looked up from the spreadsheet outlining the board's proposed budget for the second half of the year and eyed Dixie curiously. "We did it?"

"We set the wheels in motion and it actually paid off."

Dropping her pencil onto her desk, Tori leaned back in her chair, her patience worn thin by the board's ever-shrinking wallet. "Dixie, I'm sorry, I don't have any idea what you're talking about right now."

Dixie swaggered back a step, her eyes widening. "You didn't hear?"

"Hear what?" She heard the impatience in her voice, knew it was something she needed to rein in, but it was hard. Her day would have been long even if Milo had returned any of the four messages she'd left on his voice mail. It had been torturous without.

"We were right. About Clyde. He was poisoned."

She leaned forward as Dixie's words hit their mark. "Are you serious?"

Dixie crossed the room to the folding chair across from Tori's desk and sat down, the animation on her face unmistakable. "I just got off the phone with Georgina not more than twenty minutes ago. The coroner put a rush on the report and it was exactly as we suspected."

"Arsenic?"

"Arsenic," Dixie confirmed with a side order of smugness. "And I have to tell you, Georgina is absolutely fit to be tied."

Tori pushed back her chair from the desk and rose to her feet, the lack of patience she'd been dealing with all afternoon finally exploding in anger. "How on earth can she be mad? Does she honestly think it would be preferable to have a murderer walking the streets of her precious town? Does she really think that would be good for Sweet Briar and her mayoral image?"

Dixie sputtered, stopped, and sputtered again. "Good heavens, Victoria! What on earth has gotten into you?"

"What's gotten into *me?* Nothing. Except I'm angry that somehow I'm the bad guy because I think murder is wrong. That putting stock in what's real over some all-important image is seen as annoying or meddlesome."

"She's not angry at you, Victoria. Not anymore anyway."

Like a balloon pricked with a pin, Tori felt the fight leave her body. She dropped back into her chair and stared down at her lap. "Then what is she fit to be tied about?"

"That someone in her town could be so desperate to increase their business they'd resort to murder to make it happen."

She reached onto the desk and retrieved her pencil. Twirling it slowly between her fingers, she addressed the gaping hole in Dixie's statement. "And if it's someone who sits next to her at a town meeting each month?"

"I think Georgina would take that even harder." Dixie stood and made her way over to the door.

"Either way, though, I think you should prepare yourself for a good deal of wrath until this whole business is settled."

"Wrath?"

"That's right, wrath. You poked a stick into a hornet's nest, Victoria. You can't do that and expect not to have a few of those hornets coming after you."

And just like that, her fellow stick poker disappeared down the hallway, the telltale click of the back door leaving Tori to her spreadsheets and her new reality. Surely Dixie had to be exaggerating things a bit, didn't she? But even as the question circulated her thoughts, she had a sneaking suspicion she knew the answer.

Sweet Briar was a small town. The vast majority of the people who lived inside its borders had been born and raised there just like their parents and their grandparents. Ties ran deep in an environment like that. Loyalty even deeper.

The chirp of her phone brought her back to the moment and she peeked at the display screen.

Leona.

She considered giving voice mail the honor. After all, she had more than enough on her plate without adding unsolicited makeup tips and Milo advice to the mix. Then again, maybe venting her many frustrations to her self-appointed life coach would be a step in the right direction. Lord knew, keeping everything pent up wasn't doing her a whole lot of good . . .

She snapped open the phone and released the breath of air she hadn't realized she'd been holding. "How are you, Leona?"

"Well, that depends on whether you want the answer I'd have given *before* the round of threatening phone calls that came into the antique shop . . . or *after*. Because there will be a difference."

"Threatening phone calls?" she echoed over the sudden roaring in her ears.

"Technically I'm not sure four- and five-word sentences followed by angry hang-ups truly qualify as a phone call, dear, but we'll call them that for simplicity's sake."

"Tell me, Leona."

"Paris, stop! Stay away from that plant right now!"

The roaring took a sudden and decisive shift in favor of complete and utter silence. Had she heard correctly? Had Leona just snapped at Paris?

"L-Leona? Are—are you okay?"

"That rabbit is driving me nuts!"

That rabbit?

Uh-oh.

"Leona, talk to me," she pleaded. "You and I both know you're upset about something that has absolutely nothing to do with Paris."

The gasp in her ear told her that Leona's brain

and mouth had finally connected. "Oh Paris, my precious angel, Mommy is so sorry. You didn't do anything wrong, sweetheart. It was . . . it was Victoria's fault."

"*My* fault?"

This time, any and all snapping was unleashed in her direction. "Yes, *your* fault. If you hadn't insisted on coming to my meeting on Monday morning, they wouldn't be lashing out at me for this ridiculous need you have to play detective all the time," Leona thundered. "I tried to take you under my wing when you got here, tried to teach you about posture and makeup and men. But did you listen? Of course not. And where has that gotten you, Victoria? I'll tell you . . . it's gotten you nowhere. Your incessant snooping has earned you the kind of black circles no under-eye concealer will ever be able to cover. And your need to be in on everything happening around you has made you inattentive to the one man on earth who actually knows how to treat a woman. If you regret nothing else in your life, Victoria, I can promise you will regret pushing Milo Wentworth out of it."

Tori moved down the sidewalk in a veritable daze, Dixie's warning about hornets and Leona's anger-filled tirade replaying themselves in her mind again and again. In just a handful of months she'd managed to go from being the lone exception to the town's outlook on Yankees to the primo example of why Northerners could never be trusted.

To pretend it didn't hurt would be futile.

She was Sweet Briar's most hated person at the moment and there wasn't a whole lot she could do about it, short of launching a campaign designed to question the coroner's credentials. And why would she? The truth was the truth. Pretending it away for the sake of image or false peace was fundamentally wrong.

Squaring her shoulders, Tori turned left onto Maple Avenue and followed the fence line that bordered the eastern edge of the Green, the muted white gazebo in the distance bringing a smile to her lips despite the paint job it sorely needed. Once the perpetrator was found and brought to justice, everything would be fine. It had to be.

The sound of approaching footsteps derailed her thoughts and she glanced over her shoulder. "Oh, hi there, Carter. You certainly picked a great night for a run."

The diner owner stopped mid-step, made deliberate eye contact, and then turned around, the slap of his running shoes against the concrete disappearing as the distance between them grew.

Finding her breath, she resumed her walk, the obvious snub weighing heavily on her shoulders. Maybe he realized the time? Maybe his line of vision had nothing whatsoever to do with his thoughts?

When she reached the next corner, she turned left again, the shops that lined this particular end of the Green springing into view. As if guided by some sort of inner autopilot, Tori stopped outside Shelby's Sweet Shoppe and glanced at the extensive display of candy visible through the front window. Caramels, truffles, chocolate-covered pretzels, dark chocolate turtles, and a dozen or so different sinful treats lined the tiered shelf with the lone goal of weakening the willpower of even the most seasoned window-shoppers.

With barely a moment's hesitation, she gave in to the demands of her stomach and climbed the steps to the front door. Chocolate had certainly helped cure its fair share of doldrums in the past; there wasn't any reason to think it couldn't do the same now.

A step away from the front door, Shelby appeared behind the glass, her gaze mingling with Tori's for a full twenty seconds before the open sign was flipped and the shade drawn. Confused, Tori noted the shop's hours listed to the left of the door and compared them to her watch.

There was no longer any doubt.

The hornets were angry.

Officially deflated, she descended the steps to the sidewalk and headed toward home, her hand instinctively feeling around in her purse for her cell phone. She needed Milo. Needed to hear his voice. Needed to feel his warmth. Needed the reassurance his unwavering support always provided.

Milo . . .

The mere notion of the man she'd be marrying in less than six months lightened her steps. Pressing the top number on her speed-dial list, she allowed the subsequent ringing to steady her breath and calm her nerves. Milo would know what to do. He always knew what to do . . .

But as three rings turned to four, and four rings turned to five, any hope she'd foolishly allowed herself to feel fell away, leaving her exhausted and sad.

At the sound of his recorded voice, she snapped the phone closed in her hand. She'd left four messages already. If he wanted to call, he would.

Your need to be in on everything happening around you has made you inattentive to the one man on earth who actually knows how to treat a woman.

The memory of Leona's words extracted a sob from deep inside her chest and forced her from her intended path in favor of the nearest park bench. She sunk onto the wooden seat and pulled her knees to her chest. For the first time in a very long while, she was at a complete loss on what to do and where to turn.

"Miss Sinclair! Miss Sinclair!"

Lifting her chin from her knees, she turned toward the familiar voice that managed to muster the lone smile she didn't know she had left. "Lulu!"

She let her feet drop to the ground as she spread her arms wide for the hug that was mere steps away. Lulu didn't disappoint.

"Oh sweetie, you have no idea how good it is to see you." When the child finally loosened her hold on Tori's midsection, Tori tapped the child's nose with her finger. "How did you know I needed a Lulu hug just then?"

Lulu's large brown eyes swept across Tori's face, followed by a distinct nibbling of her lower lip. "You look sad, Miss Sinclair."

She shook her head. "I'm not sad, sweetie. In fact, right this minute, I can honestly say I feel happy."

Spinning around, Lulu backed her knees against the bench and plopped down next to Tori, her still-short legs dangling above the concrete below. "But you didn't have that big smile you always have when I first saw you. Are you sick?"

She captured the end of the little girl's long braid between her fingers and held it across her upper lip like a mustache. "No, Detective Davis, I'm not sick."

"Did someone rip one of the library books?"

Tori took a moment to drink in all that was good

about Lulu. The fact that colds and ripped books were Lulu's go-to reasons for why a person might be sad spoke to the innocence Melissa was working hard to preserve for all eight of her children. She released her hold on Lulu's hair and watched it fall back into position. "Nope, no ripped books."

"Then why are you sad?"

She opened her mouth to dispute the question once again, but knew Lulu was too smart to buy what she was selling. What to tell her, though, was the problem. Finally she settled on a generic version that would make sense to a fifth grader. "Have you ever done something you thought was right, only to have people get upset with you?"

Lulu scrunched her face in thought. "Well . . . one time, I guess. I think I was six. Mama left the stove on when she went to check on Sally. The fireman who visited our school told us never to leave the stove on 'cause it could start a fire." Lulu pointed her toe at a twig and tried to lift it with the top of her flip-flop. "So I pushed a chair over to the oven and shut it off."

"Okay . . ."

"Mama got mad when I told her what I did. She said I should have told her . . . or Daddy . . . or Jake Junior."

"Did that make you sad?" she asked.

Lulu nodded quickly. "I was only trying to help."

"Well, that's how I feel right now. I've been

trying to do the right thing yet somehow it's still wrong." She knew she was oversimplifying things, but the analogy worked for present company. Bobbing her head to the left and then the right, she allowed her gaze to travel over Lulu's head to the playground just beyond the bench line. "Who are you here with, sweetie?"

Lulu pointed toward the line of swings on the far side of the monkey bars. "Jake Junior and Sally. They said they'd come say hi after they finish their race."

"Who do you think is going to win?" she finally asked.

"Sally. She might be littler than me, but she can pump her legs better than any of us. Even Mee Maw says so."

"Mee Maw, huh?" At Lulu's nod, Tori laughed. "That Mee Maw of yours is one smart lady, you know that?"

"Mee Maw knows all sorts of things," Lulu boasted. "And you know what? She says the sun don't shine on the same dog all the time, Miss Sinclair."

"It doesn't?" She took one last peek at the competition taking place on the other side of the playground then returned her focus to the dark-haired girl on the bench.

Lulu cocked her head to the side and peered up at Tori. "But she says that's okay 'cause even a barren apple tree can give you shade."

Realizing the tears she'd been holding at bay all evening were no more than a few blinks away, she pulled the little girl close, reveling in the sweet goodness that was Lulu Davis. "Does Mee Maw have any sayings about being lucky?"

Lulu raised her index finger to her chin and tapped it gently. "She says someone who's really lucky could sit on top of a fence and have the birds feed him."

She closed her eyes at the description that couldn't be any more perfect for how she felt at that exact moment. "Then I guess that describes me."

"It does?" Lulu asked.

"Sure. I'm sitting next to you, aren't I?"

Chapter 22

Tori was still thinking about Lulu's words when she finally climbed into bed. No matter how many rough spots she'd encountered over the past few years, something good had always emerged from the bad.

Her former fiancé's betrayal on the night of their engagement party had seemed like the end of the world when it first happened. But in hindsight, it was for the best. Had that heartbreak not happened, she never would have moved to Sweet Briar and met Milo—the man she was truly destined to marry.

Had she been able to separate her hurt over Jeff's tomcatting from her beloved Chicago neighborhood, she'd never have jumped on various employment sites and discovered the librarian job in Sweet Briar.

Had she not discovered the job in Sweet Briar, she'd never have met Margaret Louise, and Leona, Debbie and Beatrice, Melissa and Georgina, Dixie and her beloved Rose.

Yes, Lulu was right on the money when it came to that once-awful incident. But it didn't hold up under current circumstances. There wasn't a scrap of shade she could find that would ever negate losing Milo or any one of her sewing sisters.

Rolling onto her side, she took note of the digital numbers on the clock radio and reached for the phone, her thoughts already jumping ahead to the fifth message she would leave on Milo's recorder. This time she wouldn't ask for him to return her call. No, this time she'd say everything that was in her heart and hope it fit within the time constraints allowed by his answering machine. What he did then would be up to him.

She pushed the first selection on her speed dial and waited as the predetermined number of rings gave way to the husky voice that never failed to stir up butterflies in her stomach.

"You've reached the voice mail of Milo Wentworth. Please leave your name, number, and a brief message and I'll get back to you as soon as I can."

The beep that followed his greeting gave her just enough time to find her breath. "Hi, Milo. It's me. I can only imagine how tired you are of me putting off our wedding plans for what seems like anything and everything I can find. All I can say is it's not because I don't want to marry you. The thought of becoming your wife is what gets me through everything that goes wrong in the course of a day. It's not that I think life will suddenly become smooth sailing the day we walk down the aisle, because I know it won't. There will always be dips and turns. But when we're married, we'll be taking those dips and turns together. I love you, Milo, and I'm sorry for doing a lousy job of showing it sometimes. But I want you to know that tonight, after I hang up the phone, I'm going to look through those bridal dress magazines for the perfect dress to wear when I walk down the aisle—"

A long, shrill beep sounded in her ear, cutting her off mid-sentence. She stared up at the ceiling and contemplated calling back to finish what she needed to say, but she let it go. Milo was probably trying to sleep. Besides, if all went well over the next few days, she'd be able to say what still needed to be said in person.

Closing the phone in her hand, Tori swapped it for the stack of magazines and catalogs she'd been collecting for months. Page by page she made her way through a variety of different dress styles—off the shoulder, full length, tea length, and above the knee. Some had trains, some did not. Some boasted extensive lace, others satin. Despite the vast and subtle differences between each dress she saw, though, the brides were all smiling.

She flipped the current page over and stared down at the photo spread of an actual wedding. The autumn season, coupled with the New England location, provided breathtaking back-drops for many of the outdoor shots of the happy couple and their exuberant bridal party. Slowly, she looked from picture to picture, soaking up each and every detail of the bridesmaids' dresses, the bride's wedding gown, the bouquets, the cake, and the centerpieces. But it was the photograph in the center of the spread that brought her up short.

There, smiling down at the bride as she slipped a magnificent red rose into the center of an otherwise white bouquet, was an elderly woman with so much love and pride in her eyes that Tori couldn't help but swipe at a few tears in her own. From the time she'd been a little girl, Tori had always fantasized about her wedding day. In those fantasies, the backdrop changed frequently depending on her age, as did the eye and hair color of her future husband. But the one thing that had remained constant from year to year had been the image of her great-grandmother buttoning up the back of Tori's wedding dress.

Suddenly it all made sense. It wasn't her life with Milo she was shirking. It was the actual wedding itself. The wedding her great-grandmother wasn't alive to see.

The page began to bounce in her hand as tears ran down her cheeks, unchecked. She wanted this wedding, she really did. She just didn't want the resurgence of pain she knew it would bring. There wasn't a day that went by she didn't think of her great-grandmother. But since the move to Sweet Briar had happened after her great-grandmother's passing, the bouts of pain were largely memory-based rather than visual-based. The distinction, while small, allowed Tori at least some measure of control when it came to the timing of the tears that still fell nearly three years later.

Her wedding, though, would be a different story.

They'd talked about it for years.

They'd planned out different aspects of the event through drawings and notes.

Her great-grandmother was supposed to be

there, supposed to cheer her on from the front row . . .

Pushing the magazine from her lap, Tori forced herself to reach for the next bridal dress catalog that now claimed the top of the pile. She had to do this. She had to find a dress. She owed it to Milo.

Forty minutes and six catalogs later, Tori finally found the perfect dress. For there, on the right-hand side of the page, was the kind of gown she and her great-grandmother had always envisioned. Delicate lace and tiny seed pearls adorned the fitted top. At the waist, the satin bottom draped to the floor in a slight yet classic A-line style. It was, in a word, *breathtaking*.

A quick check of the pricing in the back of the magazine, however, changed that word to *impossible*. Sighing, she shoved a bookmark inside the page and placed the catalog back on the stack. Her eyes were beginning to tire anyway. Tomorrow would be another day, another chance to find something her librarian salary could handle.

Swiveling her legs to the side, Tori sat up on the edge of the bed and put the pile of magazines on the floor beside her nightstand. At least she had a starting point for her dress now, something she could actually envision herself wearing. The fact she couldn't afford the exact dress she liked was probably a blessing in disguise. The satin buttons that graced the back of the dress would simply be too painful without her great-grandmother there to button them.

She raised her arms above her head and stretched. The next thing on her make-things-right agenda was concocting a way to smooth Leona's ruffled feathers. That, though, would have to wait until morning, when her emotions weren't so close to the surface. Instead, she plucked the notebook Dixie had given her from the top of her nightstand and flipped it open to the first page and the list of names it still contained.

Shelby Jenkins
Granville (by way of Betty) Adams
Lana Morris
Bud Aikin
Carter Johnson
Bruce Waters
John Peter Hendricks

All shopkeepers or restaurant owners. All potential suspects in Clyde Montgomery's murder. Some of them Margaret Louise was certain they could cross out—like Bud and Lana. The rest, though, were a different story. One she needed to explore in terms of access to Clyde and his food.

But first, she needed sleep.

She set the notebook on top of the stack of

magazines and switched off the lamp. With one quick hop, she was back on the bed and wiggling under the covers, her eyes heavy.

"Good night, Milo," she whispered into the dark. "I love you—"

The chirp of her phone relegated her words to a groan as she opened her eyes and rolled back toward the nightstand. With fumbling hands, she cocked the phone to the side in order to view the display screen and bolted upright.

"Milo?"

"Hey."

"I—I left you a message about an hour ago." She hated the nervousness in her voice but knew she carried that blame. "Did you get it?"

"I did."

Desperate to keep him talking, she launched into an unsolicited account of her evening since she'd left the message. "I looked through almost my entire stack of magazines after I called. And while I know it's not an excuse for my dilly-dallying, I think I figured out why I've been avoiding this part of the planning."

"This part?"

She nodded in the darkness. "Finding a dress. Writing my vows. Finalizing details for the reception."

"Basically all of it."

While she understood his frustration, she knew his words weren't entirely true. "I've picked out the cake with Debbie and discussed the menu with Margaret Louise, Milo. I know that all of the bridesmaids are going to wear autumn colors even if we haven't selected the style yet. And we just chose our honeymoon destination the other day."

"So why put off all this other stuff? I mean, the dress is supposed to be the part that women start dreaming about when they're little, isn't it?"

A wave of pain pushed her back onto her pillow. "Exactly."

"Then I don't get it, Tori."

"When I'd picture myself getting married, I always pictured my great-grandmother being there, buttoning the back of my dress and sending me down the aisle with a kiss on my temple the way she always did."

She babbled on in the wake of his silence. "I—I guess I was just having a hard time separating the two."

"Oh baby, I'm sorry." Just like that, any lingering reservation Milo harbored in his voice was gone, in its place the same warm and under-standing man she was desperate to marry. "I feel like such a jerk right now."

"Don't! Please!" She squinted up at the ceiling and tried to pick out the swirled pattern barely visible in the swatch of moonlight creeping through her bedroom curtain. "I found a dress I absolutely love in one of my catalogs. I'll be able to take the picture to some of the stores in Lawry to give them a feel for the basic style I'd really love to find."

"If you found a dress you love, why not just buy that one?"

She laughed. "Because I'm a librarian, Milo. In Sweet Briar, South Carolina."

"I'm not."

"You're right. You're not. You're a third grade teacher. In Sweet Briar, South Carolina." She pulled the sheet up to her chin and closed her eyes, the sound of Milo's breath in her ear almost hypnotic. "I can't justify that kind of money on a dress. Our wedding is *one* day. The price tag on that dress could furnish two or three rooms in our home and maybe even a swing for the front porch."

"But you love it."

"No, I love *you*. I just really, really, really liked the dress."

"I'm sure my mom would be willing to help bridge the gap between what we can afford and what we can't."

She felt the smile even before it made its way across her mouth, the sincerity in Milo's voice warming her all the way down to her toes. "I'm sure I can find something close."

When he didn't respond immediately, she found herself going over her words, looking for something she might have said to offend, but there was nothing.

"Milo?" she prompted. "Is everything okay?"

"I heard about Clyde."

Her eyes widened at the mention of the taboo subject. "Oh?"

"You were right."

Not knowing what to say, she merely tightened her grip on the phone and waited for him to continue.

"So tell me," he finally said. "Who are you looking at for his murder?"

Chapter 23

Tori was onto the second clue in the down column when the jingle of the door-mounted bell won out over the day's crossword puzzle in the battle for her attention. Glancing up, she smiled at Kate and beckoned her over to the high-topped table she had secured near the back of the bakery. While not necessarily the table she usually chose, it was the best choice for the nature of their meeting.

"Sorry I'm late," Kate said as she pushed the sleeves of her simple knit cardigan halfway up her forearms and slid into the empty seat across from Tori. "I was determined to write two pages before leaving to come here."

"And did you?" Tori hooked her thumb in the direction of the glass case on the other side of the dining area. "Can I get you a muffin or a scone? Or maybe a cinnamon roll or something?"

Kate waved off her last question in favor of the first. "It's like any writing ability I had was contingent on sitting in one particular chair, in one particular room, in one particular house . . . none of which I have access to anymore."

"How about a cup of coffee?" she asked.

Again, Kate waved off the notion. "No, I'm fine. I already had two cups this morning, and if I have another, I'll be even more jittery than I am right now. So what can I do for you, Victoria?"

Pushing the daily paper to the side, she took a quick sip of hot chocolate and then got to the point. The sooner she got her answers, the sooner she could move on to the next step. "I don't know if you've heard or not, but Clyde Montgomery's death has been classified as a murder."

Kate's face drained of all color, prompting Tori to reach across the table and grab hold of the woman's hand. "Kate? Kate? Are you okay—"

"Did you say m-murder?" Kate rasped.

At Tori's slow nod, Kate gripped the edges of the round table and made a visual effort to steady her breathing. "But—but how? And . . . *why?*" The woman's voice grew shriller as a steady stream of questions began to pour from her mouth in rapid succession. "*Who?* Who did it? Who would want to hurt such a sweet, sweet man?"

Her heart ached for Kate as the enormity of Tori's words took root and spread. "We know the how, but beyond that, everything is just speculation."

Kate's eyes bored into hers. "How? How was he killed?"

Tori took a deep breath and released it slowly, her decision to call Kate suddenly crossing into the bad judgment category. "Look, Kate, I'm sorry I called you here this morning. Maybe hitting you with this right now wasn't such a smart decision."

"You think that letting me read it in the newspaper would have been better?"

Tori wrapped her hands around her to-go cup and shrugged. "I guess not."

"So please, tell me what you know."

Slowly, she looked up, desperate for a way to fill in the blanks without making the whole situation any worse than it already was. "He was poisoned. Slowly."

"Poisoned?" Kate echoed in disbelief.

"Arsenic."

Releasing the table from her death grip, Kate raked her hands through her hair and shuddered. "But how? He didn't take any pills or anything."

"That's the thing with arsenic. It can be added

to food. How much is added at any given time determines how quickly death will occur."

"But he ate simple stuff like soup from a can, or sandwiches with virtually no condiments," Kate protested before reversing her own plea as quickly as it had been spoken. "Except for lunch! His lunch came from that meal delivery program the town started up last year!"

"Home Fare." Tori glanced around the dining area to get a feel for the bakery's clientele at that moment and then lowered her voice to just above a whisper. "I'm sure the police will be looking at them thoroughly. But from what I gather from my friend Dixie, Home Fare didn't start delivering to Clyde until after the visual decline in his health started. Do you know if that's right?"

Kate's line of vision moved to somewhere just over Tori's head as she appeared to count something out in her head. "Actually, I think that's right. He talked about feeling tired and not quite like himself in early March. I remember that because I'd just heard from a writing contest I'd submitted to, and while he was excited that I placed, his reaction seemed to leave him unusually subdued. Thinking back, it was as if the simple act of raising his hands into the air left him winded."

"So you suggested he call Home Fare?"

Kate shook her head. "I didn't, Councilman Haggarty did."

"Travis Haggarty?"

"He came over and went fishing with Clyde sometimes. He said sending the Home Fare folks over with food was the least the town could do for Clyde after all the agida they caused him."

Her curiosity aroused, Tori leaned her shoulders across the table in an attempt to lessen their distance and therefore the listening ability of any would-be eavesdroppers. "How do you mean?"

"The people in this town were always after him to sell his land. They'd bring charts and reports and ten-page pleas in the hopes of making him change his mind. I imagine it would have infuriated them to know he'd merely push them to the side of the table and drink his tea without so much as a glance their way." Dropping her hands back down to the table, Kate exhaled, blowing a random piece of hair off her face, only to roll her eyes as it returned to the same place, undaunted. "There are very few places in this whole state that are as picturesque and untouched as Clyde's land."

"Would they bring anything else?"

"Would they ever," Kate mumbled in a half laugh, half snort. "The other councilman, Granville Adams, would bring a pie just about every other day. If it were me, I'd have quit answering the door after the first few attempts, but Clyde found it all fairly amusing. He liked to tell Granville he had a different favorite flavor every time the man would show up with a new pie. One day Clyde would say apple, the next day he'd say pecan . . . or custard . . . or pumpkin . . . or chess pie. Kind of made me feel a little bad for the councilman's wife, who was no doubt tasked with making them."

"How long did that go on?"

Kate's shoulders rose and fell in a shrug. "That started once Clyde grew tired of throwing away all those charts and figures. He said it was a waste of good trees and he was done with all the pitches. He went so far as to tell the man from the resort company that he'd charge him with trespassing if he stepped foot on his land again. Even made sure his son, Beau, knew where to find the rifle in the event they didn't listen."

Tori drew back. "And when was that exactly?"

"I'm thinking it was around the middle of February because I remember Clyde asking if the pie was a Valentine's Day present or a political bribe designed to help Granville get reelected in the fall."

Valentine's Day. February fourteenth.

The timing certainly worked . . .

"Any other premade food start coming into the house at about that same time?" Tori asked.

Kate started to shake her head then stopped, her eyes widening as she did. "It doesn't work with the timing, but there were the chocolate-covered cherries from Shelby's Sweet Shoppe. Showed up every Friday like clockwork."

"And that started in February, too?"

"That's where the timing doesn't line up. He started getting those delivered late last year. But it was about six weeks ago when those boxes started showing up with a beautiful blue ribbon and a brochure."

"You mean like a sales pamphlet or something?"

Again Kate shook her head, only this time she didn't cut the motion short. "No. Like a full-fledged color brochure for the biggest thorn in Clyde's side."

And then she knew. "Nirvana Resorts?"

"That's it!" Kate said, snapping her right hand in the air. "How'd you know that?"

"Because Shelby Jenkins is the daughter of one of Nirvana's biggest executives."

Kate's mouth formed a perfect O, yet no sound came out. Instead, she rolled her eyes skyward and laughed. "And here I was thinking she must have been another person Clyde had helped along the way and that she was simply paying it back by sending him a box of his favorite treats each week."

"Did he say that they were friends?" she asked.

"No. But he never said they weren't. He'd just untie the box, toss the brochure in the trash, and dig in like a little boy who'd just gotten the Christmas present he'd been waiting on all year."

Tori took a moment to digest everything she'd heard so far and compare it with what she already knew. While none of it was new, it certainly helped bring her two top suspects firmly into the foreground. Sure, there were others on her list, but after talking to Milo the previous night, she had to admit that people like Bruce Waters and Carter Johnson didn't have as much motive. Tourists at a vacation resort really wouldn't have a need for hammers and nails, and while Johnson's Diner would probably appeal to some vacationers, the existing building really couldn't accommodate more customers. Besides, Carter was one of those people who was wary of outsiders being in his restaurant.

"Wait."

At the hushed tone of Kate's voice, Tori forced her thoughts back to the present and the woman seated across the table from her. "Is something wrong, Kate?"

Kate propped her elbow on the table and rested her chin atop her hand, her hazel eyes slowly making their way around the bakery before coming to rest on Tori. "What about the scones?"

Tori stared at Kate. "Scones? What scones?"

"The ones Beau brought when he and Clyde would have their morning tea." Kate jerked her chin in the direction of the cash register on the other side of the room. "The ones he got from *this* place."

"D-Debbie's?" she stammered as the room began to spin.

"He stopped here all the time. The box was always in the trash when I came by after lunch."

"And he just started buying those in February?"

"No. He started bringing those shortly after I began visiting Clyde on a regular basis."

"Which started after Clyde's wife died, right?"

Kate nodded. "Been almost four years now."

She felt the blast of relief Kate's time frame ushered in. "Then that pretty much negates the scones. Clyde didn't start exhibiting signs of being sick until about a month ago, right?"

"True."

"And this threat he made toward the Nirvana rep? That was when again?"

"Early February."

Early February. About two to three weeks before Clyde's health began its rapid descent . . .

She let that latest tidbit roll around in her thoughts for a moment, the time frame only shoring up what she'd already suspected. "His murder has to be related."

"Agreed," Kate whispered. "And that's why I don't think you can rule out the scones. Or the tea."

She followed the woman's gaze back to the counter. No, she refused to believe Debbie could ever be involved in something so sinister. It went against everything good about the bakery owner.

"I'm sorry," she finally said. "Murder isn't in Debbie Calhoun's makeup."

"Does that one ever do any of the baking?"

"That one?" Tori repeated before shifting her focus to the freckle-faced college student standing behind the register. "You mean Emma? Sure she does some of the baking. She's been working here since she was sixteen. Debbie has trained her well enough she could essentially hold down the fort all by herself if Debbie needed her to. And beyond all of that, the customers love her."

Kate said nothing, the woman's weighted silence making the proverbial hair on the back of Tori's neck stand at attention.

"Kate? Am I missing something here?"

Swinging her focus back to Tori, Kate's voice hardened. "Her name is Emma Adams, isn't it?"

"Yeah, I guess but . . ." Her words trailed off as reality sank in.

Emma Adams.

Granville's daughter.

Chapter 24

Tori guided the pair of scissors through the flowered fabric, each movement of her hand putting more distance between herself and the mountain of stress that made it difficult to concentrate on much of anything.

"Sometimes I wish I could be here with you every day, Rose," she said as she reached the end of the table and gathered the measured square into her hands. "When I'm here, I feel like I did when my great-grandmother was alive. Like no matter what life hurls my way, it's all going to be okay . . . because you're here."

Rose looked up from the assorted fabric pieces she was stacking on the coffee table and waved away Tori's words. "I only wish that were true."

"Trust me, Rose, it's true." Stepping around the back side of the love seat, Tori sat down beside the elderly woman. "Being here always feels good."

"You don't look like everything is going to be okay." Rose hijacked the delicately flowered square from Tori's hands and added it to the pile on her lap. "So why don't you tell me what's wrong?"

She stared down at the wooden sewing box she'd placed on the floor upon arriving and contemplated her choices. One of the reasons she'd invited herself over to sew was because she needed a distraction. Then again, she'd been in Sweet Briar long enough to know that her need to see Rose went far deeper than something so trivial.

Rose was the wisest person she'd ever known, next to her great-grandmother, of course. And at that moment, more than anything else, Tori needed the benefit of her wisdom. Especially when it came wrapped in the kind of heartfelt affection she felt for and from the retired schoolteacher. It was, in many ways, like still having a living, breathing extension of her great-grandmother.

"Oh, Rose, you don't need me showing up on your doorstep with my sewing box and an unending list of problems."

"All I've listened to over the past two years is how much I've brought to your life, Victoria. You say you enjoy sewing with me and talking to me and having me take you under my wing with gardening."

She filed away the momentary wince on Rose's face as they each shifted their position on the couch to afford direct eye contact. "And it's all true, Rose. You've been a godsend."

"That hasn't been one way, Victoria."

"What are you saying?"

Slowly Rose lifted her hand to Tori's face and smoothed back her hair. "I'm a spinster, Victoria. A spinster who has long outlived her parents and her siblings and even a few of her earliest students. That gets lonely sometimes."

"You have everyone in the sewing circle, Rose." She captured Rose's hand between her own and held it gently. "They've been a part of your life for years. They adore you."

"I think Leona would remove herself from that generality."

She couldn't help but laugh if only for a brief moment. The ongoing feud between Rose and Leona was superficial at best. No matter how many insults they hurled at each other at any given sewing circle, the simple fact that Patches—Paris's offspring—resided inside Rose's home spoke volumes. So, too, did the special project the two had undertaken together in the name of a little boy and his father over the holiday season. "I suspect you'll be getting a reprieve from her angst for a while on account of the fact she's furious with me."

"You?" Rose's eyes narrowed behind her bifocals. "Did you wear the wrong color mascara?"

"If only it were so simple . . ." She shook her head, forcing herself away from a slope that was much too slippery for a lighthearted conversation.

"No, Leona is angry because she feels like I'm somehow ruining her image around town. But I'm not . . . or I'm not trying to anyway. But forget about that. Truly, Rose, everyone adores you."

"Maybe they do, maybe they don't. But it's different with you, Victoria." Rose tugged her hand from between Tori's and pulled the flaps of her sweater more closely against her frail body. "It's like . . . it's like I have a granddaughter of my own with you. Seeing you so troubled worries me."

Tori blinked back the tears that threatened. "Oh, Rose, please don't worry about me."

"Tell me what's on your mind and I won't need to worry." Rose met Tori's gaze and held it with an air of authority. "Is it the wedding?"

She started to shake her head then stopped. "Some, I guess. But not in the way you think. Between trying to find a dress I can actually afford and ironing out everything else, I guess I'm just feeling a little overwhelmed with some of the details is all." It was on the tip of her tongue to confide her sadness over her great-grandmother's absence, but she let it go. The last thing she wanted to do was make Rose feel as if *her* presence wasn't good enough.

"It's going to be hard not having her there, isn't it?"

Her gaze skirted across Rose's wrinkled face

and down to her own hands. Rose was sharp. Too sharp at times. "I should have known you'd put the pieces together. But honestly, I didn't even know why I was dragging my feet myself until I started looking through the bridal magazines and dress catalogs last night."

"Did you find one you liked?" Rose asked gently.

"I did . . . until I saw the price tag and eliminated it immediately. But Rose, you should have seen this dress. It was elegant and romantic and classy and exactly what I wanted my great-grandmother to help me into before I walked down the aisle." Feeling the tide of emotions starting to tug her under, Tori held up her hands. "I'm sorry, Rose, I can't talk about this right now."

For a moment she thought Rose was going to argue, the woman's keen eyes searching every nuance of Tori's face. But in the end, Tori's request was granted. "If you didn't put two and two together until last night, then what else is going on? Beatrice said she saw you at the park yesterday and you were so preoccupied you didn't even acknowledge her repeated waving."

The park . . .

The park . . .

"She said she almost went over to see if you were okay until Lulu ran over to you and got you to sit down and talk."

Ah, yes. The park . . .

"Yesterday I was feeling the effects of being on everyone's most hated list." Tori turned her shoulders square against the couch and let her head drop back. "It's not exactly a fun place to be, I'll tell you that much."

"I suspected that would happen if Dixie was right about Clyde."

Without lifting her head, she addressed her friend. "I don't get this place sometimes, Rose. The only person who should be upset by what Dixie and I did is the person responsible. So why do I feel like public enemy number one right now?"

"Things don't stay quiet around here for long, you know that. People saw Clyde's death as the key to getting what they wanted. His death being classified as murder will surely push that objective back even more. Add to it the general anxiety that comes from anticipated scrutiny and, well, people are anxious. And when people are anxious, they lash out at the perpetrator."

"With that perpetrator being me, of course . . ." She didn't need to look at Rose to know the woman was nodding. Everything her friend said made perfect sense. The key was to find the person responsible for Clyde's murder as quickly as possible so all that unnecessary anxiety could go away. Or find another target.

"Dixie tells me you were right about the poison."

She scooted to the edge of the couch and stood, the same wheels that had been churning in her head all day kicking into high gear once again. "My gut tells me it was slipped into one of three foods."

When Rose said nothing, she took them both through her suspicions. "According to Clyde's friend, Kate, he told the Nirvana Resort people he'd prosecute them for trespassing if they showed up on his property again. That was in early February. Then Councilman Adams, who's been touting this project as part of his reelection strategy, began showing up with a brand-new tactic. *Pies*."

"He figured he could soften Clyde up by way of his stomach?" Rose asked.

"Something like that. Round about that same time, Shelby Jenkins started adding pamphlets about her father's resort company to Clyde's long-standing order for hand-dipped chocolate cherries." The second Tori stopped to take a breath, she found her thoughts traveling back to Debbie's Bakery and the happy-go-lucky college student who knew Tori's order before she even reached the counter.

"What aren't you telling me?"

She wandered over to the large plate glass window that overlooked Rose's flower garden and stared out at the brightly colored bulbs and flowering plants that would put even the most seasoned of landscapers to shame. "For the past four years, Clyde's son, Beau, has been showing up at his dad's house for tea and scones a couple of times a week when his work allows. It was a tradition Clyde used to have with his wife and Beau decided to continue it once she died."

The flowers blended into a blur of pinks and yellows and whites as the stress of the past few hours resurfaced. "Anyway, Emma is the chief scone maker at the bakery . . ." She let the words trail from her mouth as the enormity of what she was about to say threatened to sink her where she stood.

"And Emma is Granville's daughter."

Tori swallowed. "She knew as well as anyone that Beau picked up scones for his father twice a week. She knew because she made them and she was the one who bagged his order and handed it to him across the counter."

"You'll figure this out, Victoria. You always do."

"But what happens if it's Emma?"

Rose bent forward, releasing a loud cough that shook the woman from head to toe. "Seems to me that unless Emma knew exactly which scone was Clyde's, Beau would show signs of being sick by now, too."

She looked from Rose to the window and back again, the woman's words hitting her like a blast of cold water. "Yes! That makes sense. Dozens of people come into that bakery each morning for scones. There'd have been no way Emma could have known which scone Beau would pick for his dad." Taking a step to the side, she slumped against the edge of the window and took a deep breath. "Wow. I don't think I realized just how much the thought of Emma being involved was bothering me."

Rose patted the spot Tori had vacated and smiled when her invitation was accepted. "It'll all work out okay, Victoria, just you wait and see."

"Now if Leona could only see that I'm trying to find the truth rather than destroy her image, I might actually believe that."

Taking Tori's hand in hers, Rose held it tight. "Give Leona a little time. She hurts more easily than she lets on. But she'll come around sooner or later."

She looked down as her hand began to tremble inside Rose's. Her great-grandmother had been a gift. So, too, was Rose. Their time together could go on for another decade or it could be gone the next day. The only way to counteract that was to treasure each moment. "You're a special lady, Rose Winters."

"So are you, Victoria. So are you." Rose released Tori's hand from her grasp and retrieved the stack of precut fabric from the coffee table. She placed one piece on her lap and handed another to Tori. "Let's get started on our placemats before Milo arrives to take you on your date."

Chapter 25

Tori yanked open the passenger side door, tossed her purse onto the floor, and lifted her chin toward the vast openness that was Margaret Louise's backseat.

"I take it she's still mad at me?" she asked before sliding into the seat and reaching for the seat belt.

Margaret Louise wrapped her hands around the steering wheel and threw the powder blue station wagon into gear, sending Tori's head slamming against the seat rest as she did. "That sister of mine only has two speeds—mean and meaner. Right now, you're in the path of the second."

Tori grabbed the armrest to keep herself from being thrown across the seat as Margaret Louise sped around the corner and headed toward town. "None of this is her fault . . . or mine. I wish she could see that."

"Don't you mind none about Leona, Victoria." Margaret Louise reached up, adjusted the rearview mirror, and made a hard right toward the town square, the potholes and speed bumps that littered the road no match for the twenty-year-old car or its driver. "Arguin' with her is like a bug arguin' with a chicken. It won't do me or you or anyone else any good to try. But one of these days she's goin' to have to face the fact that Clyde Montgomery didn't poison himself."

"I think she gets that. It's really more a case of her having brought me to that meeting on Monday. Her fellow shopkeepers are now linking her with me."

"My daddy used to say you can't blame the cow when the milk goes sour."

"I'm not sure I qualify as the cow in this situation," she said. "But I definitely think I'm being viewed as some sort of troublemaker."

Margaret Louise slowed as they approached the line of shops that bordered the eastern end of the town square. "I still can't believe Shelby Jenkins closed her shop in your face the other day. I always thought it was just her father who was all vine and no taters. Guess I was wrong."

"All vine and no taters?" she echoed.

"Means he's full of himself."

"Ahhh, got it." She'd learned a lot about southern etiquette from Leona over the past two years and some of it was even true, but it was Margaret Louise's colorful expressions she enjoyed most of all.

"Now you let me do the talkin', okay? I've known Shelby Jenkins a long time and she'll think twice before she's rude to me." Margaret Louise pulled into a parking spot closest to the sweetshop and cut the engine, the car's answering shudder not much different than Tori's. "You don't think I drive like a maniac, do you, Victoria?"

What to say . . . what to say . . .

She found her breath and slowly released her seat belt. "A maniac?"

Margaret Louise pushed open her door and waited for Tori to join her on the blacktop. "That's what Leona said the other day when I took her to the grocery store to get some carrots for Paris."

"I . . . I—"

"I told her to quit her gripin' but she got me wonderin', I guess. I mean, no matter how many times I offer to bring Rose somewhere, she turns me down. And Dixie? She ain't been in the car with me since our girls' weekend in the mountains last summer. Anytime I've asked her, she gets all pale."

She looked at Margaret Louise over the top of the station wagon and waved her hand toward the sweetshop. "From what I can see, it doesn't look like Shelby's place is all that crowded right now, so maybe we should table this until after we do what we need to do."

Margaret Louise tapped her forehead with the palm of her hand and laughed. "That's one of the things I like best 'bout you, Victoria. You're always thinkin'. Helps keep us old-timers on track when we start pickin' posies."

Phew . . .

With any luck, by the time they were done with Shelby, Margaret Louise would have topics to chew on so they could make it home without readdressing the question of her driving. If not, finding a word more delicate than *maniac* would be tough.

Tori came around the car and joined Margaret Louise on the sidewalk, their destination not more than fifteen feet away. Side by side they ascended the steps, the sweet smell of chocolate beckoning to them from the open windows on either side of the door.

"I remember when Shelby first opened this place. Everyone in the circle was worried 'bout Debbie."

"Debbie? Why?"

"Because Shelby had the help of her daddy and we were afraid she'd steal some of Debbie's business." Margaret Louise opened the door and stepped inside, motioning for Tori to follow. "But they worried for nothin'. All Shelby wants to make is candy. She says it's the way to a person's heart."

"Or grave," she mumbled under her breath as they stopped halfway into the room and looked around a shop Tori had been known to frequent on occasion. During those visits, the only thing that had mattered was the smell and the selection. Today her mission was quite different. Today she hoped to get a better handle on Shelby Jenkins and her relationship with Clyde Montgomery.

"I'll be right with you folks in just a minute. I've got to wash this chocolate off my fingers."

"It's just me, Shelby—Margaret Louise. You take your time, I'm not goin' anywhere."

"Margaret Louise! I have something I'd like you to taste." Shelby Jenkins burst into the room through a swinging door on the other side of the counter and came to an abrupt stop, a flash of anger dulling the eyes that had twinkled not more than a millisecond earlier. "I'm sorry, Miss Sinclair, I'm getting ready to close right now so I'm going to have to ask you to leave."

Dipping her pudgy hand into her oversized tote bag, Margaret Louise fished around inside until she located her cell phone and checked the screen. "It's only three o'clock, Shelby. You don't close for another two hours."

Shelby wiped her hands on her apron then pulled it over her head and hung it on a hook behind the register. "I'm closing at three today."

Tori held her hands up, palms out. "I'm sorry. I didn't know. I'll come back tomorrow."

"We're closed tomorrow."

Margaret Louise rolled her eyes. "Shelby, now stop. Victoria is my friend."

"She's also trying to stir up trouble in this town." Shelby emerged from behind the counter and stopped at the front door, shooting Tori a pointed look in the process. "Clyde Montgomery is dead. No amount of snooping is going to change that. It's time everyone just moves on and sees the silver lining in his passing."

"Silver lining?" Tori prodded.

"Selling that land to one of the resort companies is going to make the lives of our residents better in more ways than you can ever imagine, Miss Sinclair."

Sensing the tension building inside her friend, Tori laid a calming hand on Margaret Louise's back while she addressed the sweetshop owner. "I know that bringing in tourists and their money will benefit our roads, our police department, our business owners, our schools, and even, potentially, my library. So, yes, Shelby, I can imagine. I've done my homework just as you've done yours."

Shelby retracted her hand from the doorknob and turned to face Tori. "Then if you've done your homework, why are you stirring up something best left alone? Clyde's property is exactly the kind of land that draws in resort companies."

"Like your dad's company, right?"

Shelby's jaw tightened. "Nirvana is one resort company, yes."

"You mean the one company that essentially harassed Mr. Montgomery until he finally threatened them with trespassing charges if they stepped on his property again, right?"

"And they left him alone after that, Miss Sinclair," Shelby said through clenched teeth.

"But you didn't, did you, Shelby?"

The candy maker widened her gaze to include Margaret Louise. "I didn't go out to that house. My deliveryman did."

"Delivering chocolates *you* made, Shelby."

Shelby fisted her hands at her side then released her left long enough to grab hold of the doorknob for a second time. "Clyde liked chocolate-covered cherries. He liked them enough he called the shop and placed an ongoing order to be delivered to his house every Friday. What I don't understand is why any of this is your business. I *do* make and sell candy for a living, ladies."

"When did these deliveries start?" Tori asked, her focus never leaving Shelby's face.

"I don't know. Six months ago, I think. What difference does it make?"

"And when did you start sending his order with your father's propaganda?"

Shelby's eyes narrowed. "I started sending along a few *brochures* after he refused to talk to anyone from my father's company."

Margaret Louise shot an elbow into Tori's side and twisted her mouth into a knowing smile. "That's 'bout the right time frame, ain't it, Victoria?"

"The right time frame?" Shelby snapped. "The right time frame for what?"

271

Lifting her index finger toward Margaret Louise, Tori took a step closer to Shelby. "You have heard how Clyde died, haven't you?"

"Of course. It was all over this town the second the report came down. Clyde was poisoned."

Margaret Louise clapped her hands. "*Exactly*. He was poisoned."

Tori took a moment to scan the candy shop's main room. The display cases were stocked with handmade chocolates, the walls adorned with photographs of the candy-making process. She looked back at Shelby. "Do you make all your own candy?"

Shelby pranced over to the main display case and flipped on a tiny interior light. "Of course I do. My favorites are the caramels but they're also the most dangerous. The cooking temperature required to make them, plus the need to constantly stir the caramel, makes it so I get burned a lot."

Tori took a step toward the display case and peered inside, the pull of the chocolate-covered caramels no match for the pull she felt to find Clyde's killer. "You make all of your candy here in the shop?"

"In my kitchen in back."

"Does anyone help you make the candy?" she asked.

"Absolutely not. That kitchen and this shop are all mine. It's all I've ever wanted to do since I was knee-high."

"I imagine you must be mighty grateful to your daddy for helping you get this place of yours off the ground." Margaret Louise waved her hand around the room. "This would be tough to do without someone helpin', wouldn't it?"

Shelby flipped off the light and crossed her arms underneath her breasts. "I thank him all the time, Margaret Louise. He helped me realize my dream, and one of these days I hope I can help him realize his."

"You mean like gettin' a hold of Clyde's property for a new resort?"

Waving off Margaret Louise's question, Tori worked to gain control of the conversation before Shelby got fed up and threw them out on their ears. "How often do you make your candy?"

"Depends on the type. Some I make every few days. Some, because of their popularity, are made every day."

She nodded along to the woman's words then got straight to the question she'd been waiting to ask since they walked in. "Do you know very much about arsenic?"

Shelby's brows scrunched upward in thought. "Not really, no. I—wait . . . *Arsenic,* right? Some guy in Texas killed his wife by putting that in lipstick, didn't he?"

"I never heard of that, but I'm sure it's possible. A little here, a little there starts to add up." Tori took a step toward the display case and peered inside. "That's why Clyde went from looking healthy back in February to looking like a mere shell of himself when he died. He was being poisoned a little at a time with something he was probably eating."

"That's a shame but—" Suddenly, Shelby staggered backward as the meaning behind Tori's words seemed to hit her with a delayed punch, draining her face of all tangible color. "Wait! You can't possibly believe I'd poison someone with *my candy?*"

Chapter 26

Tori scooted her stool closer to Milo and rested her head against his shoulder. "Thanks for humoring me tonight."

"No worries. Sometimes a brownie sounds good to me, too." Milo turned his head to hers and whispered a kiss across her temple. "But honestly? I'd rather you tell me why we're really here."

She glanced down at the uneaten brownie on her plate and knew it was time to come clean. Lifting her head from its resting spot, Tori pivoted her body around until she was eye to eye with her fiancé. "Margaret Louise and I went to Shelby's Sweet Shoppe this afternoon."

"Are you going to tell me you hit your chocolate quota for the day?"

She knew she shouldn't laugh, especially when her whole reason for dragging him to Debbie's in the first place had absolutely nothing to do with eating, but she couldn't help it. "Uhhh, no. Not possible." Then as quickly as the laugh had come, it disappeared, pushed away by a reality she knew he wouldn't like.

"I . . ." She tried to find the right words or, at least, the best way to soften them, but she was afraid.

"Hey, I was only kidding," he said before reaching forward and cupping the side of her face with his hand. "We talked about your suspects for Clyde's murder on the phone the other night. I figured you'd be paying Shelby a visit sooner rather than later."

Reaching up, she held his touch against her skin, guiding it to her lips long enough to plant a kiss on the inside of his palm. "You're okay hearing about this?"

"Yeah, I'm fine. In fact, I don't know what got into me when you first told me about Dixie's suspicions. I was acting like an idiot. One of the things I love about you is how you care about your friends. I wouldn't have wanted you to turn your back on Dixie. Our wedding will happen in October just like it's supposed to, and it'll be perfect because I'm marrying you."

She worked to keep the sudden lump from rising too high into her throat, the sensation a precursor to the tears she knew were mere moments away. "Wow," she whispered.

"No wow necessary." He took a gulp of his iced tea then set the cup down on the table. "So how'd it go? She hold up under interrogation?"

"We didn't interrogate her." She dug a fork into the double chocolate brownie and took a bite, her eyes nearly rolling back in her head as she did. "Mmmm. There was no swinging lamp, no windowless room. Just Margaret Louise and me."

Milo's deep laugh turned more than a few heads in their direction. "Same thing, isn't it?"

"Ha, ha, ha. Very funny." When she followed his gaze to her brownie, she forked up a second bite and popped it into his mouth. "She wasn't happy to see us . . . or more specifically, *me,* but Margaret Louise worked her magic long enough to buy me the time I needed to ask the tough questions."

"And?" he prompted as he liberated the fork from her hand and helped himself to another taste.

Her shoulders slumped as she found herself standing in the middle of Shelby's Sweet Shoppe, watching her top suspect slip completely off her list. "She had nothing to do with Clyde's death."

He stopped mid-chew and studied her closely. "You sound mighty sure of that."

"I saw her reaction when she realized where I was going with her candy and the fact that he was poisoned. She was absolutely mortified."

"Maybe she's a good actor."

"Trust me, no one is *that* good." She recovered the fork from Milo's outstretched hand, only to set it down next to the plate without taking another bite. "Oh, Milo, sometimes I wish I'd been too busy to pick up the phone the day Clyde died. Maybe if I had been, Dixie would have called someone else."

Hooking his finger under her chin, he guided her gaze upward until it locked with his. "You picked up because you're you. We'll figure this out."

"But what happens if the person involved is someone we all care about?" She broke eye contact with Milo long enough to assess the situation behind the bakery counter, Emma's happy-go-lucky interaction with each customer making it difficult to breathe.

She felt Milo's gaze leave her face and travel in the same direction as hers, only to ricochet back in her direction just as quickly. "C'mon, Tori, you can't be serious."

All she could do was nod, and swallow.

"Emma? But why?"

"She's Granville's daughter, Milo."

"So?"

She heard the edge to his voice, knew it seemed warranted from his point of view, but she knew better. "A couple of times a week for the past few years, Beau Montgomery has come into this bakery and purchased two scones—one for him, one for his dad. His mom used to make scones each morning for a standing date she and Clyde had for tea. When she passed away, Clyde said one of the things he missed most was tea and scones. So Beau took the tradition over, substituting his mom's homemade scones with Debbie's."

"Okay . . ."

Surprised by the confusion in her fiancé's voice, she turned back to Milo. "Those scones were made *here,* Milo . . . at Debbie's Bakery. A shift Emma works during the week. I can't look at Shelby and Granville and not consider her as a possibility, too."

"But why would she do that?"

It was the same question she kept coming back to, as well. It was also where the familial connection between Emma and the other top suspect on her list kept surfacing in her thoughts. Maybe it was nuts, maybe it wasn't. Either way, she wasn't confident enough in the nuts part to dismiss it from her thoughts entirely even if she'd allowed herself to do just that when she was with Rose.

"I mean, I still find it hard to wrap my head around Granville as a suspect, but it's possible. Emma? I just can't fathom that."

Pushing her plate into the center of the table, Tori propped her elbows on the edge and dropped her head into her hands. "I know."

"A couple of months ago, I would have shut you down on Granville, too. But with the way the next election season is shaping up, I can't be quite so sure anymore."

She dropped her hands back down to the table and gave Milo her undivided attention. "What's changed?"

"Granville likes the spotlight, the perks that come with his council seat."

"Perks?"

"The star treatment essentially. Or as much star treatment as a person can get in a town the size of Sweet Briar." Milo took another pull of his iced tea and then swirled the remaining liquid around in his cup before finishing it off completely. "Front-row seats at his sixth grader's performances, time on center stage at each and every town festival, a float for him and his family in the July Fourth parade, that sort of thing."

Intrigued, she leaned forward, hushing her voice to a near whisper. "Why? Why does that matter so much?"

"I guess you have to know a little bit about Granville's background. And Betty's, too." He set his empty cup next to Tori's half-eaten brownie and ran his finger along the edge of the plate. "From what I've been able to gather over the years, Betty came from money. The kind of money that opened doors. Granville, on the other hand, didn't. As in, he grew up in a shack out in the woods. Spent most of his life barefoot and not because he was a free spirit."

"Betty's parents must have been thrilled," she said wryly.

"Exactly. But by the time they met, Granville was on a self-made path to a better life. They fell in love, he asked her to marry him, and she accepted—much to the chagrin of her wealthy parents. So they cut her off."

She rolled her eyes but kept silent as Milo continued. "Granville got into the professional world, worked up through the ranks, and managed to buy himself and Betty a nice house not far from Georgina's place. They lived well, but he was always cognizant of the lifestyle Betty gave up to marry him. Eventually he decided to put his hat in the ring for a council seat here in town, and while a councilman in Sweet Briar, South Carolina, isn't anything terribly important, it—"

"Came with perks," she finished. "The kind of perks he felt his wife had given up to be with him."

Milo nodded. "That about sums it up."

She considered everything she'd heard up to that point, connecting new dots as she went. "Okay, so I take it he's afraid he won't get reelected?"

"Rhett Morgan is running against him this year. Rhett's lived in this town his whole life just like the guy who ran against Granville last time. The difference this time is Rhett's got no skeletons. Not even ones from his childhood. He's simply a tried-and-true Sweet Briar native and that alone is going to get him a lot of votes. A *lot* of votes."

"I'm following . . ."

"Granville isn't dumb. He knows he has to do something big to offset Rhett's bloodlines. Convincing Clyde to sell his land so Sweet Briar could profit—across the board—could have been that something big. It would have made him a shoo-in quite frankly."

Milo's news was a lot to process but it certainly added more than its fair share of underlines to the councilman's name.

"Is Emma particularly close to her dad?" she finally asked.

Milo shrugged then broke off a tiny corner of the brownie and turned it over on the plate. "Nothing over the top. But she is close to her mom, that's for sure. I mean think about it, when you see Emma outside of the bakery, who's she with most of the time?"

"Betty?"

"Yup."

Tori slumped back against his shoulder and moaned quietly. "Ugh. Ugh. Ugh. Maybe Granville isn't the only one who wants to see his wife have a taste of the lifestyle she grew up with. Maybe Emma wants it for her mom every bit as much as he does." She inhaled slowly, another thought forming behind her lips almost immediately. "Rose said something earlier about Emma not being able to know which scone was Beau's and which was Clyde's. But now, thinking about it more, maybe Emma just figured if she slipped the poison into the wrong scone, it wouldn't affect Beau as quickly. But I just don't know. I don't know what to think about any of this."

His lips returned to her temple and lingered there for several moments before dropping to her ear, her neck, and finally her lips. She tried to focus, to enjoy their moment together, but she was worried about Emma . . . and Debbie.

"It'll be okay, Tori. We'll figure this out."

"But how?" she whispered. "And when?"

"Maybe something will come out tomorrow. Something that will make all of this worrying futile, or point us in the right direction once and for all."

She parted company with Milo in order to take stock of his face. "Tomorrow? What's tomorrow?"

"The first annual Spruce-Up-Sweet-Briar event."

"Spruce-Up-Sweet-Briar? What's that?"

He gathered up his cup and their napkins and slid off the stool, the intensity of his gaze letting her know he was ready to spend a little time alone together before calling it quits for the night. "It's something Granville is organizing to get the gazebo and the square ready for Heritage Days."

"I take it he'll be there, too?" She grabbed her plate and followed him toward the trash can in the corner of the room.

"He'll probably even pick up a few sticks and take a few strokes with the paintbrush."

She felt the grin before her mouth had even twitched. "I'm pretty good with a paintbrush and a wheelbarrow myself . . ."

Chapter 27

Tori hiked the tote bag across her shoulder and took a deep breath. She had an hour before she needed to meet Dixie and Milo in the town square.

Pausing at the bottom of the steps, she did a mental run-through of everything in her bag. Over the past three years, she'd made her fair share of missteps with all of her friends—an occasional day-late birthday card, forgetting to return a phone call, being late for an agreed-upon outing, and that sort of thing. But in every one of those cases, the person who'd been on the receiving end of the misstep had accepted her heartfelt apology with grace and understanding.

None of those cases, though, had involved Leona.

Until now.

"You can do this, Tori," she mumbled before squaring her shoulders and taking the steps two at a time all the way to Leona's door. When she reached her destination, she took another, longer breath and pushed the doorbell.

Seconds turned to minutes as she waited, the lack of any discernible noise on the other side of the door leading her to believe her planning and preparation had been for naught. Yet just as she was getting ready to give up, the front door swung open to reveal Leona's mother, Annabelle.

"Victoria!"

She welcomed the warmth of Annabelle's greeting and raised it with a hug. "Annabelle, hi! How are you this morning?"

Annabelle's wide eyes moved past Tori to the comings and goings of the people who lived in the condominium complex, a hint of sadness chipping away at the woman's otherwise happy demeanor. "I wish I could go for a walk, too."

She glanced over her shoulder at the white-haired gentleman roughly ten years Annabelle's junior and couldn't help but ache for the woman. While still in relatively good physical shape for a ninety-year-old woman, Annabelle's cognitive abilities simply weren't sharp enough to allow her out on her own. "I'm sure Leona or Margaret

Louise would be happy to take you for a walk, Annabelle."

"No, by myself. But if I do"—Annabelle's eyes dulled as the familiar vacancy began to take over—"you know what happens."

Reaching out, Tori took one of Annabelle's hands in hers and peered around the woman into the hallway beyond. "Leona?" she called. "Leona? Are you here?"

When there was no answer, she stepped inside the tiny foyer and closed the door, her left hand still holding fast to Annabelle. "Why don't we go sit down for a little—"

"Victoria?" Leona appeared at the end of the hallway with Paris clutched tightly in her bejeweled hands. "Mama? Is everything okay?"

Tori met Leona's bewildered expression and did her best to smooth it over. "Hi, Leona. Everything's fine. I knocked and your mother answered." She closed the gap between them as she slowly led Annabelle toward the sitting room. "I—I think she should probably sit down for a while."

In a flash, Leona was swapping Paris for her mother's hand, taking over on the journey toward the couch. "Mama, we're just going to sit for a while, okay?" When Annabelle didn't respond, Leona's gaze dropped to the floor. "I'm here, Mama."

Once Annabelle was settled on the couch,

Leona retrieved Paris from Tori's grasp and jerked her head toward the reading alcove on the other side of the room. "What happened?"

"She noticed a man walking along the path out front and she said she wished she could do that, too," Tori explained as she, along with Leona, took turns checking on Annabelle. "And then, she slipped away." It was a statement she'd said before, as had everyone who'd come to know the elder Elkin since her arrival in town nearly six months earlier. Yet no matter how often anyone said it, or how often anyone heard it, it never made it any easier.

Watching such a wonderfully sweet woman suffer the effects of aging was painful. Watching those effects reverberate across people Tori loved as much as Margaret Louise and Leona only made it harder.

Leona lowered her voice to a near whisper. "Mama has been swiping more things lately. Big things, little things, and everything in between. It's getting harder and harder to keep up with her these days."

"Have you told your sister?" she asked.

"No. Margaret Louise is focused on her cookbook. I don't want to worry her." Leona elevated Paris until the top of the bunny's head rested just beneath her own chin. "When the cookbook is done, Mama's problems will still be there. I can tell Margaret Louise then."

Tori blinked away the sudden mist in her eyes. "I wish everyone could see this side of you, Leona . . ."

"Why? You just turn everyone against me anyway."

She sucked in her breath at Leona's words. "Turn everyone against you? Leona, please, you have to believe that was not my intention with any of this. I thought you understood this whole Clyde thing from the beginning."

Leona's head dipped forward, her wide green eyes visible atop her stylish glasses. "I understood you and Dixie wanted to play Nancy Drew. I understood that my input regarding possible suspects was invaluable. What I didn't understand was the way you were going to turn everyone in this town against me."

"Everyone?" Tori echoed in disbelief.

"Everyone." Leona looked past Tori to her mother, Tori's gaze following suit. "Everyone except Mama and Paris." Then, without waiting for a reply, Leona marched across the room, set Paris in the crook of her mother's arm, and then retraced her steps back to Tori, the anger in her eyes tempered only by her concern for Annabelle.

"Margaret Louise is mad at you?"

"No."

"Beatrice?"

"No."

"Melissa?"

"No."

"Debbie?"

"No."

"Rose?"

Leona stared up at the ceiling with her best theatrics. "When is that old goat *not* mad at me?"

She considered sharing the concern Rose had expressed for Leona less than forty-eight hours earlier, but knew it wasn't the time. Leona was angry at Tori. "Okay, I give up. Please tell me who is so mad at you."

"John Peter, that's who."

Ahhh, she should have known.

John Peter.

Leona's latest romantic target . . .

Tori dropped onto the nearest chair and pointed to its mate on the other side of the hooked rug. Leona, however, continued to stand in an act of defiance.

"Fine. Suit yourself." She leaned forward, modulating her voice so as to make sure Leona heard each and every word while simultaneously keeping the room's overall atmosphere calm for the now-dozing Annabelle. "Someone killed Clyde Montgomery, Leona. They poisoned him a little at a time until his body simply shut down. Do you think that's okay?"

Leona's chin lowered a hairbreadth.

"And while I can't be sure just yet, it seems as if someone did that to him because they didn't like a decision he'd made. A decision in regards to *his own land,* Leona." She plowed ahead, hoping her words weren't too harsh for a woman who was overly sensitive on the receiving end even if she lacked that same quality on the giving end. "Do you think it would be okay if Beatrice or Debbie decided to poison you because they were tired of you showing up to sewing circle meetings and never actually *sewing?*"

The chin shot back up to its full defiant tilt. "I am entitled to spend my time the way I see fit. I bring a dessert to share to each meeting. I'm part of the hosting rotation. I donate money to buy supplies for those group projects you're always undertaking . . ."

Once again, Tori pointed to the vacant chair. "You're right. And Clyde Montgomery was entitled to do what he wanted with his land. He paid taxes. He kept it maintained. He was the rightful owner."

Leona said nothing. Instead, the woman took the ensuing silence as an opportunity to inspect her manicure for any noticeable flaws.

"You invited me to a meeting as your friend. I'm the only one who knows you did that as a way to give me a behind-the-scenes look at some of the people most bothered by Clyde's decision. So the only thing that could be an issue for anyone—like your John Peter Hendricks—is the fact that by bringing me to that breakfast, you outed our friendship. And since I'm the one who set this autopsy and subsequent murder investigation into play, you're guilty by association. That speaks to *them,* Leona, not *me.*

"And quite frankly, in my book, anyone who doesn't want to see a killer apprehended should be more than a little questionable, if not suspect."

Slowly, Leona lowered her hands to her lap and released a long, dramatic sigh. "John Peter is an educated man. His passion, his business, is his books . . . *limited edition books* collected during his own extensive adventures overseas. Who in their right mind would have ever thought someone like that would have an interest in a person who melts chocolate for a living?"

"Wait." Tori nestled into the chair, the absolute peace emanating off Annabelle and Paris working wonders on the knots in her own shoulders and neck. "Are you telling me John Peter was upset with you because of Shelby?"

Leona's left knee began to bounce. "Perhaps I said something to make him think you were eyeing Shelby and her father in Clyde's death."

"Leona!"

"I was tired of having him leave a conversation with me to respond to one of her tiresome attempts at gaining his attention. I wanted him to know he didn't have to be so polite, that she simply isn't worth it."

"Only you found out he actually likes her? Is that it?"

The left knee stopped bouncing. "I look a good twenty years younger than she does and I wear far better shoes. *I* talk about important things like travel and—and *Paris*. And I don't stuff my face with chocolate all day long. Yet he finds Shelby more interesting than *me?* Can you believe that?"

Tori worked to keep the amusement from her voice as she gave the most honest answer she could. "No."

Leona's left brow cocked upward as an almost childlike hope lit her eyes. "Do you really mean that, dear?"

"I do. Being with you is always interesting, always fun. Any man in his right mind would be lucky to have you in his sights." And she meant it. She just wished Leona would engage her heart somewhere else one day. Thirty-five-plus years was long enough to be affected by a man who hadn't deserved her from the start.

"Anyway, I want you to know that I'm truly sorry if bringing me to that meeting on Monday made things hard for you. It wasn't my intention." She pulled the strap of the tote bag down her arm and set it in her lap, her free hand reaching inside for the peace offerings she'd tucked inside. "I brought you some presents. And some for Annabelle and Paris, too."

Leona leaned forward. "Presents?"

Tori had to laugh at the rush of excitement that pushed all other lingering emotions from her friend's face. "Sorry, no Prada. No Louis Vuitton."

"Oh?"

Wrapping her hand around the easiest item to identify by touch, she nudged her head in the direction of Leona's pride and joy. "An organic carrot for Paris . . ."

Leona beamed with pride as she accepted the offering. "She can have it when she wakes from her nap."

"Perfect." Tori reached into her bag once again and grabbed hold of the round metal tin she'd filled less than an hour earlier. "Oatmeal Scotchies for Annabelle . . ."

"She and Paris can have their treats together." Leona placed the tin next to the carrot and leaned forward expectantly. "And?"

Pushing her hand past the gift certificate to the local bookstore that no longer held any appeal for her friend, Tori, instead, grabbed for the purse-sized album she'd been planning to give Leona as a birthday gift later in the month. "This is for you."

She watched as Leona set the album on her lap and opened it to the first page and its shot of Leona in a dusty rose colored suit cradling Paris for the very first time. Page after page chronicled the pair's life together—first organic carrot, first bow tie, first trip to the mountains, first realization

Paris was, indeed, a girl, as she twitched her nose across her baby bunnies . . .

"You made this for me?" Leona said between sniffles.

At Tori's nod, the woman flipped through the remaining pages, oohing and aahing over each picture. When she reached the end, Leona closed the album and brought it to her chest, a smile stretching her collagen-enriched lips wide. "Thank you, Victoria."

Chapter 28

Tori could feel more than a few sets of eyes trained in her direction when she stepped through the opening in the fence and made her way in the direction of her fiancé. The time spent with Leona had been worth every moment, yet it had delayed her arrival at the gazebo far longer than she'd anticipated.

"Am I taking Granville or Emma?"

She paused mid-step, Dixie's question, and the volume in which it had been posed, making Tori cringe. "Dixie . . . please." Beckoning her predecessor close, she looked to the right and left. "We're not *taking* anyone. We're just here to observe. To keep our eyes and ears open for anything that might pinpoint who killed Clyde."

"How come you took Margaret Louise with you yesterday instead of me?" Dixie made no effort to disguise her displeasure. "I thought this was *our* investigation, Victoria."

"It's about finding the truth, Dixie," she reminded. "That said, Margaret Louise knows Shelby better than I do and it made sense to take her up on her offer to come along. But there's still a lot to be done. We don't have the right person yet."

Any further protest Dixie had planned to wage died on her tongue as she slumped against a nearby tree. "I'm sorry, Victoria. I'm not trying to be combative, I just want to find out who did this to Clyde. Who helps you do that really shouldn't matter, I guess."

Sensing the woman's sudden shame, Tori worked to soften her answer. "Dixie, the most important thing in all of this is that you got this ball rolling. If you hadn't been paying attention, if you hadn't spoken up, everyone would have chalked his death up to age and a killer would be forever free. No matter who fingers the actual killer, you're the one who will have found justice for Clyde."

Dixie's cheeks turned crimson with the praise. "Thank you, Victoria. That means a lot."

"It's the truth." She gestured toward the gazebo and the crowd of Sweet Briar residents assembled around its base with paintbrushes in tow. "Have you seen Milo?"

"He's over there, with everyone else." Dixie pointed her finger in the direction of the group. "I think Granville is outlining what he wants everyone to do."

"Then I say we should join them, don't you?"

They fell into step with one another as they crossed the lawn and merged themselves with the group of men and women who'd heeded the call to serve in the name of sprucing up their little town.

"For the most part, everything already looks pretty good," Granville said from his spot inside the gazebo, looking out over the crowd. "But if you look close, it's not perfect. There's spots on the fence surrounding the Green that need scraping, places where this gazebo could be gussied up. We all know that our festivals draw people from all over. We like being that town that everyone remembers come festival time. But we need those people to remember us at other times, too. Like when they're looking for a nice place to unfold a blanket and have a picnic. Or when they're thinking about picking up stakes and moving to a quieter community with a better school, a homier environment, and warmer neighbors. And we want to be that town they think of when they want to buy a present for Aunt Edna or enjoy a date with their spouse.

"People start thinking about Sweet Briar that way, and we'll all benefit. Each and every one of us."

A hand shot up not far from where Tori stood, the face attached to it vaguely familiar but not someone she knew by name. If memory served her, the man went with one of the toddlers who came to story time on a not-so-regular basis. "They keep quotin' you in the paper, Councilman Adams, for saying this kind of stuff all the time, but it seems to me you're talkin' out both sides of your mouth."

Tori craned her head over the people in her immediate vicinity, hoping to locate Milo, but to no avail. Instead, she brought her mouth to within inches of Dixie's ear. "Who is that guy?"

Before Dixie could answer, Granville filled in the blanks—or at least a helpful outline. "I believe the normal protocol for political sparring would be at one of the monthly town hall meetings we have, Doug, but since you've opted to bring your leader's agenda here, I'd be happy to address whatever issue you have."

"His name is Doug Garfield," Dixie whispered. "He grew up next door to Rhett Morgan and is now the head of Rhett's election committee—"

"You ever stop and think that maybe people livin' here in Sweet Briar *like* the quiet?"

Tori looked to the opposite side of the proverbial net along with everyone standing around them. Granville, of course, returned the volley.

"Correct me if I'm wrong, folks, but I believe I was just saying that same thing before you jumped in, Doug."

Heads nodded around the makeshift circle then turned to look at Doug.

"That's why I jumped in, Councilman Adams. Because you're pointing to the quiet and the homey feel and tryin' to convince everyone that those qualities won't change if folks start flockin' here in large numbers."

Granville's hands shot up in the air, quieting the protests of a few loyal followers inside the group. "Now, now, everyone, Doug has a right to his shortsighted thinking and a right to express it here, on town property. He, like all of us, is a taxpayer in Sweet Briar."

"Correct me if *I'm* wrong, but the last time I checked, the definition of shortsighted meant only seeing what's in front of your face at that moment. Seems to me that's exactly what you're doing, Councilman Adams, when all you see about folks flockin' to Sweet Briar is the good things—specifically the money."

"Money makes things happen, Doug. It makes the lives of our business owners more comfortable, it brings more sales tax money into the town, which, in turn, improves our roads and our services, as well as our schools."

"More people also brings more crime. Ask any police chief in any town across this country and they'll tell you the same thing." Doug slid his focus off Granville's flushed face and moved it throughout the crowd. "Is a few extra bucks really worth that quiet we all love? That hominess we all need? *I* certainly don't think so."

Granville's laugh filtered out across the grass. "If the ultimate goal was to simply get a couple folks to think of Sweet Briar when they're out for a Sunday stroll, I could see how you'd think we're talking about a few bucks. But it's not. And that's the difference between me and Rhett Morgan. I see potential everywhere I look. If I didn't, that prime land that borders Fawn Lake would still be just that—prime land that borders Fawn Lake."

"Would still be?" Dixie hissed. Digging her elbow into Tori's side, the seventy-something nearly jumped up and down.

Tori snapped a steadying hand on the woman's arm. "Shhh . . ."

"Instead, thanks to my hard work and the open-mindedness of this man"—Granville pointed to the front row and a man Tori couldn't see—"that prime land will soon play host to the kind of luxury resort that will improve the lives of our children and our residents for years and years to come."

She heard the applause, heard the verbal

accolades Granville received from the crowd, but she couldn't really focus on anything besides confirming the identity of the open-minded man just out of her line of vision. Stepping to the side of a speechless Dixie, Tori wound her way through familiar and unfamiliar faces until she was standing at the base of the gazebo's steps.

"You're selling your father's land?" she whispered in disbelief.

Beau turned to face her, his mournful eyes cast downward. "I have no use for it, Miss Sinclair. The last few years of my life have been spent commuting between here and Texas. I'm exhausted."

"But your dad loved that house."

"He loved the connection it gave him to his past . . . a past that included my mother. He found comfort in walking the halls they'd walked together, in sitting in chairs they once occupied side by side. But I never really shared that sense of comfort. In fact, as of late, that connection has been more painful than anything else."

She wanted to protest, to say something, anything to discourage the man's actions, but she couldn't. Beau was hurting. Who was she to pretend to know what it was like to walk in his shoes? Just because she craved every physical link she could find to her great-grandmother didn't mean other people dealt with loss the same way. Sometimes closing memories inside one's heart was the only way of coping.

"I didn't do it to be anyone's hero, Miss Sinclair."

"Anyone's hero?" she echoed as voices swirled around them and people parted to begin the task of sprucing up the gazebo and its grounds.

His shoulders hitched upward. "The Nirvana folks, Councilman Adams, his wife . . . any of them."

"How would selling your dad's land make you a hero to the councilman's wife?"

"She doesn't have to make any more pies."

She tried to concentrate on the painting, tried to focus on the progress taking shape with each stroke of her brush, but it was hard. On the one hand, she understood Beau's need to heal, but on the other hand, she couldn't help but feel bad for the man who'd cared so much about the property he'd lost his life in its defense.

Poking her head around the gazebo post she was painting, she smiled at Milo as he passed by with a wheelbarrow then scanned the grounds for any sign of Granville Adams or his wife, Betty. Everything Milo had told her the previous night had come full circle that afternoon. The promise of a stronger school and better town services at the hands of tourists had really moved the crowd now slapping paint across the gazebo and pulling up weeds from around its base. The councilman had been almost artful in the way he'd taken control of his chief rival's convenient plant and turned everything negative into something positive. Even as she'd talked to Beau, she'd still heard Granville pontificating about the many ways in which the luxury resort would benefit Sweet Briar.

If he shared the kinds of concrete figures Tori had found during her own research into the financial benefits realized by towns with similar resorts, Granville Adams's reelection was virtually a done deal.

Resting her paintbrush atop the closest paint can, she excused herself and went in search of Betty Adams. There wasn't much Tori could do about Beau's decision. It was his to make. But she could still try to find the person responsible for Clyde's death among her list of viable suspects.

She spotted the attractive blonde over by the picnic table laden with food for the volunteers and headed in that direction. "Wow, everything looks delicious," she said by way of greeting. "Painting makes you hungrier than I would have thought."

Betty Adams smiled warmly. "Grab a plate and dig in. But make sure you save room for dessert. The chess pie and the cherry pie are two of my husband's favorites."

Tori made a point of peering at both in an attempt to prolong the conversation. "Do you make a lot of pies?"

"Too many, according to my husband."

"Okay, sweetheart, my ears are burning." Granville stopped beside his wife and pulled her close, the smile on his face nearly as bright as the sun shimmering across the tables. "What do I say is too many?"

"The number of pies I make. You tell me all the time they're going to make you chubby."

"Going to?" He laughed. "Darlin', I think I'm already knocking at that door, don't you?"

"I plead the fifth."

Tori couldn't help but laugh at the comfortable exchange between a husband and a wife who clearly loved each other. She pointed to the pie. "I hear you sent a lot of pies out to Clyde Montgomery the last six weeks or so."

Betty's smile disappeared. "I feel so awful for that man. He always had such nice things to say about my pies."

"He kept you on your pie-baking toes, too, didn't he?" Granville whispered a kiss across his wife's forehead. "Every time you made him the flavor he said he liked best, he changed his mind and sent you scrambling back to your cookbooks. Clyde was a funny fellow like that. He had no intention of selling but he had fun toying with me anyway. I swear, I ate more pie over the last six weeks because of that man than I have in the twenty years I've been married to Betty."

Tori grabbed hold of the table's edge as the ground began to spin. "Y-You . . . *you* ate those pies, too?" she stammered.

"You bet I did," Granville said, patting his stomach as he did. "Sitting with him over pie was the only time that old codger would hear me out. Not that it did any good."

Chapter 29

Tori was onto her sixth placemat of the night when she laid down her needle and thread and moaned in frustration. "*Ugh!* Why can't I figure this out?"

Lowering her travel magazine to chin level, Leona rolled her eyes skyward. "Victoria, it's not difficult. Every woman's closet needs twelve basic items. Have those, and you have your starting point."

"Good Lord, Leona, what are you babbling about now?" Rose groused from her spot beside Paris and Patches. "Can't you see Victoria is upset?"

Leona leaned across the pair of armrests separating her wingback chair from Rose's couch and gently stroked Paris. "Every woman needs a little black dress—or LBD, for those in the know—a black blazer, a white button-down shirt, black dress slacks, a knee-length black skirt, a classic beige trench coat, dark denim jeans, black pumps, a white and black cardigan sweater, a black leather bag, a set of pearls, and diamond stud earrings. If you left your home for more than just gardening and sewing, you old goat, you'd know these things."

"My wardrobe is just fine." Rose ran a shaking hand down the front of her sweater-clad body. "I don't own a single thing on that list of yours and I'm doing just fine."

"And it's a good thing you feel that way, Rose, because if it weren't for you, I'd still be stuck on a name."

"A name for what?" Debbie looked up from her own stack of placemats long enough to address Leona without breaking a pace that had her matching and surpassing Tori's total by two.

"The faux pas segment of my cable TV show."

Needles dropped around the room as seven sets of eyes came to rest on a very smug-looking Leona.

"Say that again," Dixie demanded.

Leona uncrossed her ankles then recrossed them the opposite way. "The faux pas segment of my cable TV show."

Margaret Louise smacked her hand across her

thigh and snorted back a laugh. "Twin, you're fuller than a tick that's been suckin' on a dog all day."

"I am no such thing." Leona's chin rose into the air but not before shooting her sister a glare to end all glares. "You seem to think you're the only one who has plans, Margaret Louise. But you're not. And unlike you, I've already got a taker for *my* idea."

"Does this taker know your shirt is missin' a few buttons?"

Beatrice flipped her placemat over on her legs and continued sewing, her English accent a perfect accompaniment to her shy nature. "Her shirt doesn't have any buttons."

"Don't pay my sister any mind, Beatrice. I certainly don't." Leona waved her hand in the air then retrieved her magazine from her lap and buried her face behind it once again. "I'm done talking."

"If only we could believe that," Rose mumbled amid the stunned silence blanketing the room. "In the meantime, before she changes her mind, perhaps Victoria could finish the sentence she was trying to share when Leona cut her off in the first place."

She looked from Rose to Leona's magazine and back again, her friend's cable TV show announcement sounding eerily familiar against a backdrop that reminded her of yet another conversation she'd been too busy and too harried to revisit. "I, uh . . ."

Debbie grabbed the next precut piece of fabric from the pile beside her arm and began to stitch the edges, her needle dashing in and out of the material in record speed. "You said there was something you couldn't figure out."

Dropping her head against the back of Leona's love seat, Tori moaned a second time. "I thought for sure Granville Adams was behind Clyde's murder. But I was wrong."

"Councilman Adams is a good man," Georgina countered. "The majority of people in this town are, Victoria."

"*Someone* killed him, Georgina. The autopsy proved that." Dixie tossed her contribution onto the growing pile of completed placemats and rose to her feet, her floral housecoat shifting into place around her knees. "There's still Emma."

Debbie's head snapped up. "Emma? What about Emma?"

She tried to catch Dixie's eye, tried to ward her off a subject that would only sir up ire around the room, but it was no use. Dixie's back was to Tori. "Emma makes your scones, right?"

"Yes . . ."

"Clyde had those scones sometimes two and three times a week depending on when his son was in town."

"So . . ."

"It was something he'd been doing since his wife died four years ago."

"I'm aware of that, Dixie." Debbie's latest contribution to the growing placemat pile sat, untouched, on her lap. "What I don't understand is what that has to do with Emma."

"Maybe she put arsenic in Clyde's scone."

Tori closed her eyes and waited for the chorus of gasps that were sure to follow.

"*Arsenic?* In *Clyde's scone?*" Debbie pushed her placemat from her lap and met Dixie in the center of the room, the twinkle that usually lit the bakery owner's eyes nowhere to be seen. "First, Emma is a good girl. She is kind and sweet and way too sensitive to even think about hurting someone like that. And secondly, in order to poison Clyde, she'd have to have known the kind of scone he'd be eating in advance."

Tori's eyes flew open. "And she didn't?"

"No. Beau decided on the spot each and every time. It was part of a game he played with his father."

She felt Georgina's I-told-you-so glare before their eyes officially met but it didn't matter. No look, no words could ever make Tori feel guiltier than she did at that moment. She knew Emma. She knew Emma wasn't capable of harming someone. It wasn't in the girl's DNA.

"I'm sorry, Debbie." It was all she could manage

to say over the sudden roar of humiliation in her ears.

Leona lowered her magazine once again. "It seems to me that the most viable suspect would be the person who stands to gain in the immediate. Tomorrow can change for all sorts of reasons. But today is as close to definite as it comes."

"Meaning?"

"Meaning, a resort company can sign on the dotted line, but I would imagine it would take a while for something like that to be built." Leona tilted her head in the mayor's direction. "Isn't that right, Georgina?"

"The Nirvana people said it would take roughly two years from purchase to open, maybe longer." Georgina took the next square of fabric from the precut pile and swapped red thread for blue. "During that time they'd have to clear the land, bring in the necessary utilities, meet all the zoning and code requirements, submit a final proposal, build, decorate, and hire. None of which can happen overnight."

"Which means things can happen along the way to slow the process or render the whole thing a horrible business decision."

"Where are you going with this, Leona?"

"Who stood to gain from Clyde's death in the immediate?"

"Beau."

Tori spun her head in Dixie's direction. "Dixie?"

"I would imagine selling Clyde's land is going to make Beau a pretty rich man," Dixie said, looking out Leona's window and into the gathering dusk.

"But he's only selling the land because the memories are too painful."

"Who told you that?" Leona asked.

"Beau did." But even as the words left her mouth, she realized how naïve she sounded, how duped she'd allowed herself to be. "But Dixie"—she pleaded—"even *you* said Clyde's rapid decline first reared its head in late February or early March . . . which was about the time Clyde told Councilman Adams and the folks from Nirvana that he was not going to change his mind about selling."

"Wouldn't Beau have known that, too?"

She met Georgina's eye. "Of course, but he wasn't part of the money talks."

"I reckon the kind of money Clyde was turnin' down would have come up over tea and scones at some point, don't you?" Margaret Louise posed.

Tea and scones . . .

"Oh my God, it was the tea . . ." she whispered beneath her breath, the enormity of what she was saying making her sick to her stomach.

If anyone in the room heard her, they didn't let on.

"Why, now that I think 'bout it," Margaret Louise continued, "Kate mentioned Clyde throwin' out charts and stuff all the time, remember?"

"But when Beau came to see me at the library that day, I showed him the research I'd done on the kind of money a luxury resort could mean to Sweet Briar and he said he hadn't seen any of it." Tori knew she sounded like an idiot, but she couldn't seem to stop herself. How could she have been so incredibly blind?

"Maybe he didn't," Leona drawled. "What the town stands to gain or lose wouldn't really be any of Beau's concern, now would it? The second he sells he can take his windfall and head on back to Texas without a care in the world."

She hung up the phone, rested her head against her pillow, and waited for the jubilation she'd expected to feel at the news of Beau Montgomery's arrest. Thanks to her shared suspicions, the medical examiner's agreement that arsenic could, in fact, be administered via tea, and the chief's eagerness to close the case, the hunt for Clyde's killer was finally over, his perpetrator behind bars where he belonged, proclaiming his innocence like all good killers did.

For the first time in a very long time, Tori would finally be able to focus her complete attention on her upcoming wedding to Milo without the interruption of book festivals, holiday events, and murder investigations.

It was what she'd been waiting for ever since she agreed to help Dixie.

Yet now that it was there, she felt nothing. No elation. No sense of accomplishment. No nothing.

A ninety-one-year-old man, who was probably only a few years away from dying anyway, had been forced from his beloved home prematurely. And why? To push through a sale that could have been made just as easily when the man passed away by natural causes sometime in the not too distant future.

It made no sense. Beau Montgomery wasn't struggling financially. He wasn't rolling in money, but he wasn't destitute, either.

And now, rather than enjoy the inheritance that would have been his in a few years anyway, he'd be behind bars—void of the land *and* the money.

"Stupid, stupid greed," she said aloud, her words echoing off the walls of her bedroom as she reached for her cell phone and the lift she knew Milo's voice would provide. But before she could punch in Milo's number, the phone began to vibrate in her hand.

For a moment, she considered sending the unfamiliar number straight to voice mail, but gave in and answered the call. "Hello?"

"Is this Victoria?"

She tried to place the voice but to no avail. "Who's calling?"

"This is Kate. Kate Loggins. Margaret Louise's friend."

Closing her eyes, she willed herself to find the last scrap of energy she could muster. "I take it you heard?"

A long sigh filled her ear. "I did. And I want to thank you. I hate knowing Clyde died like that. It was so senseless."

She couldn't agree more. "I'm so sorry, Kate. I know how close you were to Clyde."

"I have my memories." Then, after a long pause, Kate got to the point of her call. "I got a call from Clyde's attorney about an hour ago and he asked if I'd come to his office tomorrow morning. He said it was important."

She closed her eyes against the image of the tea Clyde had shared with his wife juxtaposed against the tea Beau had most likely used to murder his father.

"I was wondering if you'd come with me. You're the one who found his killer."

"It was a group effort," she said woodenly. "In fact, if I'm honest, my friends put two and two together before I did."

"Will you still come?" Kate asked. "I don't want to go alone."

Chapter 30

Tori reached across the empty space separating her chair from Kate's and squeezed the woman's hand, the clamminess she felt there proof positive that she wasn't alone in her disappointment.

She'd tried so hard to fall asleep during the night, to let the promise of justice ease her into some much-needed sleep, but to no avail. Clyde was still dead. His land would still be sold if for no other reason than Beau had signed and mailed the papers before his arrest.

Whether his hands would ever even touch the money from the sale remained to be seen, but the land his father had loved so much was now gone. That fact alone made any sense of justice hollow at best.

"Good morning, Kate." Al Varnin strode into the room carrying a bulging folder in one hand and a pen in his other. "I'm glad you were able to make it this morning."

Kate smiled but said nothing, obviously waiting for an explanation as to why she'd been summoned to the attorney's office in Lawry.

"As you may or may not know, Clyde and I go

way back. We knew each other when we were kids and I became his attorney pretty much the second I completed law school. Next to my parents, he was my first client."

Tori glanced in Kate's direction to gauge her reaction to the man's buildup but saw nothing more than casual interest.

"I'm not sure why I'm here."

"I'm getting to that." Al reached inside the top drawer of his desk and extracted a sealed envelope. Leaning forward in his seat, he handed the envelope to Kate. "I think you might like to read this."

Kate took the envelope and turned it right side up. "This is Clyde's writing," she whispered.

Al nodded. "Go ahead and open it."

Tori watched as Kate slid her finger beneath the rim of the envelope and broke the seal, a folded piece of white linen stationery tucked neatly inside.

"Am I supposed to read this?" Kate asked, looking from Al to Tori and back again.

Once again, Al nodded.

With hands that suddenly trembled, Kate unfolded the piece of paper and began to read aloud, her voice breaking more and more with each passing sentence.

My dearest Kate,
Life has lots of twists and turns. Some twists we see, some turns we don't. Some

we set in motion, others are determined by fate.

Shortly before I married Deidre—the love of my life—I had a one-night stand with an extremely beautiful woman. The moment it was over, I knew I'd made a mistake. My actions, if known, would destroy a relationship that meant the world to me and rob me of the one person in my life who truly loved me.

Six years later, while attending church with my wife and young son, Beau, I saw that woman again. She was seated a few pews ahead of me with a little girl I guessed to be a year or two older than Beau.

One look at that child's face and I knew she was mine. Her eyes were the same as my mother's, her hair the same color as my son's. One fleeting look between the little girl's mother and me confirmed what I suspected.

Yet I couldn't say anything to anyone. If I had, I risked destroying the one woman who'd stood by my side for almost as long as I could remember. Deidre was my soul mate and my best friend, and I couldn't imagine my future without her.

So I kept quiet and pretended nothing had happened, but because of my volunteer work with the church, I was able to build a relationship with my daughter without fear of upsetting Deidre or Beau.

I'm sure by now, Kate, you realize you were that child . . . that you are my daughter.

She felt the gasp as it left her mouth and heard that of two others simultaneously.

As days turned to weeks, I found myself wanting to do the right thing, wanting to tell my wife of my indiscretion and beg for her forgiveness. But your mother said no. She didn't want Beau's life to be affected by what could be a nasty fallout. She felt that I could be in your life in other ways and I agreed.

Year by year I watched you grow.

Year by year my love and pride for you grew as well.

I lived a good life. A life enriched by the love of my wife and son, and by the joy I got from watching you grow and flourish.

I kept your mother's secret and she kept mine. There was no sense in hurting my wife, no sense in making her doubt herself when she'd done nothing wrong.

But it's time to come clean. You and Beau are siblings.

If you are reading this, it's because I'm dead. Beau no longer has his mother or me. You no longer have your mother or me.

My wish for you and for Beau is that you will be each other's family the way you should have been all along.

With pride and love,
Your father, Clyde

Tori stared at Kate, her heart breaking for the tears that slowly made their way down the woman's long face.

"Wow. I had no idea," Al finally said. "All these years and even I didn't know about this."

Seconds turned to minutes as Kate continued to sit there, staring down at a letter she finally folded and shoved back in the envelope. "Is this why you summoned me here? To give me this letter?"

"Yes it is. But now that you're here and I finally know the contents of the letter your father gave me in the wake of his wife's death, let me check something." Tori reached across the gap once again and rested a calming hand on the woman's back as they waited for Al to read through the paperwork contained in his folder. When he was done, he shook his head and whistled beneath his breath. "Clyde sure was right about those twists and turns . . ."

At Kate's blank expression and Tori's shrug, Al got to the point. "In the state of South Carolina there are only five requirements for a Will to be valid. The person making the Will must be at least eighteen—which Clyde was. The Will must be in writing, which, as you can see, it is." Al spun a handwritten piece of paper around for Kate to see. "It must be signed by Clyde and two independent witnesses—one I recognize as a mutual friend, the other shares *your* last name, Kate. Do you happen to know a Candace Loggins?"

"That was my mother."

Tori reached out and took hold of Kate's hand as Al continued. "The next requirement is for Clyde to have been of sound mind, which, based on the meticulous list he made outlining all of his assets, is without question. And finally, he must voluntarily sign the will—which again, needs no questioning."

Kate waited a moment then gestured toward the paper. "So what does this all mean?"

Al took one last look at Clyde's will, verbally confirmed the year Kate was born, then spun the will back in their direction. "Because of this provision right here . . ."

Tori leaned forward alongside Kate and began to read, her eyes following along with Al's finger.

318

When she reached the end of the sentence, she smiled at Clyde's true firstborn, the woman who, because of Beau's nefarious actions, was now the sole owner of the land that had touched them both in similar ways.

"But Beau sold the property already, didn't he?" Kate said in a voice void of virtually all emotion.

"His signature means nothing. Upon Clyde's death, part of the land became yours, and the remaining land and the house became his. In light of Beau's criminal actions and the exceptions Clyde put in place, the land and the property are yours alone—to sell or to keep."

Less than two hours later, as she followed Kate into Clyde's home, Tori couldn't help but feel as if they'd gotten a little closer to the justice she'd been seeking.

Yes, Clyde was still dead.

Yes, Beau had still killed him in greed.

But the one person who loved the land along Fawn Lake almost as much as Clyde was now in control of its fate.

"I still can't believe this is yours, Kate." She crossed the room to admire the same floor-to-ceiling bookshelves that had called to her the first time she stepped inside Clyde's house, the countless books and smattering of knickknacks and pictures creating an image of the man and the family who'd once lived inside these walls. When her gaze fell on the painted image of Fawn Lake as viewed from the sunroom Clyde loved, she caught her breath. "Did Clyde paint that?"

When Kate didn't answer, she peered through the series of open archways and into the sunroom. "Kate? You okay?"

Without taking her gaze from the sun-dappled lake, Kate nodded. "From that very first moment, I knew what I was going to do with this place when it finally became mine. Can't you just see the cabins scattered around the property, tucked out of sight among the trees, yet still claiming their own view of the lake?"

Mesmerized by the view, she tried to focus on what Kate was saying but failed. "Cabins? What cabins?"

"Small cabins in the woods perfect for artists and writers and musicians who want to work on their latest project. Each cabin would have a view from its very own sunroom. And me? I'd live here, in the main house. Where *I* could write while looking out at the lake for inspiration."

"I'd love to read some of your work one day." Tori turned toward the lake and reveled in its peaceful magic. "Maybe we could even show it to Colby."

Kate's eyes widened as they locked on Tori's. "Colby? As in Colby Calhoun?"

"One and the same."

"You know him? As in actually *know* him?" Kate gasped with more emotion than Tori had seen from the woman all day.

"Sure."

Kate reached down to the floor and plucked a leather-bound journal from inside her handbag. "These are some of my most recent short stories. Clyde thought they were really good."

Tori took the book from Kate and eagerly turned to the first page, the handwritten inscription on the inside front cover distracting her from the short story she was anxious to read.

> My dearest Kate,
> The best lives are the ones spent fulfilling dreams. May this book be a starting place for yours just as finally telling you the truth was a starting place for mine.
> > All my love,
> > Your father, Clyde

She felt the color drain from her face as the enormity of the inscription took root in her heart. Clyde hadn't waited to tell Kate about their connection. In fact, the date he'd written just above his note showed the knowledge of her paternity coming only a few short weeks before the start of Clyde's rapid deterioration.

So why the audible gasp while reading Clyde's

letter that morning? Why the façade? Why the games?

"You know what's ironic, Victoria?"

At the sound of her name, she willed herself to look up, to smile politely. She needed to think, to consider her options without tipping her hand prematurely. "What's that, Kate?"

"The kid who grew up here with the intact family is the kid who was more than willing to turn over the keys without so much as a look backward." Kate's voice took on an almost rambling quality as she looked past the lake to some unforeseen point in the distance. "And the kid who grew up listening to her mother cry after church every Sunday is the one who actually wants it . . . even though it belonged to the person responsible for those tears."

She made what she hoped were appropriate noises for the dichotomy Kate presented, a dichotomy that had no doubt driven the woman to take drastic measures when it came to Clyde and his land.

Clyde and his land.

Suddenly it all made sense.

Beau had expressed to his father on any number of occasions how hard it was to visit a home where his mother's face, his mother's laugh, was around every corner. He had no desire to keep the house, no desire to keep roots in Sweet Briar.

For Kate, the house forged a connection to a

man with whom she and her mother had been cheated time. If Clyde had died naturally, the house and the portion of land Beau stood to inherit would be his to sell, and sell he would.

Killing Clyde and setting Beau up for the inevitable finger-pointing that was sure to follow put Kate in the driver's seat for what might very well be the first time in her life. Unfortunately, the only direction in which Clyde's daughter could rightfully go was to jail.

For murder.

Swallowing over the lump that rose inside her throat, Tori quietly retreated her way back to the living room and the relative privacy it afforded for her second and final call to Chief Dallas.

Chapter 31

Tori set her notebook alongside the pile of bridal magazines and settled back into the crook of Milo's arm, the warmth of his nearness quieting the nagging voices that had plagued her from the moment Chief Dallas had arrived at Clyde's house.

It wasn't that she'd second-guessed her decision to call the police, because she hadn't. Murder was murder no matter how you sliced it.

And Beau no more deserved to pay for a crime he didn't commit than Kate deserved to get away with one.

But somehow it all still left an unsettled feeling inside the pit of her stomach—even with Kate's reported confession to the chief that confirmed the motive and supplied a second cup of tea during each of her visits with Clyde as the means.

"You did the right thing, Tori. You really did."

She felt the smile before it crossed her lips. Milo knew her better than she knew herself sometimes, and it still surprised her even now. "I'm that transparent?"

"Transparent—no, not always. But you're always sensitive. You know what's right and you know what's wrong, but that doesn't mean you are blind to the gray in between." He tightened his hold on her and brushed a kiss against the back of her head. "And that's okay. You just need to remember that when it comes to something like murder, it's wrong regardless of motivation. No one gets to decide when someone's time has come. No one."

Tipping her head back, she allowed herself a moment to simply study the man who meant more to her than anything else. "I know you're right, Milo, I really do," she finally said. "And regardless of how all of this turned out, it's *over*."

He kissed the tip of her nose. "Does that mean what I think it means?"

"If you're thinking I'm finally going to focus on our wedding—then yes, it does."

His lips moved on to her eyes, her cheeks, her mouth before finally engaging the dimples that made her heart melt. "So what's first?"

"I have an appointment for a dress fitting with all nine of my bridesmaids next weekend."

Milo's laugh rumbled against her head as she liberated her notebook from the opposite end of the couch and reclaimed her spot against his chest. "Did you warn the lady at the shop that the dress selection process alone could go on for days with Leona in the mix?"

"Nope."

"Don't you think it might be a good idea?"

She flipped open her notebook and looked at the first item on her to-do list for the month ahead. "I've narrowed the style of dresses to six they can select from. I'm also allowing them to choose from a few distinctly autumn-like colors. With any luck, the limited selection of both styles and colors will nip some of Leona's shenanigans in the bud."

Moving her finger to the next item on the list, she tapped the page. "Georgina has offered her yard for the reception, as has Rose. There are benefits to both settings—Georgina's is large, Rose's is gorgeous."

She moved on to number three. "While I can't pick out specific bouquets until I know exactly what everyone's dresses will look like, I can look through some floral books for ideas. So my plan is to stop by the florist in town after work next Friday and see what kinds of options are available."

"Wow."

She smiled as she looked at the fourth item on her list. "And if it's okay with you, I'd like to hire Dixie to help with the invitations. I mean, she's thrilled at today's outcome, and pleased as punch that Home Fare is adding to her route and thus, keeping her busy . . . but, still, I want to include her in our plans. Besides, Dixie has such lovely penmanship."

"You weren't kidding when you said you'd get back to planning the second you figured out what happened to Clyde, huh?" Milo reached across Tori's chest and plucked the notebook from her lap. "I think you have enough things on your list for the coming week. Add much more and you'll be a blur outside my window."

"I thought that would be a good thing," she protested.

"In moderation, yes. In overdrive, not so much." He pulled her onto his lap and buried his head in her hair. "You have to realize that in addition to not having time to plan our wedding, you haven't had a whole lot of time for me, either. And at the risk of sounding too corny, I've missed you, Tori."

She reached up and touched the side of his face, relishing the feel of his skin against hers. "I'm sorry, Milo. Sometimes I have a hard time saying no to the people I love. But know that even when I'm wrapped up in Leona's latest trial and tribulation, or worrying about Rose's latest arthritis flare, you're always foremost in my mind. I don't see that ever changing."

"I'm glad. But that doesn't mean I'm not already counting the days until we go off on our honeymoon."

"Oh?" She tilted her head and peered at him through her long lashes.

"Aside from the cabin I can't keep from thinking about, just the simple fact that Leona won't be ringing the doorbell with tales of her latest conquest is exciting."

She had to laugh. "It's a good thing she's not here right now."

"Agreed." He released his hold on her long enough to gesture toward the pile of magazines still sitting on the end of the couch. "Still hunting for another dress?"

She lingered her gaze on the nearly twelve-inch stack and shrugged. Try as she did, the image of her great-grandmother buttoning the back of the dress she could never afford flooded its way into her thoughts for the umpteenth time. "It's hard now that I found the ultimate gown. I know I have to find something else, but suddenly "nothing I see holds any appeal whatsoever."

"Give it time." He pointed at the television on the other side of his living room and then kissed her cheek. "Want to see if there's a movie on? I could make some popcorn."

At her nod, he aimed the remote at the screen and pressed the power button. Slowly, he scrolled through the channels, their options revealing little beyond news and reality shows neither were interested in watching. "It's looking a lot like a DVD night—"

A flash of Leona's face, smiling out at them from the twenty-four-inch screen, brought them both up short. "Um, Tori? What's Leona doing on cable TV?"

She slapped her hand over her mouth and stared at the screen, Leona's pageant-perfect smile rendering her incapable of forming any sort of coherent response.

"Tori?"

Slowly, she let her hand slide down her chin and into her lap. "Uh . . . she said something about a show but . . . ."

Milo pulled his gaze from the screen long enough to focus on Tori. "But what?"

"Everyone thought she was talking hypo-thetically."

"Doesn't look like that."

They turned back to the screen as the commercial that allowed them a moment to breathe ended and Leona reappeared on screen sitting in a red velvet chair, a closet of clothes her only backdrop. "Have you always wanted to dress like a princess? Have you always wondered how you can turn heads by merely choosing the right outfit? If so, you've come to the right place.

"Likewise, have you been to a party when someone's walked in wearing something too tight, too colorful, or simply so awful you couldn't look away?

"Well, I have and it's not pretty."

Tori scooted off Milo's lap to claim the empty cushion to his left. "Milo?" she whispered, staring at the screen, waiting for the proverbial train wreck she knew was coming.

"All over this county," Leona continued, "people are dressing in ways that embarrass not only *them* but also those of us who are forced to look at them across the office . . . across the restaurant . . . across the street . . . across our very own living room."

"Oh no . . ."

"But I say, no more!" Leona crossed her ankles like the royalty she believed herself to be and batted her false eyelashes at the camera and the male operator surely standing on the other side. "It's time to take a long hard look at what we put on our bodies and what those choices really say about us.

"So be sure to join us this fall when I debut my brand-new show—*Leona's Closet*. If you pay attention to what I teach you, you can rest assured knowing you won't be featured in our extra special segment—'Who Dresses You Anyway?' And believe me, you don't want that."

And just like that, Leona and her red velvet chair disappeared from the screen.

"I don't believe it," Milo mumbled.

"I wish I could say the same thing . . . but I can't. We are, after all, talking about Leona."

"Wow."

"*That,* I'll second." She flopped back against the couch, the description of Leona's show making Tori more than a little uneasy.

"Um, Milo?"

"Don't say it. Talking about Rose on cable TV would be low even for Leona."

Oh, how she hoped Milo was right.

For Leona's sake more than Rose's . . .

A knock at the front door brought her to her feet just as she realized she was in Milo's house rather than her own. "Oh, sorry. Do you want to get that?"

"No, I think you should."

Shrugging, she made her way across the room and over to the door, a friendly face on the other side of the glass taking her by surprise.

"Rose?" she asked as she yanked open the door. "Is everything okay?"

The retired schoolteacher shuffled into the room, a familiar magazine page clutched inside her wrinkled hand. "Everything is fine. Or it will be if you don't argue."

She caught the wink that passed between Rose and Milo and knew something was afoot between the two. "Okay, what's going on? Why do you have a picture of the dress I want?"

"Because I'd like to make it for you if you'll let me."

"M-Make it for me?" she stammered. "You can't be serious. Rose, a dress like that will take you months."

"I can do it, Victoria."

She rushed to explain her words. "Oh, Rose, I don't doubt you can do it. Your sewing is beautiful, you know that. But . . . it's too much to ask. Especially with your—"

Rose stamped her foot. "Don't say it. I'm perfectly capable of making this wedding dress. All you have to do is say yes."

Tori felt the tears just before they began the journey down her face, Rose's offer making it difficult to do anything other than cry. "Are—are you sure?" she asked in the steadiest voice she could manage amid all the emotion.

"I just ask one thing in return."

"Anything," she whispered.

"I'd like to be in the room when you put it on that day. And if it's okay with you, I'd like to button the back of your dress . . . if my hands will cooperate."

She allowed her gaze to leave Rose long enough to mouth a thank-you to the man who not only *listened,* but also *heard*—a rare but winning combination she was truly blessed to have found in a lifelong mate. Then, turning back to her cherished friend, Tori gave the only answer that felt right . . .

"It's a deal."

Reader-Suggested Sewing Tips

From Sandra
in Slidell, Louisiana:

- Small hair scrunchies are superb for putting around spools of thread and keeping the thread from coming unraveled. In addition they are just the right size for slipping around partially used packages of rickrack/bias tape, etc. to keep them from coming undone, as well.

- Use an old medicine bottle for dull needles and pins. Put them in the bottle until it's full then throw that away instead of the separate pins and needles that might fall out and harm someone. You can even melt a small hole in the top of the bottle so you don't have to open it each time. To melt a hole in the bottle, use a nail and a pair of pliers. Heat the nail on a burner, use the pliers to hold the nail, and melt an opening for the pins, etc.

From Martha L.
via my Fan Page on Facebook:

- Transfer all of your craft paper patterns onto cardboard (I used the lids and bottoms of old gift boxes). Then cover them with clear packing tape to protect them from spills and tears.

From Megan B.
via my Fan Page on Facebook:

- Use a lanyard to keep your trimming scissors handy.

From Marlene W.
via my Fan Page on Facebook:

- Change the needle in your sewing machine after about ten hours of sewing. A new needle makes for much smoother sewing. Always change when starting a special project.

Placemats

Pattern

Placemats, like Tori and the gang make in *Remnants of Murder*, can be made of most any fabric—plain, print, whimsical, or serious!

Simply take (and cut) two pieces of fabric. A good rule of thumb on size is 15 inches by 21 inches per placemat.

Place the fabric pieces with the right sides together and pin in place. Stitch, leaving a 3-inch opening that will allow you to turn the work right side out. Once it is right side out, press the edges and stitch the opening closed.

Placemats can be decorated with paint, glitter, cutouts, and special occasion detailing (a child's handprint for Thanksgiving, or snowflakes for winter, etc.).

Center Point Large Print
600 Brooks Road / PO Box 1
Thorndike ME 04986-0001 USA

(207) 568-3717

US & Canada:
1 800 929-9108
www.centerpointlargeprint.com